For a fellow who smelled of ling[...] train stuck to his skin and clothes[...] his scent intoxicated.

She stared out the window into the night, putting a hand atop his arm.

"God did I need this." Surfer Boy rested his chin on Rhea's crown.

". . . How long has it been since your last girlfriend?" she asked.

When he didn't answer, Rhea couldn't decide if that meant it had been a long time or if he'd recently been relieved of a relationship.

Or perhaps he'd lied about not having a current girlfriend.

Or wife. Just because he's not wearing a ring doesn't mean he's not married.

"I've . . . had the occasional date but it's been a year or so since my last actual relationship."

Rhea bobbed her head. If he wasn't lying, his story matched one of her assumptions.

"Am I a rebound screw?" he asked her. "It doesn't matter to me, I'm just curious."

If it didn't matter, she thought he wouldn't have asked. "You're not," she assured him. "Yes, my divorce was recent, but I hadn't been invested in that relationship for years." *If ever, actually.*

Surfer Boy shifted his head from Rhea's crown to her shoulder and nodded.

"Why were you so reluctant to ask me to snuggle? I thought for sure you were gonna ask me to shit on you or maybe masturbate with a broken beer bottle or something."

"I like this kind of thing. But I never trusted my girlfriends not to laugh at me for asking—*especially* Sally. Because, you know, real men don't snuggle. I was supposed to fear commitment and intimacy."

"So . . . you . . . trusted *me*?"

"Sure! Why not? I trust you—sometimes strangers are more trustworthy than friends—and I figured with you, I've got nothing to lose."

Rays of Sunshine (*Tales by Rails* and *Smiles by Trials*) is a work of fiction. Names, places, characters, and incidents either are the product of the author's imagination or are used fictitiously. Any resemblance to actual persons, living or dead, is entirely coincidental.

2016 Newget Press Paperback Edition

Copyright © 2016 by Jewel E. Leonard

All rights reserved.

Published in the United States by Newget Press using CreateSpace Independent Publishing Platform.

Leonard, Jewel E.
Rays of Sunshine / Jewel E. Leonard
ISBN-13 978-1535234276
ISBN-10 153523427X

Printed in the United States of America.

Cover design by Scott M. Leonard, images used with permission from bigstockphotos.com and pixabay.com.

> "Be careful who you call your friends. I'd rather have four quarters than one hundred pennies."
>
> — Al Capone

Al Capone is probably not the first person to come to mind when you think of quotations about friendship, but here we are . . .

DEDICATED TO MY FOUR QUARTERS
(in alphabetical order)

Ashley, Christina, Lo-arna, Vania: for all the ways you've helped me—in real life, with my writing, and with this book especially—for all the laughs we've shared, for staying at my side through my lowest lows and many woes, for putting up with my general craziness. In other words, for being Level 10 Friends.

AND TO MY LOVING HUSBAND

Scott: for the same reasons as above . . . and many more.

Rays of Sunshine

PART 1

TALES BY RAILS

By Jewel E. Leonard

"If a train doesn't stop at your station, then it's not your train."

— Marianne Williamson

The Facebook update announcing her divorce was one of the hardest things Rhea had ever done. Saying "I do" at nineteen had been a breeze. Saying "I sure as hell don't" at twenty-three was a nightmare wrapped in a special hell tortilla no self-respecting hopeless romantic should ever have had to experience.

Still looming for Rhea was a trip to the local Social Security office to reclaim her maiden name. And then it would be off to the Department of Motor Vehicles to handle her driver license and vehicle registration, followed by the United States Post Office for an address change—which posed its own problems she really didn't want to think about at present. Hadn't she been hurt enough without having to deal with a whole hell of a lot of waiting in line at government offices?

Despite that awful to-do list, all Rhea could do was sit and stare at the status update she was preparing to make in her Facebook app: *The divorce is final.* It lacked emojis, emoticons or any other indication of how she felt about it, but she found it weird to add anything to the statement.

"What emoji would someone use on a blindsiding announcement like that?" Rhea wondered. *I'm divorced. Just thought you should know, winky face. I'm back on the market, open-mouthed smiley with tears.* Maybe it needed an *LMFAO*.

She didn't know why it needed any of that stuff.

So Rhea relied on nothing but her words and left their interpretation to her friends list.

She pressed the blue *Post* button and waited for the first

"I'm sorry."

The first misplaced joke to celebrate.

The first frowning emoji without words accompanying it.

The first "call me if you need me" empty offer of support.

And Rhea would dutifully press *Like* on each—even the ones that pissed her off, whether or not her anger made sense—knowing behind the hollow acknowledgments of her failure were scads of judgment she deserved for having been a stupid kid who was looking for a quick escape with the first man who'd glanced her way sporting an interested smile.

That's just what Mark Coleman had been: An interested smile and a four-year mistake.

The first alert buzzed on her phone. *Charmed Mooregood likes this*.

The daughter of hippiecrites, Charmed was the quintessential frenemy, someone whom Rhea followed on social media—years ago—and who typically made no remark on Rhea's activities except when she couldn't pass on the opportunity to *Like* a bad day. A flat tire. Or that visit to the emergency room for an EpiPen when Rhea discovered her kiwi allergy.

Despite that knowledge, Rhea whipped her cellphone across the living room with an agonized scream.

She knew she shouldn't have said anything about the D-I-V-O-R-C-E, but she also knew people would notice Mark's absence of thinly veiled participation on her Facebook wall. Her closer friends with better attention to detail would notice how all Mark's family members unfriended her in a blitz of social media abandonment.

Rhea stood with a sigh, retrieving her phone from where it landed on the beige carpet after bouncing off the adjoining beige wall. Mark bathed them in beige; that should have served as a prediction of the beige life they would share. In reality, those choices did nothing more than to make the selling of their condominium a little bit easier.

Rhea turned the smartphone over in her hand. Its screen had shattered. "Of course. Why *wouldn't* it?" She ran her finger across the screen to wake it. No response. She double-tapped it. Still nothing. She pressed the inset button on its back. When that too failed, she tapped its screen harder in fury which disappeared as quickly as it flared.

Upon further consideration of her broken phone, Rhea smiled. No phone, no phone calls. No well-meaning yet still somehow obnoxious texts. "I *have* always thought about taking a break from technology. Might as well start now."

With little fanfare, Rhea dumped what used to be her cellphone into the kitchen trashcan.

"*Rhea?*" The front door of the condo eased open. "Ready to go?"

Rhea puffed out her cheeks with an exaggerated exhalation. "Come in, Cass. I'm just waiting for the movers."

Cass let herself in, walking down the short hallway and into the living room. "Mark's leaving you the couch." She crossed her arms over her chest and thumped her shoulder against the wall. "Generous."

"Hey. He could've left me with nothing."

"I'm not giving that asshole credit for nothin'. He hurt my bestie. He can rot in the hottest, foulest-smelling corner of hell for all I care. He should hang out in the sulfur pit where the devil hard-boils his eggs—"

"I really don't need your animosity toward him. It isn't helping anything."

Cass tilted her head, regarding Rhea with a pout. "It helps *me*. I want to hate him. Look . . . It's not like you need to put on a happy face for your kids."

"Thank God for my IUD, right?" Though Rhea never told anyone, condoms broke on Mark routinely. She wanted children someday, she supposed, but was grateful in retrospect there were no unplanned pregnancies. They couldn't even agree on how to care for pets the few times they broached that topic.

"Right." Cass smiled stiffly. "So what are you going to do now?"

"I figure I'll stay in a hotel for a few nights. Return to work on Monday and start searching for an apartment I'll barely qualify for. Live paycheck to paycheck. That's the

American Dream, isn't it?"

"Stay with us! Jack won't mind. We've . . . kinda . . . already discussed it."

Rhea turned away from Cass to hide her scowl. Who *hadn't* talked about her in the last few months? "I couldn't." At the moment, she didn't want to live with her best friend, let alone talk with her.

"Why not?"

"I—I just—can't be around other couples right now. I'm sorry."

"It kills me a little to think of you, all alone in a hotel room—"

"I'll figure something out," Rhea snapped. "Don't worry about me."

Rhea spent Friday night in the Holiday Inn down the street from where she'd lived with her ex-husband. She stepped out only to get food from McDonald's—lamenting their lack of all-day breakfast because she believed the only thing worth eating there was the Egg McMuffin with sausage—otherwise lounging in bed with the television on the local evening news. If there was anything more depressing than Rhea's life, it would be on the local news.

By noon on Saturday, Rhea ventured to the hotel lobby. She perused the rack of travel pamphlets, picking through them for something new to do in the area. Sea World. San Diego Zoo. Disneyland and Disney California Adventure. Balboa Park, Hotel del Coronado, El Campo Santo Cemetery and the neighboring Whaley House. All of which she'd visited, many of which she visited enough to justify having annual passes.

Once the prune-skinned, white-haired, shaky-limbed gentleman left the lobby computer, Rhea settled down at it. She supposed she should search for apartments though what she wanted to do instead was to sit around and do nothing for a month or two. Procrastination sounded wonderful.

RAYS OF SUNSHINE

She double-clicked on the browser icon and it pulled up from being minimized in the taskbar. The previous user left the Amtrak website open. Rhea blinked and glanced around the lobby. The gentleman was nowhere to be seen. She returned her attention to the website, pursing her lips. Her voice was a mere whisper: "Dare I . . .?"

Rhea approached the Southwest Chief at Los Angeles Union Station, suitcase wheels clacking on the ground behind her to the rhythm of concrete and mortar joints.

She'd never been that close to a train and was surprised by how big it was.

It would not have taken much for its size to intimidate her into tucking tail and running home—well, to the Holiday Inn, anyway—so she set her mind to dwelling on that later. If she gave it more than a passing consideration this was the first time she'd done anything of this caliber by herself, she was afraid she would be out the two hundred-some dollars her coach ticket cost her.

She wasn't going to dwell on the cost, either. If Amtrak didn't issue refunds—and she doubted it did—that money was long gone either way. A sunk cost.

Might as well use it.

With a deep breath, Rhea allowed the attendant to help her onto the train. He set her luggage into a compartment with other suitcases, and directed her up a tight staircase into the upper level coach seating. The car was damn near empty with only three other passengers aboard. They were settling in and gave off vibes of having no interest in socializing. So Rhea set her backpack on the seat beside hers and sat, looking out her window.

When the train pulled from the station—so smoothly Rhea didn't notice the sensation of moving, only the station as it slid by outside her window—she gave a small start. It was too late to back out now, regardless of the throat-clenching anxiety rising in her chest, so she thought it prudent to stave that off by pulling out her small laptop. Okay, so it went against her technology break. She still wasn't getting on social media, though, so in her opinion it wasn't cheating.

Day one, she typed.
I have an overwhelming feeling this is going to be a quiet, lonely trip.
And maybe that's a good thing. I needed time away from everything.
I don't know what I was expecting but the Amtrak attendant was nice enough.
The people in my car so far are quiet and keep to themselves.
I think I might go find the lounge car and see about getting myself a snack.
I kinda miss having wifi already though it's nice to not have the temptation to get online. What would I do? Check social media, get pissed off and wish I hadn't looked? I don't yet miss my phone. I hope that won't change. I wonder if anyone will even notice I'm gone? Doubtful.

Rhea closed her laptop and stuffed it into her backpack which she stowed on the overhead storage shelf. Praying it would be there upon her return, she went hunting for the snack car.

Situated on the lower level of the lounge car, the snack car was something akin to a musty deli with limited stock that could accommodate no more than two customers at a time. Three if they didn't mind getting personal or if they were all far skinnier than she was. Rhea bought a bag of Fritos and a can of Pepsi; after all, what good was vacationing without eating poorly for at least part of it? Still, she promised herself her next meal would be at least a little bit healthier.

The train stopped at Riverside station while Rhea sat by herself at one of the small tables adjacent to the snack bar, first devouring the bag of chips before polishing off the soda like a frat boy drinking beer. For the sake of appearing feminine near the snack car attendant, she swallowed a burp.

The carbonation stung her nose.

Once the train departed Riverside station, Rhea ascended the narrow staircase to the observation car where she settled into an outward-facing seat to watch the unimpressive view of Southern California chug by.

Train rides, Rhea mused, *involve an impressive amount of sitting. I should really figure out what there is to do at the end of the line. Maybe see if anyone has any ideas—of course, that'd involve talking with someone. Good luck with that, Rhea.*

But then she would have something to look forward to during her humdrum train ride.

Two hours done. Forty-six to go.

Had she put another few hundred dollars into her tickets, she would have had a private cabin in which to pass the time by getting herself off. In two days, she was sure she could find her G-spot: an endeavor Mark never had any interest in. And so they didn't bother because they always did whatever he wanted in bed. Why she hadn't done it on her own, Rhea didn't know.

"That was an awful big sigh for such a pretty girl to make."

Rhea glanced up with a start, her face growing hot—not as if the man could have somehow known what was on her mind.

Pointing with a beer can in hand, he asked, "This seat taken?"

More than half the observation car's seats were unoccupied, yet he pointed at the one adjacent to hers. She thought to send him away.

What if he needs companionship? If the passengers in this car—or his—were as disinterested in conversation as the ones in Rhea's car had been, well, she couldn't blame him for coming to her to talk.

She offered him the kindest smile she could muster. With a nod toward the seat in question, she invited him to sit: "Go ahead."

He sat beside her, gripping the can with both hands. He squeezed it until it crunched before releasing it again and telling her, "Thanks."

Rhea attempted a casual sideways glance at him. He had sandy blond hair trimmed short, pretty grey eyes, and was surprisingly tan. If she had to guess, she assumed he'd spent recent hours on a surfboard in the Pacific Ocean. What was a surfer doing on an eastbound train?

"Where are you heading?" Surfer Boy asked.

"Chicago," Rhea replied. "You?"

He nodded. "Same. I make this trip each year."

"By train? Really? *Each year?*"

"Yep. I . . . don't fly."

"I've never met anyone who doesn't fly," said Rhea in disbelief. Those were the friends who genuinely believed people who didn't fly weren't to be trusted. She had friends who believed non-flyers were modern-day urban legends. Everyone flew. *Everyone.*

"Never have." He ran his left hand over his head, his hair feathering back into place. It looked too soft to have been in the ocean recently. She also noted the distinct lack of wedding band, but moreover, the small tattoo on the inside of his wrist: an innocuous semicolon. "Lost my dad in a plane crash about a decade ago. Or . . . Longer, I guess. I don't like to think about how much time's gone by since then."

"Oh. I—I'm so sorry."

They were silent for a while before Surfer Boy spoke again. "Amtrak's got an unfortunate reputation. But I've personally never had a really bad trip. Of course, some trips are better than others, but never anything bad enough to keep me from booking tickets again afterward. I've been thinking about driving there sometime, too."

"This is my first time on a train," Rhea admitted.

Surfer Boy finished off his beer. "This is a doozy of a trip to make for your first one."

Rhea laughed despite herself. "My motto is 'go big or go home.' I like adventure."

"I like adventurous types."

Her mouth ran away without her: "Was that a pick-up line?"

"It's just conversation. Small talk." His tanned cheeks

acquired a hint of red.

"I . . . just got out of a disastrous relationship." Her gaze dropped to her ring-less left hand. "That's why I got on this train. I'm running away." *From a home I don't have*, Rhea finished silently.

"Cool." Surfer Boy bobbed his head.

Cool?

She expected he would vanish. When he didn't, she allowed herself a more thorough physical assessment of him.

He was trim, and her height within an inch; a little above average for a woman, therefore a couple inches below average for a man. Not as though height mattered to her. Nor did appearance, though Surfer Boy was an exceptional specimen in that department.

Upon further investigation, he reminded her a little of Chris Hemsworth. *A lot like him, actually. Nice.* But a Chris Hemsworth lookalike wasn't what Rhea was looking for in a future relationship.

What Rhea wanted in her relationships was emotional availability.

She was swift to correct herself: she wanted nothing. Not for a few years, anyway, after getting the *yuck* of failed marriage off her skin and out of her system. How long did the typical divorce-flush last? A year? Year-and-a-half? Was there a ratio of time spent in a relationship to the time it took to recover? Rhea could check the internet on her phone—*No, wait. I broke that.*

Surfer Boy gave her a fleeting smile revealing nice teeth. He may well have been perfect and that made her even more suspicious of him.

"We're all running away from something."

Judging by the look he was giving her, Rhea could tell he expected her to run.

And yet she remained in her seat. *Why?* She cleared her throat. "So what's waiting for you at the end of the line?" Rhea shifted toward him as much as her seat allowed.

"Memories," said Surfer Boy after a long silence.

Rhea considered how to move along a stalled conversation she hadn't wanted to engage in to begin with.

He came to her rescue with small talk which was marginally better than uncomfortable silence. "What do you do for a living? No. No, wait. Let me guess." With a tilted head, he studied her.

Rhea had cut her light blonde hair a few days ago in an act of defiance because her ex-husband had been vocal about disliking, as he called it, "the militant dyke look." She, on the other hand, referred to her cut as a pixie bob and had longed for that style for years. Her build was a mesomorphic one that took on muscle well when she properly tended herself. In recent months she hadn't been to a gym more than a handful of times, so her toned belly was on the softer side. Everything was rounder than she preferred, but she was nothing a hot-blooded straight man would boot from his bed.

Of everything about Rhea—spunky hairstyle, full breasts, shapely legs—Surfer Boy's gaze trained on her hands.

"You're a writer," he guessed.

"It's a hobby," said Rhea. "And nothing more."

". . . *Pianist?*"

"My long fingers fooled another person, I see!" she laughed. "I used to play flute though."

"Do I get another guess? I'll get it this time."

"Sure." Rhea smirked. *He'll probably peg me as an artist.* "Why not?"

"*Vampire hunter.* You look like a badass Buffy." Surfer Boy added hastily, "Oh *please* get the reference!"

"Excuse me? Sarah Michelle Gellar was already pretty damned badass!"

"I'm glad you get the reference. But you'll have to excuse my assessment, she was a cheerleader. *You* look badass."

"She was pretty damned badass, excusing her being a cheerleader." Rhea added, "Cass—my bestie—is a huge Buffy fan. I don't watch it much, myself, but she's exposed me to it a lot. Actually, I'm a massage therapist."

Surfer Boy's face lit up and his response was predictable: "I have this cramp in my back—"

She stood.

"Please don't go." He cleared his throat. "It was a dumb joke I'm sure you've heard tons of times before—"

"Once or twice," lied Rhea, walking around to the back of his seat. "But I have this obnoxious thing where I have to prove myself to the unbelievers." She held her hands over his shoulders. "Do you mind?"

He tipped his head back to glance at her. "For real?"

"Yeah."

"Pleasant conversation and a free massage? This may be the best vacation I've ever had!"

Rhea began the massage on Surfer Boy's shoulders, and his head dropped as if he'd lost consciousness for a heartbeat.

Yep, she thought. *Muscular*. Rhea corrected him with a wide smile, "Free? Ha! I charge a hundred per hour."

He groaned when Rhea hit a knotted muscle. "And I'll bet you're worth every penny."

Rhea let that slide; she'd heard worse over her years as a therapist. His groan, however, stirred something inside her. She bit her lip and forced herself to ignore the unwelcome tug in her lower abdomen.

She discreetly glanced around and noticed heads turning toward that noise.

"No joke . . . I give a far more effective massage in private," she said. "And whether or not you were teasing me—" she leaned in, gently pressing a muscle in spasm with her thumb until he winced. "You need this."

The other passengers resumed their business. They were reading books or paying attention to tablets and phones. Two were actually engaged in conversation with each other. *Good for them.*

Surfer Boy sighed. "Oh, I can't afford you."

"That's a shame." *Why the hell am I still touching his back? And why the hell isn't he stopping me?* "I'd have considered it my good deed for the day to do you for free." Rhea realized how bad that had to sound. "To *massage* you for free!" she blurted louder than she intended. "Free massage!"

Heads turned to them again.

His head tilted toward her so fast she was amazed he didn't give himself whiplash. "I have a roomette downstairs!"

"I'm sorry?" Rhea choked on her phlegm.

"I've got a sleeper room downstairs." Watching the horror spreading across Rhea's face, he added, "I swear, I'm not a creep!"

She smiled despite herself. "I believe you but just in case you get any felonious ideas, remember: I'm a badass vampire slayer."

Surfer Boy led Rhea from the observation car. They walked two coach cars toward the engine and down a cramped staircase. His was the small cabin adjacent to the stairwell.

"Tight squeeze," Rhea remarked as she peered into the cabin from the little corridor. They would both have to be sitting across from each other if they wanted the door closed.

Neither closed it. As she stepped into the room, Rhea said, "Please don't murder me." To lessen the impact of what sounded harsher than she'd intended, she added, "If you strike me down, I shall become more powerful than you can possibly imagine."

"Did—did you just quote *Star Wars IV*?"

Rhea's cheeks went hot. "No."

"Yes." He flailed at her, his face alight. "Yes, you did!"

She was still blushing, but given his excitement, Rhea could at least smile. "Come on, who doesn't know at least one line from at least one *Star Wars* movie?"

"I get the feeling you know more than that."

"Shut up and let me massage you."

"*Anyway*, why on earth would I kill someone who gives such stellar massages?" Surfer Boy sat, resting his thigh on the seat as he turned his back to her.

"This is still not optimal. Better than being the center of attention out in public, anyway." She continued her massage more or less where she'd left off in the observation car. "There are some real weirdos out there. 'Least, that's what everyone thinks."

He groaned between the words: "How can I . . . prove

to you I'm . . . a nice guy?"

"I guess time will tell."

They fell silent. Rhea concentrated on what she was doing, and Surfer Boy made the occasional noise that fell somewhere between pleasure and pain. Each time it was more the former, she felt that excited twinge in her gut and an unwelcome clenching of muscles further south of there.

As the train rolled into Victorville, Rhea was overwhelmed by her reaction to him. She yanked her hands away, curling them into fists and struggled not to choke on the lump of desire lodged in her throat.

Surfer Boy shifted toward her in his spot, failing to conceal his pants as they tented with glorious and generous blood flow. *How big is he if he looks like that beneath his clothes?* Following her intrusive thought, Rhea stammered, "L-look at the time, I should be going—I need to go—"

"Oh my god," he gasped, "I am *so* sorry—"

She turned and smacked against the opposite train wall, which couldn't have been more than two feet away. "It's not you, it's the—it's me." Her face ached under its flush. "I've got a seat I paid hundreds for, and I—I can't have spent more than a half hour in it—"

Rhea stumbled up the stairs without another word. She spent ten minutes going car to car searching for her seat before she located it, collapsing into it with a hard exhalation.

Day Two.

I woke about a half hour outside of Gallup, NM. The train car is full now.

Last night was restless. Bearded man behind me has a loud, intermittent snore. If he snored continuously, at least that might eventually act as white noise and I could sleep through it.

Coach chairs are modern-day torture devices. I have half a mind to offer discount massages to the folks in this car for some quick spending cash but I feel that's unethical as fuck. Which reminds me . . .

Surfer Boy: Handsome as fuck. This blond-haired, grey-eyed, tan, ripped guy who sat down next to me in the observation car . . . we had a nice chat last night. I gave him a solid massage for which my muscles still ache, and I freaked out at his boner. How many times have I seen tent poles in my career, and I've never acted so unprofessionally! He must have been so embarrassed—I think he apologized to me? I'm not even sure now—and I couldn't even muster the coherence tell him it's normal. I am the worst massage therapist ever! I'm torn between wanting to see him again (good conversation, gorgeous, I mean hello?! I'm divorced, not dead!) and being too embarrassed to face him.

Hell, I was so embarrassed, I didn't bother changing out of the underwear I soaked while giving him a massage. That probably didn't help me sleep last night. They're dry now, but . . . yuck.

I've got another 30 hours on the train.

What are the odds I'll see this guy again?

It's just one more overnight. I can do this. Hopefully tomorrow night will be better. Last night, when I was actually able to sleep, I kept dreaming I was in an earthquake. It must've been the motion of the train sneaking into my unconscious, but I still wonder if it's a sign I need to move the hell away from California already.

I guess I'll go see what the dining car is all about while I can still get breakfast . . . I totally missed dinner last night and I'm freaking starving.

The dining car had tables situated down its length on either side of the train's narrow walkway—five tables on either side, what looked like an open kitchen area, and an additional four tables on either side in the back half of the car.

Each booth accommodated parties of four and Rhea was warned that with nobody else accompanying her, she would have to share with at least one stranger once she was seated.

So she waited to be called in the busy adjacent observation car, staring at the seat in which Surfer Boy with the fantastic erection received the first part of her massage last night.

It was a good thing he wasn't there. Rhea didn't think

she needed to make such a staggering mistake so soon after finalizing her divorce; she often failed to consider her marriage had been dead for a couple years before the "D-Word" was first uttered.

Had it ever been alive, for that matter?

An attendant from the dining car called for her: "Rhea, party of one?"

She exhaled, supposing she'd better get used to that "party of one" business and followed the attendant into the dining car. Rhea was surprised to be deposited at an empty table; not just for having the table to herself but because she fully expected to be taken to one already occupied by Surfer Boy.

As she sat facing the direction of travel, she counted her blessings. *A nice quiet breakfast is what I need to set myself straight. Straighter, anyway!* Rhea was certain—it was her luck, as luck would have it—she'd have been forced to share a table and an uncomfortable meal with Surfer Boy.

She bit her lip, rested an elbow on the vibrating table, her chin on her fist and watched the New Mexico desert roll by outside the train window.

It wasn't unattractive per se, but Rhea preferred dense forest to desert. Something akin to the Pacific Northwest, perhaps, but without all the plate tectonics bullshit. Three earthquakes in excess of 6.5 magnitude in her area since she was born was three too many.

She'd never been to the Northeast and thought she should correct that. Maybe she would spend a few days sight-seeing in Chicago—while Surfer Boy visited with his memories, not as though he or anything he did factored into *her* trip at all—and take a connecting train further east.

Pennsylvania? New York? Massachusetts?

She'd heard tales of extended family out that direction but had no clue where anybody lived, nor how to contact them. Her family was expert in the art of disowning.

The sound of the car door sliding open behind Rhea got her attention; those doors were far from quiet. She turned in time to see Surfer Boy being escorted into the dining car. *Oh shit.* Her heart flew into her throat as she scanned the other tables. Those which weren't in use by parties of four were already seating three. She had ample space. *Please God no. Not here.* She prayed fervently he wouldn't be seated with her: *Oh please, please, please!*

"Excuse me ma'am, do you mind having company?" the attendant asked Rhea.

Fuck. Of course. Rhea knew the attendant was being polite but had no intention of giving her any choice in the matter.

Surfer Boy—*poor guy*—stood behind the attendant looking sheepish as hell; he had to be as miserable about the arrangement as she was.

What kind of an awful bitch would I have to be to say no? She assumed he wished she would pass on his company as much as she was considering it. "No," Rhea said, her voice thin. "I don't mind at all." She gritted her teeth and hoped it would come across as a pleasant smile.

Surfer Boy sat across from her. "'Morning."

Rhea turned her attention to the single white carnation in the hand-sized glass vase set against the train window. "Did you sleep well?" she asked, her voice still high and thin.

"I go back and forth . . . between being surprised and not surprised by how hard I slept. It's difficult to sleep well on a moving train, and their beds kinda suck. But . . ." He swallowed, then cleared his throat. "I was real relaxed."

She was desperate to not smile. *Not all of you was 'real relaxed.'*

Rhea cleared her throat. "I'm so sorry I took off like that last night. It was royally unprofessional of me. I should've told you what happened was—" *Normal? Typical?* "—something you should in no way be embarrassed about." Especially not when considering the size of his bulge. Rhea's face grew hot again, whether or not she wanted it. "As you can see by the color of my cheeks, blood will flow wherever it damn well pleases."

With a wide smile, Surfer Boy regarded his blushing companion. "That's mighty big of you."

"I could say likewise—" Rhea clapped a hand over her mouth with a squeak. What the hell was with her inability to censor herself around this guy? She hadn't had any alcohol in forever.

"So it wouldn't be a stretch to assume we're both far too uncomfortable with each other to introduce ourselves?"

She chuckled from behind her hand. "*That's* a safe bet."

He hesitated before telling her, "Please don't hide your pretty smile."

Rhea lowered her hand. "Oh. Wow."

"Do I want to know what that 'wow' was about, or will it be another joke made at my expense?"

"It's . . . been a real long time since I smiled. I mean *genuinely* smiled. Not like the 'hi, how are you,' 'oh I'm fine,' polite-but-totally-fake smile." Rhea forced herself to meet his gaze. He had such attractive eyes and a stare so attentive it made her insides tilt in exhilaration. "So. You know what *I* do. How are you paying for your own little cabin downstairs?" *Old money?*

"I robbed a bank a few years ago and I'm slowly but surely spending the small, non-sequential, unmarked bills."

Rhea's smile fell and the flush washed from her cheeks.

"Hey, didn't I tell you I'm not a creep?"

"And didn't *I* say only time would tell?"

"I'm an artist," said Surfer Boy. "And . . . one who apparently sucks at teasing."

"Better to suck at teasing than to tease at sucking." Her eyes went wide. Ribald comments were so unlike her yet she'd made more of them in the last twenty-four hours than she'd probably thought of in her entire lifetime.

When his eyebrows jumped and a smirk grew across his sexy lips, she blurted, "So you're an artist, huh?"

"Yep. Mostly I use pastels. I'll park myself on the beach and do landscapes. Lately I've been dabbling in portraiture."

"You make enough doing that to take these trips?"

"Sure." He shrugged. "I made friends with a gallery owner in Laguna Beach. He hosts my work for me, takes a surprisingly small cut of my sales, and I don't pay a penny otherwise for sky-high space rent." He smiled at Rhea pointedly. "It pays to be nice. As I told you I am."

A waiter came by to take their orders. While Surfer Boy waffled over his options after Rhea placed her order, she searched through her purse for a pen and the small notebook she kept in there for occasional reminders she liked to leave herself. The last note was nothing more than a single word scrawled in the nicest cursive she could muster: *smile*.

After the waiter left their table, Rhea slid the notebook to Surfer Boy, holding the pen out for him. "Would you draw me something?" she requested with a wicked little smirk. For added measure: "Please?"

"I suppose I owe you some thanks for a fantastic massage." He took the notebook and rested it on his lap, then took the pen and went to work.

A few moments later, he handed the open notebook to Rhea. He capped the pen with an exaggerated snap of his wrist and handed that to her as well.

Beside her single-word reminder to smile, Surfer Boy had drawn a stick figure with a smile taking up half its face. Beside it: a scribble he may have considered his signature.

"Hang onto that," he told her. With a wink came the boast: "That autograph is worth money."

Rhea couldn't stop smiling though she wasn't trying hard not to. His doodle would serve as a wonderful reminder of him long after they parted ways.

"Listen." Surfer Boy lowered his voice. "I *do* have some of my smaller pieces with me. I'm trying to get into a few art galleries in Chicago."

"I thought you said you were going to Chicago for memories."

"Oh I am. And while I'm in the area, I'll do some networking, too."

"Good luck with that."

"Thanks." Surfer Boy bobbed his head. "Will this be your first time in Chicago?"

"Yeah. I was so eager to escape, y'know, that I put all my energy into *how* I was running away, rather than into what I would actually do once I got to . . . where I was running to."

"Are you open to suggestion?"

"Absolutely."

RAYS OF SUNSHINE

"Of course I'm gonna say you need to go to Willis Tower."

"Exacerbate acrophobia, check." Despite her fear of heights, Rhea wrote *Willis Tower* into her small notebook on a fresh page.

"Maaaaybe," said Surfer Boy, his smile growing inappropriately affectionate for a woman he'd known for less than twenty-four hours, "I shouldn't suggest Adler Planetarium, then."

She jotted that down, as well. "That sort of stuff doesn't bother me."

"Got a fear of sharks?"

"Nope. Cass is the—oh, what's the word?" Rhea tapped her pen to her lips in thought. She was well aware Surfer Boy was staring at them. She drew her bottom lip behind her upper teeth and bit down gently. He exhaled. "Is that galeophobe?"

He shrugged. "'Unno."

"Anyway, she's afraid of sharks, not me."

"Go see Shedd Aquarium, then."

Rhea wrote it down. "Anything else?"

"Navy Pier, but go at night. Have a Chicago Dog at Wrigley Field."

Their meals arrived.

"If you have any time," he added, squeezing preserves onto his toast from a small rectangular plastic tub, "go see Millennium Park and the Art Institute."

Rhea made notes of those and lifted her mug, the pen clinking against its side. "You just added those to sound artsy." She sipped her coffee, struggling not to make a face; it wasn't Starbucks.

"If I was going to sound *artsy*, I'd have offered to accompany you to the art exhibits as an unofficial docent or something."

The coffee mug came down a bit harder than Rhea intended. It was silent for far too long under the weight of stares that challenged each other. ". . . *are* you offering?"

He jammed the toast into his mouth, pointing to it in indication he couldn't answer.

Rhea tended her food with far more decorum, yet she couldn't resist the gentle tease: "I'll bet that toast tastes better than a foot does."

He swallowed and cleared his throat before replying, "I bet you'd be surprised. You can make most things edible with a liberal application of jelly."

She cut her sausage link into quarters, sparing a passing thought to Mark. "Not *everything*."

"That sounds like a story if ever I heard one."

Tell hot train stranger about my aversion to orally servicing my ex-husband, no matter how he coated his genitalia in sweets to entice me? No, thanks. "It is. And that's all you're getting of it!"

"So . . . Are you enjoying your first train trip so far?" Surfer Boy asked.

"It's been . . . Different. The guy behind me has one hell of a snore."

"And now you see why I get my own room on years my art has sold well. That, and the coach seats are impossible to sleep in." He added casually, "Although . . . it might not be so objectionable if I had a personal masseuse to help me rub out the kinks."

It wouldn't be so objectionable to help him rub one out. Rhea fought with her blush and lost. *Dammit.* At least she was successfully holding a guilty smile at bay.

"I didn't mean it like that . . ."

But Rhea *did* mean it; that was terrifying. Her mind wandered to how she might trick him into letting her give him a hand job. She'd never given a happy ending with her massages but there was a first time for everything. "We masseuses prefer to be called massage therapists."

Surfer Boy groaned, his head dropping back. "Is there any other way I may inadvertently offend you before you're done with breakfast?"

Her plate was somehow half-empty. "It may offend me if you didn't share your portfolio with me."

"I'm not comfortable taking it out in coach." He winked at her.

Rhea smirked. "You're not an exhibitionist. Too bad." She certainly could have been under the right conditions.

Any. Any conditions, if I'm being honest.

He made another groan, his head falling forward this time. He covered his face. "Oh my *God.*"

"Hey." Her voice was soft. "All joking aside, I don't blame you for being protective of your art. There are some skeevy people out there and probably all of them concentrated in coach. Nobody seems to want to chat with me. I mean . . . Except you. And . . . You're not exactly riding coach, big spender."

He dropped his hands, flashing Rhea a charming smile. "Their loss. Don't let that deter you from taking other train trips. I ordinarily find some interesting folks on my travels. This particular trip? I met a sexy . . ." His next words were deliberate. ". . . *massage therapist.*"

Rhea was smiling so hard she feared she might split her lip. "What are the odds *two* massage therapists would be on the same train?"

"Oh just take the compliment already."

"That's easier said than done." She forced herself to add: "But thanks."

"You're welcome to come to my roomette to look through my portfolio once we're done eating."

"I'd like that."

After breakfast, Rhea followed Surfer Boy down to his small cabin. It was significantly less peculiar to do that now than it was last night—which was, in itself, peculiar.

Then again, Rhea was traveling alone, which she'd never previously done. The constant swaying and jostling of the train didn't faze her so much anymore. And she wanted to grab that man's ass a little bit. *I could pinch it and explain to him afterward it looked tight and in desperate need of some kneading.* Because it *did* look tight in fact, and her desire dictated it *did* require loads of kneading. That was factual.

Surfer Boy moved a large, flat, black briefcase from where he'd left it halfway buried by the sheets he'd slept in overnight while she suffered in coach, and maneuvered his bed into a pair of seats situated across from each other. He sat and Rhea squeezed in to sit across from him.

"Hey, would it freak you out if I closed the door?" he asked.

Rhea shook her head, though she wondered if she should at least think better of it. Space was so tight in the roomette she imagined there wasn't enough room for him to murder her anyway. Hell, there wasn't enough room in there to grab his ass without employing some Kama Sutra style techniques.

He slid the door closed and opened the portfolio, resting the back cover on his lap and the front cover against the roomette door. "How about that, it was facing the right direction! Like USB drives: fifty percent chance of plugging it in right, have it upside-down ninety percent of the time."

She laughed the laugh of someone who knew that annoyance all too well. "First world problems, am I right?" Rhea leaned forward, resting her elbows on her thighs.

She was unsurprised to see Surfer Boy created a lot of seascapes; there was even one with landmarks she recognized from her occasional trips from Irvine to Laguna Beach. His oil pastel landscapes had the appearance of brilliantly colored photographs with a soft-blur filter applied to them. They were nothing short of stunning. How he could ever have a bad year selling his art, she didn't know.

Surfer Boy Who-Actually-Maybe-Was-The-Artist-He-Claimed-To-Be-And-Then-Some—whose nickname would remain Surfer Boy regardless of its inaccuracy because Rhea fancied it that way in addition to its being far shorter—was talented. His artwork demonstrated a keen eye for color and a gentle touch.

He also had a few landscapes in his possession on which he'd used watercolors.

"These are fantastic," said Rhea. "You're amazingly talented!"

"Well . . . Don't be too disappointed by my portraits. I haven't been doing portraits for as long as I've done landscapes."

If she were to judge by his expression, it wasn't false humility; not unless he was—in addition to being a great artist—a great actor as well.

His portraits didn't have the refined touch of his landscapes but they were still excellent in their own right. Rhea couldn't even begin to figure out how such things were done.

"This is my mom," Surfer Boy said of the second to last piece in his portfolio. "I don't think I've ever worked so hard on anything in my life."

"She's a beautiful lady." Rhea smiled, glancing at him. "I can see a resemblance."

"She . . . *was*."

"Oh—oh my God, I am so sorry—" She impulsively rested her hand on his knee.

He placed his hand atop hers; it felt so natural.

They were silent for a while, the beautiful eyes of Surfer Boy's deceased mother gazing up from his painting and looking full of life.

Because she couldn't think of anything else to say, Rhea filled the silence with the stupidest words ever: "I'm recently divorced."

"I'm sorry." He paused. "Your choice or his? Or . . . *hers*?"

She snorted. "It was a him. And it was mutual. He showed interest in me when we met in high school. I jumped at the opportunity, although I wasn't attracted to him. When what little interest he had in me waned, we were left with . . . a condo." Rhea was blushing. "You totally didn't need to hear all that." *Or any of it, for that matter.*

"So you're over him?"

"Oh *yeah*. Though I now have the lingering weirdness where I know the state said we were married. Next time? Next time, I'm marrying in a church."

Surfer Boy squeezed her hand. "Good for you."

"Good for me?"

"For not being scared away from the institution by a bad experience."

"Oh. It's the fatal flaw of a hopeless romantic I guess."

She pulled her hand back to turn to the last page in his portfolio. Her jaw dropped. "*Oh my God!*"

"It's—real sucky, I know—I—I never meant for you to see it—"

The last piece was a distinct departure from the rest of his artwork: a graphic novel style pencil sketch of Rhea as Buffy the Vampire Slayer.

"This—it's—*amazing*—" She was otherwise at a loss for words. Rhea glanced at him; he was inches away, his body heat searing into her.

The train slowed into the Albuquerque, New Mexico station.

"*I need to kiss you*," she whispered.

Surfer Boy closed his portfolio and set it against the window in wordless concession.

Rhea pressed her lips to his, ignoring the noise of the passengers detraining right outside the cabin door. Surfer Boy's lips were soft and reverent as he obliged her.

That wouldn't be nearly enough. However, she leaned back. "*Wow.*" Never, not in all her years with Mark, had any kiss excited her as did the brief closed-mouth smooch she'd shared with a man whose name she didn't know.

"I guess it's safe to tell you now, I think you're hot as hell," said Surfer Boy.

"To be perfectly fair, I . . . I dreamt about you and your hard-on last night." She shook her head. "I lost my shit over it because it was this unexpected but flattering thing, and *oh, my God* . . ."

"I couldn't stop thinking about how I freaked you out."

"Well if it makes you feel any better, it wasn't your stiffy that scared me. Not exactly. It was . . . It was how badly I wanted to play with it."

Surfer Boy hesitated. "You over that?"

"The fear? Or the desire?"

He chuckled. "Both, I guess."

"Totally. And . . . not at all."

There were shouts from outside the train. It was much too easy to forget they weren't inhabiting their own planet. Rhea sat back with a shaky breath. "What's going on out there?"

"It's what Amtrak calls a layover. The train sits here for an hour or so. They turn off the a/c and the less lazy passengers take the opportunity to get out and look around Albuquerque."

"Is it worthwhile to get out?"

"Not since the tamale people stopped selling here."

Rhea frowned; that must have made sense to him at least.

"The view in my roomette is *far* better, too."

"You're biased." She chuckled. "Y'know, since I complimented your dick."

"I'm only partially biased." Surfer Boy opened the blue curtains over the roomette window.

Rhea made a face when she saw what was outside the train: the wrong side of the tracks.

"Folks sell stuff on the platform. Poke your head outside, get some fresh air. You'll regret not taking advantage of the stop if you don't do it."

She considered it. Surfer Boy said they'd be there for an hour and she figured she wouldn't have another chance to see Albuquerque. On the other hand, Rhea thought they could give a whole new meaning to the term *layover*. On the *other* other hand, it was only an hour at the station, versus another twenty-seven hours stuck on the train with nowhere else to go, and nothing else to do but make out.

Make out . . . or whatever.

"Will you still be here if I step off the train for a bit?" asked Rhea. *What am I doing? I got on the train for adventure, not to find a man.*

He thought briefly. "Y'know what? I'm gonna step out, too. We'll meet back here around noon?"

"Okay." Rhea grabbed her purse and led the way off the train.

Surfer Boy winked at her before sprinting away down the platform.

She watched him run, exhaling a breath she was certain she'd been holding from the minute he plopped down in the observation car beside her. That was a hell of a long time to not breathe.

A cluster of passengers on the train platform pored over card tables lined up against a brick wall as well as blankets spread out on the ground. The items being peddled were variations on a theme—primarily Southwestern style turquoise jewelry. Rhea guessed the merchants were Albuquerque locals who took advantage of Amtrak's restless riders during these layovers.

It was a massive relief when nothing they brought to market appealed to Rhea as she didn't want to deal with the temptation of wasting her money on frivolous expenditures. A pretty turquoise necklace: frivolous. Admission to an art museum recommended by a hot stranger on the train? That was compulsory.

She walked to the door nearest Surfer Boy's room and there she paced, considering what she would write the next time she had the opportunity to sit with her laptop. What would she say once she got on Facebook?

Rhea smiled; for the first time since she publicly admitted her marriage was dead, she didn't care what people would say. Yes, she hoped her friends and acquaintances would be happy to hear from her, and happy she wasn't miserable following her divorce. But she found it far more important she could post something happy and not be 'faking it.'

It would be the first time she hadn't faked something regarding her love life since—

Ever.

Rhea blinked. That she considered a kiss with a stranger anything related to a love life was unnerving, not to mention sad.

She would not allow herself to get attached to this poor guy. She might let him occupy her time while they were trapped in a seventy-mile-per-hour sardine can with nothing better to do than to have idle chat that danced around deeper issues they both battled. But once they got off in Chicago, she would shake his hand, thank him for making her first train ride much more enjoyable than it would have been otherwise, and high-tail it to her hotel without a lingering thought of him.

Rhea debated if she should give him her email address.

Oh, what would that accomplish? This was, if it needed classification—which it didn't—a one-night-stand. A one-night-stand at most; Rhea was no expert on such things, but she was under the impression one-night-stands involved an actual sex act. *A kiss* didn't qualify.

Perhaps Rhea was giving some serious consideration to getting into Surfer Boy's pants, but she was more likely to leave it at a single enthralling kiss. That was more her speed.

She saw Surfer Boy step onto the platform down by the train's engine.

Old Rhea would stop at a single kiss.

Train-riding, chopping-off-her-hair, abandoning-her-life-because-why-the-hell-not Rhea was unsure she would stop there. Surfer Boy was so handsome it was unreal. And in a slim-cut T-shirt highlighted by the midday sun, his chest and arms looked as good as they'd felt, maybe even better. She'd made herself pay more attention to giving him an awesome massage than to studying his physique, which may have been a judgment error. It *did* pose the question: why was an artist so well-built?

"Hey. You like Kit Kats?" Surfer Boy asked Rhea as he approached. "I stopped by 7-11 for a couple things but didn't want to return without something for you. What kind of asshole does that?"

Mark did such things to her all the time but she knew he was an asshole and she'd known it for years.

Rhea herself preferred Reese's Peanut Butter Cups to Kit Kats, but chocolate was chocolate *was chocolate*; all these quibbles being beside the inarguable fact that the gesture was so considerate it hurt.

In light of new evidence, maybe she'd give him her email address after all. Laguna Beach wasn't so far from Irvine—if she was going to stay in Southern California.

He'd make a halfway decent guy to hang out with sometimes, she thought.

"Thanks," said Rhea. "They're great."

"I *almost* got you Reese's but then I worried you might

have a peanut allergy so I figured Kit Kats were safer."

Rhea swallowed a deep sigh. Of course he did. And of *course* he did.

He took a long breath. "I overestimated how far away the convenience store is and ran when I didn't have to. Not to sound out-of-shape for a girl I'm trying to impress, but I didn't stretch it out and now I've got a cramp in my thigh."

She gave him a sympathetic smile. "All for a Kit Kat bar for me?"

"That . . . and a couple other necessities." Surfer Boy gestured to the train. "Ladies, first."

Rhea led him onto the train. "You're watching my ass, aren't you?"

"I could say 'don't flatter yourself.'" He waited until she sat in his roomette and he closed the door— "But that'd be a lie."—followed by closing the curtains on the windows.

"Y'know," said Rhea thoughtfully, "I could help your muscle in spasm with another massage. I feel like I owe it to you for embarrassing you last night. That was uncool of me."

Surfer Boy's eyes twinkled delightfully. "Don't feel obligated to, but I'd be a moron to turn down your offer."

"Shall I start with your leg or work my way there, top-down?"

"Do whatever works best for you."

Rhea smiled. "You'd make a kick-ass client."

With a bit of maneuvering, Surfer Boy turned around and knelt on his seat. There was the glancing of his hand against her knee, and as she repositioned herself, her breast brushed by his shoulder. Neither commented on the contact, but each touch left Rhea tingling. Her mind churned away, searching for more excuses to touch him aside the massage. *What would he say if I asked if I could touch it?* She shook the thought from her head. *He'd call me crazy.*

When she could dedicate her full attention to the subject, she thought she should thank God for leading her to her current career—for this point in time alone. Who cares about the new babies her touch soothed? Screw the women whose pregnancy aches she'd eased, or the sports stars she helped get back onto their respective fields of play. It was all about finding an innocent means to a sexy end with a man she didn't know from Adam.

Now it was about the Actually-An-Artist Surfer Boy on the train with her. Rhea began with his neck. He tensed at her touch, or maybe it was from the jostling of the train as it continued its journey to Chicago. She slid her fingertips into his short hair, massaging from the base of his skull to his crown.

"Oh," he groaned, "this is so much better than what my barber does."

"And it doesn't hurt that it's a woman doing it to you?"

"My barber's a woman, too. The difference being she doesn't know what the hell she's doing without her clippers in hand."

Rhea gave him a long caress down the back of his head for the flattery.

"And although she's pretty, I'm not wildly attracted to her."

Rhea paused.

". . . That was a compliment."

"I know," she whispered. After a hard swallow, she added in an even tinier voice: "Thanks."

"I'm gonna go out on a limb and guess your ex wasn't the complimentary type."

Rhea's hands traveled to Surfer Boy's shoulders where she transitioned into a deep tissue massage. He groaned, bracing himself against the seat. She otherwise failed to acknowledge his statement. She preferred to leave Mark out of this.

Unlike last night, Rhea watched what she touched, the way his T-shirt pulled and puckered over his skin. She clenched her jaw, making a conscious effort to keep her arousal at bay. But—as they both demonstrated previously—blood was apt to flow wherever it damn well pleased. Her core throbbed despite her efforts to repress it; the best she could do was to focus on him with what little concentration she had to spare.

She alternated between deep tissue and Swedish

massages, at times doing nothing more than running her hands over his muscles and lamenting he hadn't taken off his shirt first.

"God you are so good," Surfer Boy murmured. "But . . . my thigh's really cramped."

"Oh, sure, sure, I'm on it. Face me again."

He repositioned himself so he was sitting in the seat the way its designers intended. Rhea leaned forward and rested her hands on his knees, her V-neck T-shirt gapping away from her chest. When Surfer Boy inhaled, she saw his eyes locked onto her exposed skin. "That's . . . *swell,*" he breathed.

Her gaze dropped to his crotch: That was swell, too. She smiled. *Maybe last night's hard-on wasn't as accidental as he pretended.* "So which muscle is giving you grief?" Her hands slid along the length of both thighs, stopping so close to his crotch that she felt the fabric of his shorts straining over his erection.

"That one." Surfer Boy nodded to his left leg.

She slowly assessed his muscle spasm with both hands, her smiling broadening. "You *are* aware I can totally tell you're faking your cramp."

"Well how else was I gonna get you to touch me there and still look cool about it?"

"You don't need to play these games." Her thumb slid across his zipper. He pushed back from beneath it. "I'm alone in a confined space with you already. You closed the door and the curtains and I didn't protest either." Rhea raised her eyebrows pointedly with a smirk.

Surfer Boy lifted her face by the chin, meeting her gaze. "Kiss me."

She leaned in, pressing her lips to his; she swore there was a spark between them, but it was equally possible the result of static electricity. Albuquerque—or the air aboard the train, anyway—was dry.

He tilted his head, gliding a hand up the nape of her neck. Rhea sighed and she felt him smile against her lips.

". . . What?" she asked, pulling away.

"I liked that sound. I wanna hear you make it again."

"I'm sure there are plenty of ways to make me sigh. Or .

. . ." Rhea bit her lip. "To get me to make even better sounds."

"Is . . . that . . . an invitation?"

Oh just screw me already! She chose a more diplomatic reply instead: "As a general rule, I don't touch my clients' willies."

"As a general rule?"

"Allow me to translate . . . I've *never* done that." With a coy little smile, she added, "I also don't go around kissing strangers. You're the exception to all those rules, so . . ."

"So." Surfer Boy brushed back her hair, sliding his hand down her neck to her collarbone. Further down he went until he cupped her left breast through her shirt and squeezed it with restraint.

She moaned, her head tipping back. "*Yes*."

"Oh that *is* a better sound." Surfer Boy kissed the side of her neck. His kisses turned to sucking and she leaned into him with a deeper moan.

Rhea was having the inarguable need to be free of her underwear; not so much from her desperation for sex, but because the growing wet spot was uncomfortable. With a fleeting glance, she saw he was having a similar pre-cum issue. And the sight of the small dark circle on his shorts brought with it an obnoxious realization. "*Oh*."

"O—oh?" He frowned.

"I've got an IUD, but—and I'm sure you're clean, please don't be offended—I don't have a condom, and—"

"I *do*?" Surfer Boy fished around in his right pocket and produced a wrapped Trojan. "The Kit Kat wasn't the only thing I bought at the 7-11."

Rhea blinked. "You just *knew* you were gonna get into my pants, didn't you?" She tried to sound offended at his cockiness.

"What can I say?" He returned her feigned offense with an aloof shrug. "I'm an optimist."

"Or I'm that easy."

He answered firmly, "*I'm. An. Optimist.*"

"Fine. Whatever. Want help on with that?" Rhea flicked the Trojan packet.

"Are—" Surfer Boy faltered. "Are you ready? That was

fast."

"Hey. I'm easy." With a playful smile, she unzipped her jeans and pushed them below her butt. She took the fingers of his left hand and guided them along her panties, his fingers dipping between her lips through the damp fabric.

If there was any bit of Surfer Boy left unaroused, that action vanquished it. His voice was husky and starved: "*Fuck*, babe. I need you."

She shimmied the rest of the way out of her denim while Surfer Boy opened his fly and manipulated his swollen cock out of his boxers.

Rhea's breath caught in her throat at the sight of it. *What for the love of all things sacred am I doing?*

She was opening the condom packet and unrolling the rubber down his shaft, that's what she was doing.

She was marveling at his firmness, that's what she was doing.

She was smiling at the way it seemed to beckon her as she encircled it with her hand.

Surfer Boy grabbed her around the waist, pulling her toward him. She straddled him on his seat, sliding against the length of his erection with her slit. Her panties still being on made the sensation even better. They moaned in unison.

Rhea rubbed up and down him, emulating as best she could the lap dances she'd seen at strip clubs. She probably looked ridiculous but he wasn't watching anyway; his head was pressed into the seat padding behind him, his eyes squeezed shut. The tip of his cock was spreading her lips through her underwear's fabric. "Do you like this?" she whispered.

"God yes."

"Do you want me?"

"So fucking much, please."

She chuckled. "I could be a tease." And she was teasing herself at least as much as she was teasing him. Her desire was palpable and she slipped the soaked crotch of her underwear off to the side.

"I'm willing to bet you're not. Teases don't go this far for sport." Surfer Boy squeezed her thighs and ran his hands along them, grasping her butt. "Your ass is divine." He manipulated her hips and thrust into her.

She gasped.

"Oh—*shit*—! Did I hurt you?"

"No, no." Rhea lifted most of the way off him before lowering herself again. The fabric of her underwear slid against her clit, shooting sparks all through her body.

"You're so tight." He exhaled. "I wouldn't have been surprised."

"Shut up and screw me already. Please!"

Surfer Boy kissed her hard as she gyrated against him. If only she had the soundtrack to go with releasing her inner adult film star. Rhea's moans and panting would suffice where porn groove lacked.

When he didn't respond with an explosive climax within a minute of penetrating her, Rhea went still.

He grunted. "Why'd you stop?"

"You—you liked that? Why haven't you come yet?"

His brows furrowed. "Because we just got started? You're gonna have to work me harder than that, Sunshine." He yanked her to his chest, whispering in her ear, "I'm gonna make you *ache*." Surfer Boy rested his hands on her hips, guiding her motions.

Rhea, comfortable against his wall of muscle, wrapped her arms around his shoulders and marveled in the friction between them. How great it was to be on top for once!

Surfer Boy kissed her shoulder and peppered kisses on the side of her neck, Rhea turning her head when they reached her jaw; their lips met. She beckoned him inside with coy flicks of her tongue and rewarded his reciprocation with a deep moan.

He guided her to ride him harder and faster while the train slowed into a depot. And as it stopped, Rhea's climax gained momentum at break-neck speed. So he kissed her harder, muffling her moans.

People rummaged about in the luggage area on the other side of the roomette door, loud chatter leaking into Surfer Boy's cabin.

"Oh God I'm coming," she panted against his lips. "I

can't stop—" Rhea's back arched, her head kicking back with an elated cry.

Surfer Boy's climax followed hers; he burrowed his face between her breasts and moaned into her shirt.

They fell silent, catching their breath.

The loud chattering didn't seem so loud anymore.

"Wow . . ." he whispered. "You're a hellion."

Rhea glanced toward the roomette door, realizing it was closed but unlocked. Thank God nobody walked in on them. "You think anyone heard us?"

"Well . . ." Surfer Boy frowned. "If we can hear *them* . . ."

"*Oh my God.*" She hoisted herself off him, slipping the uncomfortably wet crotch of her panties in place with a grimace while he tended the used condom.

"No reason to freak out . . . *Maybe* the folks outside were elsewhere all this time. Maybe anyone who could've heard us got off in—" He checked his smartphone before zipping his shorts. "Lamy, I guess." Surfer Boy looked at Rhea, still without her pants. "You're *really* a massage therapist?"

"*Yes* I'm really a massage therapist." She perched on the seat across from him so the wet spot wouldn't rest on the cushion; not for sanitary reasons as much as for her comfort. Rhea considered how miserable it would be to put her jeans on with wet underwear beneath them. She needed a change regardless of who was outside the roomette and what they had to think of her. "Why? Didn't I prove myself to you? Or are you hunting for another free massage?"

"Oh—no—I wouldn't imagine massage therapy would be so great for your physique. You could be a model with curves like those."

A plus-sized model. Even in her fittest or leanest times, she would have been considered plus-sized. It wasn't a negative thought, just a factual representation of that industry. "Yeah, well, how does an artist look the way *you* do?"

Surfer Boy smiled. "I work on the beach. Running over sand, playing beach volleyball . . . Excellent work-outs, pretty much every day. Can't beat nature with a gym, if you ask me."

Rhea nodded. "I can see it. And for what it's worth? Give deep tissue massages eight hours a day, five days a week. See what *that* does for your body."

"Any chance I could?"

She watched his expression, trying to decipher an ambiguous statement. *Is he asking for a work-week-long massage or—*

"I'll bet your tits are magnificent, we've got about twenty-five more hours before Chicago, and I've got two more condoms."

Rhea's eyebrows jumped.

He flinched. "I . . . realize how that must've sounded. They came in a three-pack. Dammit, I'm sorry—"

Rhea got to her feet, teetering with the swaying of the train. "I need to grab something from my luggage."

"You're not coming back, are you? I wouldn't blame you."

She bit her lip. ". . . Surfer Boy . . ."

"*Surfer Boy?*" he asked with a crooked smile.

"That's what I figured you were before you told me you're an artist. I'm sure you've got a name for me."

"Sunshine."

Rhea snorted.

"What?"

If she decided to give him her email address after all, he'd understand why she snorted. "I'll be honest with you. That was the first orgasm I had that wasn't the direct result of my own hand."

"—since . . .?"

"Ever."

"Since *ever?*" Surfer Boy gasped. "Whoa."

"And you're telling me I have the chance for two more of those? I'm coming back." Rhea slid open the roomette door and stepped out into the train corridor. Two women of advanced age sitting in the cabin at the end of the car had left their door open and watched her with utmost disdain. She slunk into Surfer Boy's roomette and dropped to her seat with dark cheeks. Rhea slid the door closed with a heavy sigh. "They were listening. I'm pretty sure I even heard a '*well*

I never!'"

"Well." Surfer Boy grinned wickedly. "If they 'never,' I'm willing to bet they're wildly jealous of you. That O sounded amazing. And hey. If you're too embarrassed to go out, you're welcome to stay here with me. I'm enjoying your company."

The corner of Rhea's mouth crooked upward. "Mind if I open the shades?" She tipped her head to the cabin window because opening the curtain on the roomette door wasn't happening.

"Sure, sure. This area isn't much to look at, though." He spread open the curtains for her.

The New Mexico desert was unimpressive where the train was traveling: a few hills with sparse brush and nothing much else.

"Oh."

"It gets better," Surfer Boy promised, "going into Colorado."

Rhea nodded, gazing out at the terrain. For a while, she watched, her mind going silent. When she snapped out of her meditation, she looked at Surfer Boy. His head was bowed, a book open on his lap.

Mark had never been into cerebral endeavors like reading; he preferred to fish with his friends or spend money at Barona without her. Rhea had no idea what he played at the casino but judging by their bank account after his trips there, he wasn't much good at it. Thankfully he seldom went.

It crossed her mind on any number of occasions he could have been cheating on her. She hadn't cared enough about him—or their union—to investigate. While her ex-husband had, ironically, missed the mark on a great many aspects of their relationship, Rhea hadn't invested much effort either.

It was hard not to compare Mark with Surfer Boy. Well, what she knew of Surfer Boy, anyway.

Rhea wondered what the point of this whole exercise even was. She was happier now—on the train with a sexy stranger and without any ties to her life—than she had been for years in what masqueraded as domestic bliss. A twinge of guilt struck her; she should have at least missed her family.

Her companion remained engrossed in his reading and turned a page.

Was she staring at a chance encounter whose memory would always bring her a smile? Or was this the beginning of a life-long friendship? Maybe he was even future husband number two.

Surfer Boy glanced up following the little peep Rhea hadn't meant to make. He smiled. "I hope you don't mind I was reading. You looked like you didn't want to be disturbed."

"I, uh—" Rhea shrugged. "I was enjoying the scenery." With a chuckle, she added, "The scenery being what it is. So whatcha reading?"

He flashed her the cover. "*Stranger in a Strange Land.* It's one of my favorites. I always bring it with me on these trips."

"Heinlein." Rhea bobbed her head in appreciation of his choice. "Nice."

"Don't tell me. 'S one of your favorites, too?"

"What are we, in middle school?" Her smile grew and she bounced in her seat like a first grader eating a chocolate cupcake. "Let's say our favorite subject in school on the count of three!"

Surfer Boy stuck out his tongue. "It would have been cool to share tastes in literature. That's all." He muttered, "I've yet to find another person who's as into Heinlein as I am."

"I enjoy Heinlein, yes, and *Stranger in a Strange Land* is my favorite of his. I generally prefer lighter fare."

"Romance?"

It startled Rhea there was no judgment whatsoever in his guess. Everyone sneered at the genre when she admitted to reading it. Of course, aforementioned 'everyone' didn't know the full truth: "Erotica." And she had no idea why she'd told *him*.

"You're fun," Surfer Boy surmised.

Nor did Rhea have any idea why she was admitting this: ". . . I like porn, too."

He closed his book and set it aside, leaning in, rapt. "Tell me more!"

She laughed. It was a good, solid laugh: the kind from which it took several deep breaths to recover.

Surfer Boy smiled, though he asked, "What? It's not every day I meet a girl who watches porn, let alone admits to liking it."

She sobered. "I'm doing a lot of things I don't do every day. Like . . . anonymous sex."

"My name's—"

Rhea clapped her hand over his mouth. "*Don't.*"

His eyebrows quirked but she felt his lips form a smile against her palm.

"I . . . Kinda . . . Like it better this way." She pulled back and added sheepishly, "I hope that's okay."

He nodded. She couldn't decide if he was appreciative or a bit disappointed. "Can I have your name?"

"Joan."

"*Liar.*"

"I liked your nickname for me. It reminded me of a time when I liked myself better."

"Sunshine it is, then. Sounds a bit . . . whore-y, though."

Rhea stuck out her tongue at him but didn't argue his assessment.

"Would you at least consider calling me Artist Boy?"

"Sorry. You're stuck with Surfer Boy. I like it too much."

He sighed with a dramatic shrug. "I guess I'm just gonna have to learn to surf when I get home." He winked. "After all, I can't be misrepresented by my own name."

"You have a girlfriend." Rhea swallowed hard. "Don't you."

"Are you applying for the position?"

His casual demeanor toward that concept put her off a little.

"No. I just can't see why such an awesome guy is single."

Surfer Boy leaned back and closed his eyes. "Sally didn't like how I wasn't a manly man. She also didn't like that she wasn't the center of my world."

Rhea frowned; he'd been ridiculously attentive. To *her*, anyway. Mark could have certainly made the same inattentive gripes of her.

"When I'm working on a painting, it can be . . . difficult . . . to get my attention. A few too many times, I guess, I failed to drop everything to cater to her random whims . . . and she dumped me. Before her, it was Tracy. That chick kept a lot of secrets from me and was always a bit too attentive of other guys for my tastes." He added hastily, "I don't have hang-ups about sex—obviously, right—but if I'm exclusive with a girl, well . . . Don't be fucking my friends behind my back. Common courtesy y'know?"

"Mark hated to spend time with me," countered Rhea. "I don't need for my man to be there twenty-four, seven. In fact, I prefer my space. It's hard to have a relationship with someone who is *never* around and who takes no interest in anything you do. He knew I was a massage therapist and that's about it. He took advantage of it, too. Not by getting free massages from me, mind you! He preferred to get discounted massages at the office where I work. He . . . always asked for Amanda."

"What an asshole."

"Outside my job, he knew nothing about me." Rhea shook her head. "He rarely bothered to comment on my Facebook status updates with anything significant. Never replied to my tweets. Between him and my family, I'd pretty well convinced myself no one wanted me to talk."

"How did you end up with such a jerk, anyway?"

She took a deep breath. "He was the only one in high school who showed any interest in me."

"Oh come *on*!" Surfer Boy flailed at her. "Bullshit nobody was interested in you! Not unless you attended the Braille Institute or something!"

Rhea hesitated. "Have you seen *The Princess Diaries*?"

He laughed, but apologized for doing so.

"I wasn't *dorky*," Rhea defended herself. Except she kind of was. "I didn't have contact lenses back then and my glasses were . . . Let's say they were unflattering. They were what my parents could afford, not what actually worked with my face and hairstyle." Her hairstyle, of course, being the blunt cut provided by her father himself rather than by an actual stylist. And he'd been plenty vocal that he thought no glasses looked good on her so they didn't waste time trying to find any. "And I wore hand-me-downs. From my *brothers*."

Again, Surfer Boy laughed. "No."

"Who would make this crap up?"

"Someone looking for a laugh? Someone who *got* laughs from it?"

Rhea glanced out the window. "My therapists thought I was joking, too." She regarded him in time to see the blood drain from his face. With an impish grin, she nudged his foot with hers. "That *was* for laughs."

He mustered a weak smile. "Phew."

"There was only the *one* therapist."

After several minutes, Surfer Boy ventured a comment. "Your ex will be sorry for losing you."

Doubtful. Rhea again looked out the window as the train slowed into a station. "I never realized there was a Las Vegas in New Mexico. Weird." There was a long silence before she ventured what seemed to be an unrelated remark. "Sex was always over *real* quick. He was in it for his own climax."

"Ohhh," said Surfer Boy in realization. "That's why you were confused when it took me so long to come. In his defense, they claim a guy who comes quickly has an evolutionary advantage over those of us who've mastered the art of prolonging ejaculation."

"They?" she asked, her face hot. Even her ears burned.

"Yeah. The mystery 'they' who say these sorts of things." He laughed. "If you ask me, it makes better sense us guys with a shorter rebound time have the advantage."

Rhea watched as the train departed Las Vegas.

"So you like porn and erotica." Surfer Boy leaned in again, resting his forearms across his lap. "And you write, too?"

"I keep a journal. I doubt any real writer would consider that legitimate writing."

"What else can you tell me?"

"Well . . ." Rhea took a deep breath. "I prefer coffee to tea. I like my sodas flat."

He wrinkled his nose.

"I know, it's gross. Well, not to me. I'm a Sagittarius—which may or may not matter depending upon your personal beliefs on how the alignment of celestial bodies affects us—I like lilies, and long walks through dense forests. Well I like the concept. I've never gotten to do that but I imagine I'd enjoy it a lot. I listen to things like Fall Out Boy and Linkin Park during the day—when I'm not at work, I mean—and I like falling asleep to Mozart."

"And you're from—"

"Orange County originally. You?"

"New York. I moved to Orange County when I was eighteen. Fell in love with the beach."

"What else?" Rhea asked.

"I like playing volleyball and tennis. I was picked on mercilessly in school because I never learned to ice skate. I watch the Red Wings. They're an—"

"Ice hockey team." Her eyes narrowed. "*I know.*"

"Shit!" Surfer Boy laughed. "Lemme guess: you're an Anaheim Sucks fan?"

Rhea found the situation a little less funny than he did. "Quack. Fucking. Quack."

"Selanne sucks."

"You're just jealous he hasn't moved to your team to decay with the rest of the *Dead* Wings before he retires."

"Dead Wings. I've never heard that before." Surfer Boy was smiling, but he rolled his eyes. They regarded each other in strained silence. "God you're hot. Wanna go grab lunch?"

"Sure." She reached for the door. "*One* last thing on the topic of ice hockey, though."

"Mmm?"

"Kiss my fat ass."

"Bend over and I'll do more than kiss it."

Rhea was sorely tempted to see if he would if she complied. Instead, she slid the cabin door open and took a step outside. The living fossils at the end of the car were still there, still with their door open. And still with their stink-eyes. She retreated into Surfer Boy's roomette, bumping into him. "Sorry," she whispered.

He shrugged it off, taking the unabashed opportunity to cop a feel.

"Looks like I'm stuck here 'til the judgmental bags go to sleep or get off the train."

"We can have them bring our meal here if you want."

Rhea blinked. "Wait—*what?*"

"Cabins get room service if we want it. When they come around for dining car reservations, we order our meals and they'll bring 'em down here."

"Yeah, that tears it. Next time I take the train, I'm springing for a sleeper."

"I've always thought they were worthwhile."

Rhea settled on her seat; Surfer Boy did the same. He motioned to her feet. "Why don't you put those up here?"

"Okay . . ." Rhea kicked off her sneakers and rested her feet on the sliver of Surfer Boy's seat beside his right thigh.

He moved her feet from the seat to his lap, rubbing them through her socks. "No judgment," he requested. "I'm not a professional."

Rhea took a deep breath; that was the first time anyone had done that for her. "I honestly can't decide if this is some sneaky reverse-psychology punishment or karmic apology."

"Maybe it's nothing more than some nice guy who kinda sorta maybe wants back in your pants a little bit?"

She closed her eyes, smiling. "If that's true, I appreciate his honesty."

"Does that score him any brownie points?"

Rhea pulled her right foot from his hand, pressing her toes into his crotch gently. She rolled her ankle. "It might . . ." Her head cocked and she gave him a wicked smile.

"You keep that up, I'm not gonna be able to concentrate on you."

She shrugged, feeling his manhood push back against the ball of her foot.

There was a knock on the door. *"Taking reservations for dinner,"* said the attendant outside.

RAYS OF SUNSHINE

"Oh—yeah—" Surfer Boy struggled, knocking Rhea's feet to the floor and grabbing a pillow to cover his lap. He was blushing so hard, she imagined that's how he looked after a day in the sun. He slid the door open, telling the attendant, "We're ordering room service."

The attendant smiled without a hint of suspicion and replied, "I'll return for your order."

Rhea leaned out of the room, peering down the corridor. As the attendant leaned into a neighboring room, she caught sight of the old ladies shaking their heads at her in disapproval when their eyes met. She straightened with a sigh. *I suppose there are worse places to be trapped.* "Do you know what you want?"

He looked sheepish as he replied, "Same thing I always get." With a nod toward the train window and a reposition of the boner-concealing pillow, Surfer Boy said, "Menu's in there."

Rhea pulled it from between the folded tray table and window, and made her decision following a quick review of the few dinner options. "So." She rested the menu on her thighs, sneaking her foot between his legs and resting it against his erection. She tapped it with her toes. "We should probably cool it 'til after dinner."

Surfer Boy gripped the pillow, hissing inward through his teeth. He whispered, "We could totally get in a quickie."

Rhea pulled her foot away, crossing her right leg over her left, rubbing the outside of his right calf with the top of her right foot. "I'd prefer not to," she said simply. Quickies were all she ever got from Mark. Maybe someday she'd learn to appreciate them, but she was in no rush to acquire that taste.

"Are you two ready?" asked the attendant.

Rhea and Surfer Boy exchanged purposeful looks, answering in unison: "*Yes.*"

Surfer Boy requested the Vegetarian Pasta. And while Rhea knew she should have done likewise, she opted for the Herb Roasted Half Chicken. It was close to a thousand calories more for her entrée than for his, but Rhea knew she had a considerable amount of walking ahead of her in

Chicago; she had no plans for renting a car or taking taxicabs during her trip.

She slid the door closed once the attendant left. "I haven't eaten yet and already I'm having calorie guilt."

He smirked. "We'll just have to help you burn some calories to make up for it." With the train stopped in Raton, Surfer Boy pulled out his smartphone and did a quick internet search while it had enough signal to do so.

"Kissing," he read, "burns sixty-eight calories per hour. Undressing, at least eight." He glanced at Rhea. "I'd sure as hell enjoy watching you burn at least eight calories."

She giggled. "I'm sure it could be arranged." Her gaze shifted toward the cabin window. A few people were milling about on the train station platform.

"Massaging burns at least eighty calories, but I'm sure you burn far more; you're stronger than you look."

"Thanks?"

"Sex itself is at least a hundred forty per half hour. If you're straddling me again, it's at least two hundred. For you, anyway."

Rhea glanced around the roomette in disbelief. "This thing can't be more than four by six! How else could we do it if I'm not straddling you again?"

With a small motion of his free hand, Surfer Boy replied, "These seats convert into a bed."

"Oh." She considered the possibilities—though she was shamefully uncreative—and it still didn't leave them much space. Rhea was flexible if nothing else and she wagered he was as creative with sex as he was in other endeavors, like painting. Pairing his creativity with her flexibility, she was confident they could figure out positions that would school the Kama Sutra. "Ohh." Lost in thought, she mused aloud, "Wonder what oral burns?"

Surfer Boy fumbled with his phone.

Rhea arched a single eyebrow. *This could be fun.*

"A—a hundred," he stammered after a quick check of his phone. "But . . . you don't wanna go down on some guy on the second day of a cross-country train trip."

"Why not? What if I did?"

He gawked. "Are you for real?"

"Are *you*?"

"If . . . If you're serious, at least let me go freshen up first. Though I'll be honest . . . Much as I'd enjoy a BJ, it seems like a waste of a condom."

Baffled, Rhea replied, "It doesn't have to be. Give me a heads-up—" she chuckled at her innuendo, "—and we can always switch to a less . . . *wasteful* use of the condom. I'm getting hot just thinking about this, so it's not like I wouldn't be ready for a traditional finish."

"Goddamn I like the way you think." He exhaled, lifting the pillow to reveal he was at full mast.

Had he gone flaccid and gotten aroused again, or had he been hard the whole time? Whichever case, the vein in his neck strained. So she leaned over, drawing lazy circles with her fingertip around his dick through his shorts. "How long until our food arrives?"

"I don't know," he moaned. "Ohhh I don't *care*."

"What happens if they bring it by and we don't answer the door?" asked Rhea.

"Don't know, don't care."

Rhea watched Surfer Boy's expression, thinking she had a solution to their situation. "Want a hand job, then?"

"Please—"

She drew his zipper down so slowly she thought she felt the release of each individual tooth. Rhea coaxed him out of the fly of his boxers. "You didn't happen to buy any lube at 7-11, didja?"

"I didn't see any. I didn't even think about it. Son of a bitch."

"No worries." She leaned over, rifling through her purse where she'd left it on the floor at her feet. "C'mon . . . It's in here somewhere . . ."

Surfer Boy glanced at Rhea, his brows furrowing. ". . . you . . . carry KY in your purse?"

She giggled. "No, but how hot would I be if I was always prepared for the possibility of sex?" Rhea located the travel-sized container in her bag and pulled it out. "It's regular lotion. Not great, but better than nothing. I don't mean to start a fire with your wood."

With a shake of his head and a chuckle, Surfer Boy told her, "It's not gonna be the lotion getting me off."

Rhea applied some of the generic-brand lotion to her hands, rubbing them together a few times to absorb the excess and to warm the remainder. She drew a few light circles with her fingernail around the tip of his cock and it quivered. As she played with him, she thought to warn him she was inexperienced in this type of massage but figured such admissions would be a turn-off. Besides which, the plan was to enjoy herself. She hoped he would enjoy himself as well, but this was self-indulgence at its purest.

She wrapped her fingers around his shaft, feeling his pulse throb against her palm. "Tell me what you like."

"I like you touching me."

She melted a little. "I might do better with some guidance."

Closing his eyes, he leaned back as much as the train seat permitted. "Surprise me, Sunshine. I like women who take control."

Of course he did. In theory, Rhea didn't object to running the show; she'd just never been with a man who let her do it. She had many ideas but no experience. "You'll tell me if I hurt you, right? Remember: I'm stronger than I look."

"You're not gonna hurt me." One eye popped open. "If you want a way out, all you have to do is say so. I know this isn't exactly everyone's favorite pastime."

Rhea paused to apply more lotion to her palms. "Enough talking for now." She leaned in to kiss him sweetly while caressing him with a warm, damp hand along the underside of his shaft.

Surfer Boy sighed against Rhea's lips. She moved a hand up and down his hard length, twisting at times, squeezing at others. When he stopped returning her kisses, she straightened, alternating her hands as if milking him and trading slow, long strokes with fast, short ones. The hand beginning to cramp cupped his nuts and kneaded them gently. Rhea bit her lip; she loved their size and weight against her palm.

Before long, Surfer Boy's breathing changed from slow and deep to rapid and shallow, his hands white-knuckling the edge of the seat. Rhea leaned back, narrowly avoiding his cum stream.

He moaned quietly in appreciation while Rhea continued to fondle his sac.

"Your hands are magic," he murmured.

"Thanks. My hands are my business."

Surfer Boy glanced at her.

"You know what I mean." Rhea leaned over to grab the bottle of hand sanitizer from her bag. "Oh!"

"'*Oh!*' what?" he asked, grabbing some of the train's complimentary tissues.

"I got my first souvenir of the trip!" And it was all she could do to keep from laughing about it. "You Lewinsky'd my bag."

"I—what?" Surfer Boy followed Rhea's stare, seeing his ejaculate decorating the handles and one side of her purse. And a little bit of the train's floor. "Oh, Christ, I am *so* sorry! I mean, who cares about the floor—you take a black light to this place and I bet there isn't a spot that wouldn't glow— but your *bag*! I want to replace it. Gimme your address, I promise to send you a replacement."

Rhea smiled, sighing quietly. "I've no doubt you would." She wiped the bag with her fingertips, wiping them into a tissue before using some hand sanitizer. "Problem being, I don't exactly have an address." Rhea continued without giving him the chance to gawk, "Don't worry about it. This was a gift from Mark and serves as a reminder of him I neither need, nor want."

"It should be paid for, at least." He arranged his junk inside his boxers and zipped his shorts.

"What if . . ." Rhea said, thinking it through, "you give me a self-portrait? This was a fifteen buck purse and I'm sure a sketch from you would be worth far more. Wouldn't that absolve you of any lingering guilt?"

"I came. On your *bag*." Surfer Boy hesitated. "Technically, by-the-way, I Clinton'd on it."

LEONARD 47

"You're splitting hairs and it's my fault for how I . . . aimed the nozzle. Besides, *I* see it as approval of my technique."

Surfer Boy shook his head, a disbelieving smile on his face. He looked at the window as the train entered Trinidad, Colorado. "The curtain's been open all this time?"

"I'm sure nobody saw anything. And if it makes you feel any better . . ." Rhea crossed her arms over her stomach and grabbed the lower hem of her shirt. "A little tit for tat?"

The attendant knocked on the door. "Dinner service."

"Maybe after dinner, I guess." Rhea thought, *I wonder what the attendant would do if I opened the door without a shirt on?*

Surfer Boy pulled open the roomette door as Rhea strategically placed a foot over the spunk on the floor. Her socks were thin enough it seeped right through but she said nothing of it.

He pulled out the table between the two seats in the roomette, and the attendant left them with their bagged meals.

"So." Surfer Boy put their food on the table between them and set the paper bag at his side. "We've got twenty-one hours before we get to Chicago." He poked at his Vegetarian Pasta. "Assuming the train's on schedule."

Rhea didn't want to think about parting ways with Surfer Boy. She also didn't want to think about *not* parting ways with him. In under twenty-four hours, she'd gotten a little too fond of him when what she should have done instead was anything else. Why hadn't Rhea taken the opportunity to step outside his roomette and have dinner on her own? She cast a casual glance at him. Would it be so objectionable to be pen pals who, on occasion, got together to fuck each other silly?

It was just that: fucking. Because he couldn't love her so soon after meeting her, and she sure as hell refused to love him already.

Or ever. "How often is the train late?" Rhea asked as casually as she could. They had two condoms left. Would twenty-one hours be enough time to lay waste to them? Then again, he'd already gone twice in about four hours. She couldn't admit to herself running out of screwing time was what worried her.

It was that she was going to miss him.

Shit.

"More times than not." He took his first bite of pasta.

"Then I'm super glad I'm not taking a connector train." She laughed stiffly.

"What are you looking forward to about getting to Chicago?"

Rhea took a long breath, straightening in her seat. She gave it some thought while cutting her chicken. "I'm looking forward to starting the arduous process of figuring out who the hell I am."

"Whatever comes your way in that process, remember one thing: *smile.*"

She did. "I *will.*"

"Were you serious about what you said earlier? That you don't have an address?" Surfer Boy asked. "Or was it a polite way of declining to give me it? I won't be hurt if it's the latter. Honest."

"I . . . Actually, honestly don't. My original plan was to find an apartment after my stuff was moved to storage. But I procrastinated and the next thing I know, I'm at a Holiday Inn without a place to live. No plan. I went to start the apartment search on a public computer and the last person who used it must've gotten train tickets. Or at least considered getting them. I was already down a condo and a smartphone, so I figured why the hell not? I thought so often over the years about running away and here was my chance."

"Did your ex take your phone, too?"

"Oh, no. It, uh, kinda . . . had a rapid unscheduled disassembly." She smiled sheepishly. "Against the living room wall."

"Because of your ex?"

"Again, no. That was a case where—well y'know the episode of Family Guy where Lois posts a Facebook update about someone dying or whatever, and a frenemy likes it?"

Surfer Boy nodded and crossed his arms over his chest.

"You read Heinlein, watch porn and Family Guy. You're into ice hockey—granted, your tastes there are questionable—and you volunteered a hand job. You also drink beer, by any chance?"

"Haha, no. I draw the line at beer."

"Oh."

Rhea smirked. "I prefer tequila." When it came to tequila, she could drink most men under the table. She had on more than one occasion referred to it as her superpower.

"You're perfect."

It would have been all too easy to regale Surfer Boy with all the ways in which she was imperfect. Rhea opted, instead, to finish her dinner and try to convince herself there would be no difficulties in saying good-bye to him when the train arrived in Chicago.

When he finished his pasta and Rhea was done with her chicken, Surfer Boy decided he should work on the self-portrait she'd requested.

She took the opportunity to retrieve her laptop from the luggage in the compartment above her seat in coach. Nobody there gave her a second look; she assumed they couldn't care less where she'd been, what—or whom—she'd been doing, or whether she was coming or going.

She giggled to herself: She certainly *had* come, and was planning on doing so again. Maybe even a few times! Rhea thought it wise to get all the horniness out of her system while she had the chance.

Who knew when another sexy stud would fall into her lap the way Surfer Boy had? She glanced around. The average train rider was just that: *average*. Like Rhea, no one looked primped for the trip. Chances were, she wouldn't encounter another Surfer Boy on the train. Maybe not anywhere.

She wondered how many Rheas he'd had in his travels.

Not as though it matters. It sure as hell doesn't matter to me . . .

Says someone who's in total denial.

Rhea bristled at her thoughts.

With her laptop in tow, she paid a brief visit to the snack car where she bought herself a bottle of orange juice. She got

RAYS OF SUNSHINE

halfway up the stairs to the observation car before turning back to purchase a beer as well. After all, she didn't want to return with nothing for her companion. Rhea wasn't an asshole.

Upon her return to Surfer Boy's cabin, she found him hard at work—paper on the table, pencil in hand and a selfie on his phone for reference. She halfway expected he would doodle something for her the way he had in her purse notebook but this looked like he was investing some genuine effort in it.

"Hey," she greeted him, offering the beer.

He took it. "You rock."

"Oh that's just the motion of the train." Rhea jutted out her hip and winked.

"Thanks," Surfer Boy said with a chuckle and a small shake of his head.

"Mind if I take the upper bunk? I don't wanna disturb you."

"You're not disturbing me, but if *you* want privacy—" he motioned to the bed above him, "—by all means."

Rhea set her laptop on the upper bunk and hoisted herself onto it. "Thanks for being so cool."

"*Likewise.*"

She settled on her stomach, lifted the laptop's screen, and opened her word processing program.

"Hey, would you object to some music?" asked Surfer Boy.

"Never." Rhea reviewed her last journal entry. She put the cursor on a new line below the last thing she'd written that morning. "Go right ahead."

The silence in the cabin broke when Imagine Dragons streamed from his phone.

She nodded although she knew he couldn't see it. "I approve."

"I thought you might."

While considering what she would write, Rhea switched which font she was using for her document. And then she adjusted the font size. Followed by adjusting its color.

She used to do similar things when she kept a

handwritten journal: flicking the clips on pen caps with her thumbnail until the clips snapped off, unscrewing tops and removing ink cartridges. Putting the purple ink cartridge into the green pen casing, and swapping the green cap with a red one.

She referred to it as writer's roulette but it was nothing more than filthy, naughty procrastination.

Rhea liked to decorate her lined notebook paper with little ink dots of whatever random color was in the pen she selected. She often felt like writing, but no words were there.

That was sort of true now, except she wanted to write and the words were there.

She just didn't want to put them down. To document them, even with the availability of the backspace and delete keys made them feel so concrete.

She inhaled.

We fucked.
Rhea rapidly tapped backspace seven times.

screwed.

She pressed her lips together into a thin line of disapproval, highlighted the line and pressed delete.

There were shenanigans. Sexy, sloppy, memorable shenanigans.
I was never one for love-at-first-sight bullshit. The closest I got was my ninth grade crush on Brianna that subsequently sent me into a depression which lasted the length of the school year and made me so confused that I questioned not just my sexuality but my whole existence.
I still don't believe in love at first sight.

She flat-out refused to.

When I think about reaching Chicago,

Rhea covered her mouth. Between lying on her stomach so soon after a meal, and the jostling of the train, she felt ill. Only after the feeling vanished did she continue:

RAYS OF SUNSHINE

I have to remind myself I still believe there are good men out there. Surfer Boy, however, may be too good to be true. Much as I want to take him (at face value), his too-good-to-be-trueness makes me too suspicious of him to enjoy his companionship. His companionship on the train. His continued companionship going forward? I don't even fucking know anymore.

What harm is there in giving him my email address? I mean I know it'll take away the whole anonymous sex business . . . which I hate to admit is really turning me on. More than screwing while still fully clothed.

What if this is The Guy? When we're talking and he's looking at me, I sincerely believe he could be The Guy. That's not quite right. He isn't looking at me. He's looking into *me. Surfer Boy has the most intense stare when I'm talking to him, like he's looking at my very soul. It makes me feel like even my insides are blushing! Like I want to curl up and die but in a good way. That makes no sense but it's how he makes me feel.*

What if Surfer Boy and I go our separate ways and I never find a better match for myself? Can I really let fate decide? Maybe this encounter is fate clubbing me over the head. "Hey dumbass, here's your soulmate!" Would I miss my chance and try later to find him on Craigslist's missed connections? Or take a photo of myself pouting and holding a sign asking for people to help me find a guy whose name I don't even know? Hope it goes viral? Ha!

Because anyone cares enough about me to help find the random guy I fucked on a train trip when I ran away from a home I technically didn't have. When I didn't bother to tell any of them where I was going or when I would return? Hell, I didn't bother telling anyone I left.

They probably haven't even noticed I'm gone.

I really wanted to give myself alone-time. I need it. I don't know who I am, and I don't see how I'll be able to find myself while I'm too busy trying to mold myself into the ideal mate for another guy. I did it once, and I don't want to be that kind of girl again. Or anymore.

Can we have a standard friendship going forward after starting it with sex?

My God, it's practically something Carrie Bradshaw would write. Let me try:

I couldn't help but wonder . . . could Surfer Boy and I have a standard friendship after starting off with sex?

"Hey Surfer Boy?" Rhea asked, saving her document and snapping her laptop closed. She leaned over the edge of the upper bunk as he scrambled to cover his artwork.

"It's not done yet!" he yelped.

"I'm not looking, I promise. Any way you could grab my notebook and pen from my purse?"

He flipped the paper over before rummaging through her bag. He made no comment on her pepper spray, the hard clamshell glasses case, half-full prescription bottle of aripiprazole, or the Softcups—though she guessed the unmarked purple packets didn't scream *danger, danger, menstrual cup!* to him. He handed the notebook and pen to her. "Here you go."

"Thanks."

They regarded each other in silence. After a brief hesitation, he leaned in for a closed-mouth kiss. Surfer Boy sat back down at the table, waving toward her. "Don't look 'til it's done."

"I . . ." Rhea squeaked. "I won't." She repositioned herself on the bunk, turning to the center page of her notebook. She gave herself a minute to recover from that peck before she wrote:

Dear Surfer Boy,
I'm making no plans for my future, immediate or long-term. I don't need another husband, or even a boyfriend. But I could always use another friend who makes me smile and laugh.
I've enjoyed our conversation and if you wanted to be fuck buddies, well, I don't think I could find myself a more capable guy to fill the position.
If your offer to accompany me to the art museum still stands, I would like to take it. I don't currently have a phone or home address, but my email will work any place I go. I hope you'll use it.
rheaofsunshine90@gmail.com

Thanks for a great time.

"Sunshine"

Rhea spent the rest of the ride into La Junta, Colorado trying to convince herself not to give her companion that piece of paper.

At the train station, Surfer Boy knocked on the bottom of the bunk. "It's a ten-minute stop here. Wanna go outside for some fresh air?"

What Rhea really needed was to stop by the lavatory. Since it was only ten minutes, she chose to accompany Surfer Boy off the train, instead.

They milled about beside the train on the station platform, shoulders touching, hands brushing, but neither reaching for the other.

"I, uh . . . I've got a favor to ask you," said Surfer Boy, his voice low. "And I feel gross for even thinking of asking it."

Rhea gave him a lingering side-eye, taking a large step away from him. "Oh *please* don't tell me it's anything . . . Fifty Shades-y."

Surfer Boy stopped mid-stride. "What, exactly, would that entail? The only thing I know of the franchise is that it's Twilight fanfiction written for horny moms."

She lowered her voice to match his; the people milling around them didn't need to hear about her kinks—or, in this case, lack of them. "I'm not into having anyone else remove used feminine products from my gash." Tampons were one thing. The feminine cups she relied on, however, would be a whole different nightmare. Something akin to elevators in *The Shining*, a scene from *Carrie* or the menstrual equivalent of Gettysburg.

His eyes went wide.

They regarded each other in silence.

He exhaled. "That sounds awful."

"Glad we're on the same page. That was my assessment, too. A friend braver than I am read it and reported back to me."

Surfer Boy nudged her playfully in the shoulder with his several steps later. "Sure, your *friend* read it. Isn't that the type of book *you* enjoy?"

"Okay, I'm not even gonna pretend your use of air quotes on 'friend' wasn't insulting. But yes, I have my standards. So what was that favor you wanted?"

"Maybe, sometime before we get to Chicago you would indulge me . . ."

Rhea leaned in, her eyebrows arched. ". . . *in?*"

"Say like . . . if we were to sit close together on the same seat . . . maybe with my arms around you. Like . . . just, you know, relaxing, with no expectations of sex."

She frowned. "Are—are you asking me to cuddle with you?"

"I believe the technical term is snuggle. But . . ." He dipped his head, his face flushed and expression bashful. ". . . yes." It was as if he was asking for an orgy. Or anal. Or furry play. Or to pull a used tampon from her twat. "Please?" Surfer Boy added when she didn't respond immediately.

Rhea blinked, watching him somberly. What had he been through that he was so ashamed of asking a girl to snuggle? She smiled. "I'm sure something like that could be arranged."

"Thanks. I'd really fucking appreciate it."

She tried not to laugh at his use of the expletive. "So . . . You wanna—" She nodded toward the train.

"It's not urgent," he said. "Maybe something we could do in the room with the lights out and the curtains open. I could hold you and we can watch the night pass us by."

"Are you . . . are you planning on me spending the night in your cabin?"

"You're welcome to." He paused. "You don't need to, either, of course. But that bed is far more comfortable than a train seat. I think you know what I mean since you spent a night in coach."

She pursed her lips. "I'll think about it." Rhea had little doubt this would make her resolve crumble in regard to giving him the note. She should have said no to snuggling and already regretted it.

They reboarded the train and Rhea excused herself to use the restroom—restrooms being what they were on the Superliner: a toilet not so different from a Porta-Potty, a single sink set into a countertop made of some material which hoped it might be some distant relative of granite—thrice removed—and barely enough standing room between the toilet and the sink to get anything done. There were so many silver railings, Rhea wondered if Amtrak used them to compensate for the lavatory's lack of room. And the toilet had a flush loud enough she considered taking her headphones to use as earplugs the next time she had the misfortune of needing to relieve herself.

Maybe it'd be worthwhile to dehydrate myself for the remainder of the trip.

Upon her return to Surfer Boy's roomette, he requested a little more time to work on his self-portrait. Rhea obliged, climbing into the top bunk and settling down with an eBook loaded onto her laptop.

It wasn't until the train departed Lamar, Colorado over an hour later that Surfer Boy knocked on the bunk again. "I'm done with my drawing for now. I promise I'll finish it for you before we part ways tomorrow. I do good work way early in the morning. If you stay here tonight, I'll try not to disturb you."

"'K."

". . . Wanna join me down here?"

Rhea nodded, reaching to close her laptop.

"Hang on a sec. Let me fold out the bed down here." He slid the door open for the much-needed space another couple feet of walkway afforded him.

"'K," she squeaked again, her hand poised at the top of her laptop screen. It had to be the most ridiculous thing ever that his mention of the word 'bed' catapulted her heart into her throat; they'd had sex and she'd given him a hand job, so why did the addition of a bed make things in any way more significant?

Is he going to get romantic with me?

Why was that scarier than saying '*I do*' to someone she

hadn't loved?

Rhea was a hopeless romantic: she ate, slept, and breathed *love*. This should have made her overjoyed, not fearful. She shook her head to clear it, closing her laptop. *It will be okay. It will all be okay.*

She took a steadying breath, reminding herself that regardless of his overtures, *she* was in this for an anonymous one-night-stand with a hot guy and nobody would change that. Not unless she decided to—and he agreed with her.

Oh God, he just might.

She was resolved she would change nothing.

"All right, it's ready," said Surfer Boy. "Join me?"

Rhea dropped from the bunk without a word. All the tiny train pillows—and the normal pillow in its plain blue pillowcase that Surfer Boy, in his experience, must have brought with him—were propped against the wall on one end of the bed.

He was sitting cross-legged, smiling at her as he opened his arms. "I can't tell you how much I appreciate you indulging me here. I'm . . ." He lifted his right shoulder in a shrug. "I'm a little starved for affection. And not the euphemistic kind of affection."

"Euphemistic affection? You mean the word 'affection' as a substitute for the word 'screwing?'"

"Yep."

She cleared her throat. "Mind if I get out of my jeans? I snuggle best when I'm comfortable."

"I want you to be comfy. By all means, do what's necessary." He nodded in encouragement. When she sat on the bed, he closed the door. The curtain over the door's window followed it.

Rhea slipped out of her pants and turned to him. Surfer Boy pulled her into his embrace, reclining against the pillows and the wall behind them. He squeezed her with a deep, satisfied sigh and she allowed his warmth to envelop her. For a fellow who smelled of lingering sex—and had a day of train stuck to his skin and clothes—his scent intoxicated.

She stared out the window into the night, putting a hand atop his arm.

"God did I need this." Surfer Boy rested his chin on Rhea's crown.

". . . How long has it been since your last girlfriend?" she asked.

When he didn't answer, Rhea couldn't decide if that meant it had been a long time or if he'd recently been relieved of a relationship.

Or perhaps he'd lied about not having a current girlfriend.

Or wife. Just because he's not wearing a ring doesn't mean he's not married.

"I've . . . had the occasional date but it's been a year or so since my last actual relationship."

Rhea bobbed her head. If he wasn't lying, his story matched one of her assumptions.

"Am I a rebound screw?" he asked her. "It doesn't matter to me, I'm just curious."

If it didn't matter, she thought he wouldn't have asked. "You're not," she assured him. "Yes, my divorce was recent, but I hadn't been invested in that relationship for years." *If ever, actually.*

Surfer Boy shifted his head from Rhea's crown to her shoulder and nodded.

"Why were you so reluctant to ask me to snuggle? I thought for sure you were gonna ask me to shit on you or maybe masturbate with a broken beer bottle or something."

"I like this kind of thing. But I never trusted my girlfriends not to laugh at me for asking—*especially* Sally. Because, you know, real men don't snuggle. I was supposed to fear commitment and intimacy."

"So . . . you . . . trusted *me*?"

"Sure! Why not? I trust you—sometimes strangers are more trustworthy than friends—and I figured with you, I've got nothing to lose."

And everything to gain, Rhea realized. "I think I'll stay here tonight." She prayed she wouldn't regret the decision. "I'm comfy."

Surfer Boy squeezed her. "Thanks. You still don't want my name?"

"Nope."

"And I still can't get yours?"

"Whore-y or not, I like Sunshine."

"Okay." He kissed her cheek.

She drew in a deep breath; he was going to decimate her heart if she allowed it.

And she was allowing it.

Well, fuck.

Rhea was succumbing to the exact same idiocy that scored her a loveless marriage from which she had nothing but regrets. Did she shy away here for fear of history repeating itself and risk what might have become the love affair of a lifetime?

He shifted his arms down and rested his hands on her lower abdomen.

She could defer everything about their future together to him. An eyebrow crooked upward. *Actually, that'd work quite well.*

It was no longer her decision to make.

For the span of an entire heartbeat, that was a satisfactory solution to her dilemma.

"What are you thinking about?" asked Surfer Boy.

Rhea didn't skip a beat: "World blights, the economic ceiling. Ebola. Global warming. How I'll never get to be Pope."

"Sexy."

"If I didn't think unsexy thoughts, I wouldn't be able to keep my hands off you. And I'm respecting your desire to snuggle."

"What a considerate sacrifice."

Rhea smiled.

"Would you tell me about your perfect date?"

Rhea turned slightly and cast a sideways glance at Surfer Boy. "I'm not particular. I'd want to enjoy myself." She shrugged, her shoulders sliding against his chest. "A quiet, candle-lit dinner at home. Comedy in a movie theater. Bike ride on a boardwalk. Snowboarding followed by hot cocoa. Brunch at a place that knows how to brew a proper cup of coffee. It all boils down to being with someone I actually want to be on a date with. Someone who wants to talk to me and listen to me."

Surfer Boy was drawing figure-eights with his fingertip through Rhea's shirt below her navel. There was a laziness to his actions that awakened her desire the way fire wicked along streams of gasoline in movies. She choked on her excitement.

The cabin was getting a little too warm for Rhea's preferences.

"W-what about you?" she stammered. "What's your ideal date?"

"Well, I sure like what you described."

"You're just saying that."

"No. Really." He paused. "I'd enjoy a meandering stroll through an arboretum or botanical garden. Go find one of those amazing hole-in-the-wall restaurants. Maybe spend a day sharing a Sea-Doo."

She thought that sounded incredibly fun. She could have said so but didn't want to encourage him.

"Of course, going to art museums would be fun for me."

"You're just saying that because you think I expect it." Rhea smiled.

Surfer Boy laughed; it made her want to dissolve into absolute nothingness—but the best kind of dissolving into absolute nothingness.

"Yeah, I *did* say it for that reason, but that doesn't make it any less true. Hey . . . y'know what I've always wanted to do? One of those single-day beach-to-desert-to-mountain trips. Pack a cooler and have a hell of a time." He sighed. "Maybe throw some sleeping bags in the trunk and camp out under the stars."

If he was being honest about that too, they were compatible in more ways than just with sex. Rhea resented him a little for it. She wanted to tell him to knock it off already.

"Not a camper, huh?" he asked.

"Oh I'd love to go camping more in the future. Mark was no fun to camp with." *He was no fun for much of anything.*

They were silent for a while.

Rhea broke the silence: "What's been the best part of train travel for you?"

"It's always been about the destination. I was more concerned about getting there, getting home."

"That sounds familiar."

"*Buuut* . . ." Surfer Boy said. "This time it's different. I found the best lay I've had in . . . a real long time."

His hesitation pushed Rhea to consider inquiring about it. It made her think maybe she was the best he'd ever had and she could certainly use the boost to her self-esteem. Instead, she smiled. "Does it still count as snuggling if there's kissing, too?"

"I think, strictly speaking, no." Surfer Boy kissed her on the shoulder, and again on the side of her neck. "I'm really enjoying this. Thanks for indulging me."

"You're welcome."

Surfer Boy toyed with the elastic waistband of Rhea's underwear.

She closed her eyes. "You're a tease—"

"—says the woman who insisted on snuggling in her underwear," he pointed out.

"I wasn't teasing. I wanted to be comfortable. Just like I said."

"So I guess you're going to hold me responsible for finding you so damn attractive?"

Rhea was going to rebuke him when he slipped his hand down the front of her white cotton panties. Instead of a snappy retort, her breath caught in her throat. A single finger sank into her slit, sending a jolt of arousal through her abdomen. Her thighs snapped together.

"No?" asked Surfer Boy. "I'll stop."

Her voice a husky whisper, Rhea said, "I wish you wouldn't stop."

"You're gonna cut off circulation to my hand if you don't loosen up."

It was a conscious effort to relax her hips for him.

His slick finger circled her clit, rubbing her tender lips on either side of it. Surfer Boy whispered in her ear, "I get the idea you were never told how sexy you are."

"*No*," Rhea moaned, shaking her head against his chest.

"I get the idea you've never been gently teased to the brink of orgasmic bliss, and dangled mercilessly over the precipice of resolution." His voice was silken arousal flowing over her every peak and valley, wrapping her soul in ruttish seduction.

"When I thought you could be dangerous . . ." She struggled to string the words together. ". . . I worried about my body. I think I should fear for my heart . . ."

"I'm not in the business of breaking hearts, honey." He slipped a couple fingers into her far enough that she jerked and gasped. "I'm in the business of libidinous pleasure."

Surfer Boy's breath warmed her neck and his teasing caress was driving her rapidly to a climax he had, in no uncertain terms, told her he was going to prolong. As her voice rose, he retreated, leaving her gasping for air.

His hands slid along her quivering thighs and beneath her shirt, stopping at her bra band.

"When will you let me come?" she breathed. "When I cry?"

"No," Surfer Boy replied.

"When I scream? When I can no longer take it?"

"No." He kissed her ear, taking her lobe between his teeth and tugging. "When *I* can no longer take it." His lips traveled down the side of her neck and across her nape. "Can I see you naked?"

"Will you do me then?"

"In good time, Sunshine. Though . . . it might help speed up the process a little."

That was good enough for Rhea, who was as impatient with her orgasm as the train trip was long.

"Turn to face me, please. I want to watch."

She repositioned herself on the lower bunk of Surfer Boy's roomette, checking out his crotch. He managed to restrain himself so well Rhea was worried her relief was nowhere in sight.

"Will you get undressed, too?" she asked.

"If you want me to."

"Of course I do."

He nodded at her. "Oh, but ladies first."

She slipped out of her underwear and lifted her shirt over her head, revealing an unlined white cotton bra which matched her panties.

Surfer Boy's eyebrows lifted; he was staring at her right breast.

Rhea glanced down. She scarcely thought about the horizontal barbell piercing her right nipple.

He motioned with his left hand to touch it, but hesitated. The piercing seemed to stun him into a brief silence.

She popped open the hooks around the back of her bra and shrugged the straps down her arms.

Surfer Boy couldn't stop staring. "*May I—?*"

"Not until you've undressed, too." She smirked. "It's only fair."

Rhea never saw anyone undress so quickly. In the time between moving from his embrace and pulling off her bra, his cock had gone from flaccid to full attention. And it was magnificent when he was fully undressed.

He either groomed himself or was naturally fairly hairless, which Rhea liked. Mark was a human Wookiee and it grossed her out to no end.

Everything about Surfer Boy was magnificent. His shoulder to hip ratio, his biceps, and the definition of the muscles across his chest.

My god. He's fucking perfect.

And he was staring at her with a carnal hunger that was nothing short of ravenous. Rhea thought he might devour her, and she was thrilled to invite him to her buffet.

As opposed to ravaging her, he caressed her right breast, running his thumb over the tip. "Did it hurt?"

Rhea thought back to that visit to the tattoo studio. It was so long ago she didn't remember much about it beyond how she had to psyche herself out to open her bra for some strange man. Funny how that didn't apply here. "It was . . ." She tilted her head, smiling as Surfer Boy fondled her pierced nipple with a gentle hand. "It was kind of a . . . a hurts-so-good sort of pain."

He took a deep breath. "What did the ex think about it?"

She shrugged. "He never said anything, never played with it."

"Would it hurt if I played with it?"

"It healed a long time ago. Play away. Who knows . . . it might even feel good."

Surfer Boy kissed his way from her neck to her breast, then to her nipple which he sucked into his mouth.

"Mmm," Rhea sighed.

He flicked the barbell with his tongue, back and forth, up and down. He bit gently, tugging until her entire body stiffened and she groaned.

Rhea was warned the piercing might cause her to lose sensitivity; it turned out to have the opposite effect. "You're making me so wet."

"Tell me more," Surfer Boy murmured, continuing to play with her piercing with his hand. He was moving closer to her, kissing her neck, sucking the skin in the hollow of her collarbone far harder than he did when her nipple was between his lips.

Rhea was afraid of what she might say, so she kept it simple: "Your lips feel so good."

"And?" A hand dropped between her thighs.

"I want you inside me. Drill me mercilessly."

Surfer Boy turned his wrist to rest his open palm against her slick lips.

"*Oh god.*" she gasped.

He slid fingers between those luscious folds, and she arched her back, pressing her chest to his. He brought her to the brink of climax, alternating between long, slow caresses and fast ones which circled her clit. Surfer Boy pulled away.

Rhea cried out her frustration. "Oh, come *on!*"

He paused to roll on the condom, flashing a suggestive smile her direction as he pushed her onto her back and slid his body along hers. He peppered Rhea's face with kisses, rubbing his hard-on against her clit. Each motion evoked a moaned plea for release.

"Not until *I* can't take it anymore," Surfer Boy reminded

her.

The friction between them brought her to the brink again, and at long last, he thrust into her. Rhea's fingernails sunk into the flesh of his back, her orgasm crashing through her body. With each thrust, smaller climaxes followed.

Surfer Boy's climax some fifteen minutes later was an act of mercy for Rhea, who could hardly take any more stimulation.

She didn't notice when he pulled out, nor when he nestled against her. It was as if she'd temporarily died in his embrace. She came to with the sensation of his fingers raking her hair.

"Oh. My. God . . . Holy. Shit."

Surfer Boy whispered in her ear, "I still can't tell you my name?"

"Not right now," Rhea breathed. "Not if you want me to remember it."

"I'd remember yours."

"Well it's still Sunshine."

He huffed, but nuzzled her.

His bare chest to her back was sublime.

It was as if being naked with him deprived her of their anonymity, names aside; it no longer felt like a one-night-stand. Rhea wondered if he felt the same way. Of course, she had no omniscient narrator who could hop into his head and whisper his thoughts to her without his being aware of her presence. If she wanted his thoughts and feelings, she'd have to ask but she was afraid to. If that question came out, she was sure her dinner might follow it.

Rhea felt the shades of drowsiness being drawn over her eyes. She moved to leave the bed, but his embrace tightened.

She was afraid if she stayed in his arms overnight, she would stay in them forever. That wasn't problematic, per se, except for destroying her previously laid plans.

"Excuse me," she insisted, wrenching herself from his grip.

"You're leaving?"

Rhea smiled at him. "Just for the top bunk. If I'm gonna use one of these beds over a coach seat, I wanna take full advantage of it and do an ugly sprawl."

He slipped on his shorts and she put on her jeans and T-shirt without bothering to put on her undergarments first. He slid the door open when she was dressed and remarked as she climbed into the bunk above him, "Nothing you could do is ugly."

"Sweet dreams, Surfer Boy," she chuckled.

He slid the door closed again and locked it. "You, too."

She stripped and snuggled beneath the covers, praying they were sanitary as they were touching her privates.

They turned out the lights and Rhea took a deep breath, enjoying the noise of the train as it cruised along its track somewhere in Kansas, enjoying the uneven sway she hoped would lull her to sleep, enjoying the relative darkness the roomette afforded that coach could not.

Before her eyes adjusted to that darkness, the telltale glow of a smartphone illuminated the cabin from below her bunk. Rhea bristled. Mark used to like fiddling with his phone in bed at night as a way of avoiding intimacy with her. That wasn't the case here, but it served as an unwelcome reminder.

The quiet strains of Mozart's String Quartet in D Major filled the air. A rush of warmth flooded Rhea's body; she couldn't decide whether she wanted to laugh or cry. So instead, she thanked Surfer Boy and rolled onto her side for much needed sleep.

Rhea roused periodically throughout the night. Several times she awakened with a start following more earthquake nightmares; she thought she should purchase some melatonin prior to her trip home. That is, if she didn't decide to take a plane instead.

The last time she closed her eyes—at five in the morning—yielded her longest stretch of uninterrupted sleep and an erotic dream starring Benedict Cumberbatch as Sherlock. A fiction idea?

She woke a little after eight, hearing Surfer Boy rummaging below. She stretched with a quiet moan.

"'Morning, Sunshine," he said. "How'd you sleep?"

"It's no Serta, but so much better than coach," she replied. "Where are we?"

"We just left Kansas City, Missouri. We should be in La Plata in about two hours."

Rhea ran a quick calculation in her head; she had seven hours to decide what she was doing with the note she'd written to him. Seven hours to use the remaining condom, which was a less significant issue in comparison to the note conundrum.

"If you want to get breakfast in the dining car, we'd better get going."

She kind of hated herself that his use of 'we' made her smile. "I think I'll get some pastries or whatever from the snack car. If you'd like to go to the dining car, please, feel free."

"I'd rather have a small bowl of cereal from the snack car, myself. So that works out."

Rhea narrowed her eyes. "You're not saying that to make me feel less guilty because you changed your plans for me?"

"I was hoping you'd pass on the dining car. Scout's honor."

"I trust you're holding up a hand in pledge down there."

"No," Surfer Boy laughed. "It's down my pants."

Rhea tried to peer over the edge of the bunk, knocking the top of her head against the door instead. "Ow!"

"You okay?"

"*Yeah*," she grumbled, rubbing her crown. "It's just my pride." Rhea cleared her throat. "You mind too terribly passing me my bra?" She wasn't sure where it wound up but guessed it was somewhere on his bed. He'd probably snuggled with it last night. She smirked.

"You seem like a practical girl," Surfer Boy observed, passing her not only her white cotton bra, but the matching pair of panties as well.

"Huh?" She wiggled into her underwear, but not without

kicking the roof of the cabin by accident.

"That—The white cotton bra?"

Despite herself, Rhea laughed. "I'm on a fucking train, dear! I wasn't exactly expecting to have sex this trip. The Cosabellas are at home." Upon further thought, she augmented, "In storage. I didn't want to ruin my nice lingerie. But..."

"But?"

"But the kinds of sexy underthings I have would blow your mind."

Rhea had to become nothing short of a contortionist to put on her outerwear while still in the bunk.

"Ahh, you're killin' me," replied Surfer Boy.

She giggled.

"I'd prefer you with *no* underthings. If I took you out for a night on the town and you whispered to me that you were going commando . . . I'd probably need a change of pants right on the spot."

"I find it hard to believe you could come so quickly. And after what you did to me last night? It'd serve you right."

"You dressed?" Surfer Boy asked.

"Yep."

"So I can open the door?"

"Uh huh."

The door slid open and Rhea climbed down, plopping beside him on the bed. "So. Did you finish the sketch?"

"It needs some fine-tuning before I'll even pretend to be satisfied with it. I'll finish it after breakfast if that's okay with you."

"Of course it is."

"Hey . . . Thanks again for last night. You have no idea how bad I needed that."

Her cheeks dimpled as she slipped on her shoes. "You're a phenomenal lover. Er—that is—you're a real great lay." Rhea prayed he would dismiss her first comment if she prattled on a little bit: "Can men be classified as lays? Laids? Is it lains? Or is there a special classification where it's like men are the lay*ers*? I mean, I was on top the first time, so you were the one laying. Well actually, neither of us were laying—"

"*Thanks.*" Surfer Boy helped her to her feet. Without further comment, he escorted Rhea to the snack car. They bought what loosely qualified as breakfast and took their food to eat in the observation car.

Rhea shook her bottle of orange juice. "Y'know . . . I kinda forgot about the rest of the world last night . . . It was nice."

"I'll take that as a compliment," he replied, starting on his small bowl of Cheerios.

"I should add, though—and I'm hesitant to do it—this isn't what I wanted. I got on the train to see the world. Well the US, anyway."

"I thought," he replied between bites, "you got on the train to run away."

"You *would* throw that back at me." Rhea polished off her orange juice. "Do you really mean to tell me you actually pay attention to the things I say?"

Surfer Boy said, "It's not *that* weird is it?"

"I guess I'm not used to it." Rhea watched the landscape for a few minutes before she made the off-hand remark: "I'd love to tour haunted places . . . The Myrtles, Winchester Mansion, Gettysburg. And while I'm there, Eastern State Penitentiary. It's a total guilty pleasure that I'll park myself in front of the Travel Channel and watch all those *Most Terrifying Places* shows. I love it when October rolls around."

Surfer Boy nodded. "Sure, sure, that'd be fun." He finished off his cereal, setting the empty container and plastic spoon on the small table between their seats. "Y'know what would be an amazing trip?" He leaned forward, resting his elbows on his knees. "Driving up PCH with the canvas down and seeing all the haunted places along the way. Whaley to Winchester and everything in between."

Rhea thought about it; she'd never taken anything amounting to a true road trip. It sounded daunting, exhausting, and fun all at the same time. She glanced at him, trying to figure out if he was inviting her on such a terrific outing. She wouldn't have declined.

He gazed out the train windows.

"I bet it'd be a hell of a trip," she replied.

Surfer Boy watched her with a smile.

"So . . . What else is there to do on a train assuming you're by yourself?" asked Rhea. "I didn't know what to expect so when I was packing I went light on the entertainment. I got real lucky to run into someone who wanted my company. Because otherwise I suspect the boredom would have been . . . catastrophic."

"The magnitude ten-point-oh of boredom?"

"The EF-five of boredom."

It wasn't appropriate by any stretch of the imagination to classify boredom with the Enhanced Fujita or Richter Scales, but there they were: both laughing about it harder than they should. It wasn't even especially funny.

As their laughter died down, Surfer Boy glanced at Rhea with a particularly affectionate smile. "Y'know, I was *so* afraid of approaching you when I saw you sitting by yourself here," he confessed. "I thought, there's no way in hell she's alone. She can't be single. She'd never talk to me. We'll have nothing in common." He hesitated before whispering, "I'd convinced myself you were a humorless bitch because you're that damned hot."

"Wow," said Rhea. "That was . . . The most ass-backward compliment I've ever received."

He winked. "And I meant every word of it."

"Still, it's one of the sweetest things anyone's ever told me."

The affectionate smile on Surfer Boy's face faded. "I'm sorry."

"Don't be." She cocked her head, gazing at him. "Your kind comment means more to me because, well . . . It's remarkable in its uniqueness."

"You were pretty seriously mistreated."

"Don't hold my ex accountable. He wasn't the only one to treat me poorly. With few exceptions, I can't pick my friends for shit. And my family . . . Well . . . They laid the foundation. I can't, for the life of me, imagine why anyone would pursue me. Not until I fix myself."

"Maybe some of us like fixer-uppers. I've always thought about flipping houses."

Rhea squeezed her eyes shut. What the hell were they doing? She tilted her head upward and opened her eyes. "You, uh . . . You never told me how else you stay occupied on a forty-four-hour train ride."

"Books. Movies on a laptop. I sketch a lot, and when I'm feeling sociable, I try to make friends. And when I'm *really* lucky, I . . . get lucky." Surfer Boy winked at her.

"And how often does that happen?"

"This trip. Just this one. But it's more than made up for all the others."

"Maybe I'm setting a precedent for your future travels."

He didn't reply.

"So we've got what, about six hours 'til Chicago?"

Surfer Boy nodded. "Yep. And I still have to do finishing touches on the portrait you asked for. I'm gonna head back to work on it." He stood. "You joining me?"

Rhea hesitated. Her laptop was still in his roomette; she kind of *had* to return, at least for that. It worried her she didn't think she'd be able to leave him, even if she were following him for the sole purpose of retrieving her belongings. On the other hand, she didn't want to return to coach.

"It's a huge decision," he teased her, "I know."

"Yeah, yeah," Rhea decided, sticking out her tongue at him. "I'm coming."

Surfer Boy led the way. "Now *where* have I heard you say that before?"

Rhea lifted a hand to swat at him in playful retaliation but stopped herself in time. There was a flash of horror in realizing the familiarity of such behavior. She didn't want familiarity; how many times would she have to remind herself before it stuck? "I'm gonna let that slide."

He snorted; nothing more.

RAYS OF SUNSHINE

Back in the roomette, Rhea hoisted herself onto the bunk while Surfer Boy folded the bed into two seats and dropped down the small table between them so he could finish his self-portrait.

Above him, Rhea settled in front of her laptop and typed. It was neither journal entry nor fiction, the document treading ground somewhere in between. And she had no clue what she would do with it. Two pages in, she saved the file to her desktop, naming it: *From LA to Chicago*. She took a deep breath and continued to type.

They were two hours outside Chicago when Surfer Boy's head popped up beside Rhea in the top bunk. She startled at his unexpected appearance and snapped the laptop shut. Her face flooded pink.

A smiled crept across his face. "Were you writing about me?"

"No!" Rhea yelped. "Of course not!"

"Because I'd be flattered if you were."

"It's nothing. I just . . . Thought . . . I might try my hand at some fiction. Because I needed to prove to myself I can't write for shit."

Surfer Boy shook his head, having to brace himself against the wall when the train hit a rough stretch of track. "I'm willing to bet you're better than you give yourself credit for."

Rhea chewed her lip, staring at the laptop's lid. "Someone once told me the reason I'm such a good listener is because I've got nothing of value to contribute to conversations."

He gaped at her, the swaying of the train still jerking him around.

Her eyes met his. "What?"

"What kind of absolute *douche-canoe* would say something like that?"

Her father. "Does it matter?" Besides which, she had kind of lied about the original statement; the time she had the audacity to point out he was talkative, he'd told her he dominated their conversations because she had nothing of significance to discuss. She hadn't meant for her observation to be hurtful, but never convinced herself he hadn't intended to cut her to the quick with his rebuttal. That was the day she'd decided to get a certification for massage therapy rather than go to college for a journalism degree.

That was the day she accepted what became her first date with Mark; it was no fluke those events coincided.

"Sunshine?"

"I thought I'd try my hand at some fiction. A random line of narration popped into my head, so I typed it. And then the line that followed it. And another. And the next thing I know, I'm ten pages in, I've got a full plot and realizing I've got all sorts of parental issues . . . That I'm currently spewing to a stranger who doesn't deserve me dumping all my emotional baggage on him."

"You've got a whole plot already?" Surfer Boy asked in disbelief. He snapped his fingers. "Just like that?"

"Yeah I can't believe it either." It was yet another thing about the trip that was so unlike her.

"So . . . Will this story have a happy ending?"

Rhea studied his face, as if she would find an answer there. "I dunno yet. I guess we'll have to wait 'n' see."

"Is there any way I could help ensure a happy ending?"

"Well technically," said Rhea with a smirk, "that's *my* responsibility as a masseuse. And I've given you one."

"What about *you*?"

"What *about* me?"

"You deserve a happy ending, too." Surfer Boy smiled at her. "And I'd like to help. To . . . Be a part of it, somehow."

Rhea wondered if they were on the same page anymore. She doubted they were even on the same planet. She had no idea how to respond to his declaration.

In her silence, he said, "We've got less than two hours before we reach Chicago, part ways, and never see each other again."

Rhea swallowed hard; she didn't know how to respond to that either. Was his saying that an assumption it was what she preferred? "Y-yeah," she stammered.

"Let's not spend it being sad. Would you like to join me down here?"

RAYS OF SUNSHINE

She nodded.

As Rhea dropped down, Surfer Boy told her, "Just so we're clear, I *would* like to keep in touch. It's up to you if we do. And . . . in what capacity. As friends or fuck buddies or . . . *whatever.*"

She smiled at him, wrapping her arms around his shoulders. "Thanks for clarifying."

Surfer Boy inhaled. "For a chick who's spent a couple days on the train, you sure do smell good."

"I smell even better when I'm fresh from the shower."

"Goddamn, I'll *bet* you do." His hands slid down her back and he cupped her ass. "I can imagine taking you in a shower." He pulled her hips toward his. She felt his heat through their clothing.

Rhea kissed him, her lips brushing softly against his. "Oh? What would that be like?"

"I'd lather you up with whatever fragrant soap you use . . . Over your shoulders, down your arms." He demonstrated with his hands. "Soap-down your back, of course, maybe massage you a little—if you promised not to mock me."

Her voice husky, Rhea said, "Maybe I'd have given you some pointers on back massage before we hopped in the shower together. Maybe . . . Your touch is already amazing as it is."

"*Maybe* . . ." he continued, caressing her breasts through her shirt and bra, "I'd make sure your rack is *really* clean. Wouldn't want that glorious piercing to get infected now, would we?"

She sighed. "No . . ."

"Soap down your stomach, your legs." He kissed her briefly. Kneading her ass, he said, "And I'd clean *this* thoroughly . . . And everything around the front, too."

"Uh huh . . ."

"Ever been eaten out in a shower?"

Rhea shook her head, her heart thundering. "I've never been orally serviced. *Ever.*"

Surfer Boy reached between her thighs, massaging her through her jeans. "I'd drop to my knees at your feet, spread your legs with my face. Dip my tongue between your lips and taste your nectar." He demonstrated with his mouth on hers, moaning.

On the average day, Rhea enjoyed her showers; but she'd never wanted to be in one more than she did now.

Did she dare ask him to go down on her? *No.* She hadn't bathed in three days and it must've smelled reminiscent of a bakery on the beach down there. *Make that a fuck no.* It was nothing a little Summer's Eve couldn't fix, but until she could shower . . . ?

Until when? She drew in a sharp breath, pulling away from Surfer Boy's lips.

"What?" he asked, his voice tight with apprehension. "Is it something I said? Something I did?"

Yes. No. Rhea dreaded the arrival in Chicago more with each passing minute. "Take me," she begged. "Take me slow, take me long. Make it last a lifetime, for the love of God."

Surfer Boy nodded, converting the seats in his roomette into a bed and closing the door. "I'll be glad to, but . . . One question first."

". . . Yeah?" Her phlegm thickened.

"If you don't know my name, what will you scream when I make you come?" He lifted her T-shirt off over her head before reaching around to unhook her bra and pull it off.

"I . . . Guess . . ." Rhea smiled, pleased with her quick thinking. She'd have to remember the exchange for her story: "I'll just have to blaspheme the hell out of myself."

He chuckled, giving her a big nod of appreciation. "I'll make an angel out of you yet."

Rhea wriggled out of her jeans and underwear, reclining on the bed. She gazed at him, aiming for an innocent expression which had to be more porn queen than nun.

Surfer Boy undressed under Rhea's watchful eyes. His physique, if imperfect, was so close to perfection she didn't see any flaws: nothing but smooth, tanned skin over the fine lines of well-defined muscles. She'd massaged him, and given him the handy-j, but she had yet to explore his body with her mouth. She bit her lip, staring at his erection.

There she was, making plans for future encounters with him. Rhea thought he'd be great fun to suck on in the shower like a big, vanilla ice cream drumstick. Nuts, and all.

"What's that look for?" Surfer Boy asked, his lips crooking upward into a smile.

"*Nothing*," Rhea lied. "I'm just taking in the sights."

He rolled on the condom. "Promise you'll remember me."

"You've already given me so much that I couldn't forget you even if I wanted to."

Surfer Boy lowered himself to the bed, wrapping his body around hers and kissing her on the neck. He drew Rhea's skin between his lips and sucked. She inhaled sharply and moaned.

His cock rested against the inside of her thighs and she squeezed it between her legs.

"Oh yeah," he told her, his lips against the sensitive mark he'd left on her neck. "That feels so good."

So she squeezed him a bit harder and he moaned, his voice reverberating against her neck. Surfer Boy peppered her collarbone with pecks and he kissed a trail down to her breasts.

Rhea raked her fingers through his hair, trying to cling to him as well as her composure without it being too obvious she was well on her way to losing control.

He flicked the barbell in her nipple with his tongue, squeezing her left breast. Rhea clenched her eyes shut as his lips scorched her skin. She knew it then: He was branding her.

"I want to taste you," he whispered.

Rhea was certain he'd been teasing her with the shower talk, as if it had all been sexual bravado during foreplay to get her juices running—which it had.

"I *need* to taste you."

There was such urgency in Surfer Boy's voice that Rhea could do nothing but indulge him, cleanliness be damned. "Who am I to say 'no?'"

He acknowledged her statement with no words but with actions: kissing a meandering trail down her torso to the tops of her thighs. And then from her right thigh, kiss by kiss, he nestled his face between her legs, greeting her pussy with a long slow lick the full length of his tongue.

The sensation filled her whole body with a sizzle of excitement unlike anything she'd ever experienced. "Oh my *God*—" she gasped and the remainder of her articulation collapsed into a long, deep moan.

"You are so fucking sexy." He licked again.

"Don't—stop—" She praised him with another moan between staggered gasps, gathering what loosely qualified for bedding into fists.

After a little bit of repositioning, Surfer Boy teased her with his fingertips, sneaking the tip of one into her white-hot center, his tongue tracing circles around her clit.

Rhea whimpered. She'd have told him whatever he was doing to her pussy was unabashed cruelty, but while she was coming, her words were not. Just sexy, delightful moaning and sighing as wave after wave of unparalleled bliss imparted by his tongue washed over her.

When pleasure gave way to oversensitivity, Rhea tried to close her legs on Surfer Boy. He chuckled and backed away, wiping his chin with the back of his arm. Her chest heaved and he reached out to caress her right breast, circling her nipple with his thumb.

Focused on her piercing, he told her, "This is so damn cool."

"You—gonna—waste—" Rhea managed a deep breath to finish her question. "—the condom?"

Surfer Boy gave her a big smile and a simple answer: "Nope." He slid along her body, positioning himself before easing into her.

She closed her eyes, compelled to commit this moment to memory and forget it all at the same time. Rhea ran her hands down his sculpted back, settling them on his ass, where she enjoyed the rhythm of sex from yet another vantage point.

He kissed her neck, working his way to her jaw. But he hesitated putting his lips to hers.

"*Kiss me*," Rhea said.

He grunted between thrusts. "I taste like you."

"You could taste like my ass. I don't give a shit." She put her hands on either side of his face and drew him down to her, pressing her lips to his softly. Rhea found nothing objectionable there. So she parted her lips, and he did the same, their tongues dancing around each other, exploring each other's mouths. It was only then that she tasted herself on him, but she didn't care. The things he did with his tongue, wherever he did them, were marvelous.

He broke their kiss. "Will you ride me 'til I come? Please, Sunshine?"

Thinking of his stamina, she worried she would get a saddle sore from such endeavors; but oh, would the pain ever be worthwhile! She smiled at him. "Sure thing. Just . . . Don't make it too hard for me."

Surfer Boy dismounted her, glancing at his cock as it jutted away from him. "I'm pretty damn sure it doesn't get any harder than this."

In the cramped quarters, they maneuvered around each other. He reclined on the bed and she straddled him, her dripping slit mere inches from his erection. She watched it quiver beneath her as he adjusted his position between her thighs. Rhea gave him a devious smile.

He lifted his head, watching her. "What's that look for?" he asked, his eyes and voice wary.

"You really tortured me earlier, y'know?"

Surfer Boy dropped his head back on the pillow. Though he was smiling, he groaned: "Do your worst."

Rhea reached around behind herself, curling her fingers around his balls. "Is that a challenge?"

He moaned, closing his eyes with a wide smile.

She lowered herself until the tip of his dick parted her folds; it tortured as much as it teased and she was sure she felt the anticipation as much as he did. Rhea lifted herself off him, sliding her heat against the full length of his cock— which served to make her even wetter, and him, somehow even harder. She thought to point out he *could* get stiffer but instead, she repositioned herself facing his toes, backing up toward his face. She wrapped her hand around the base of his cock, and brought her mouth to its tip.

He grunted. "You're a tease!"

Rhea wrapped her lips around him, rotating her slick hand and sucking. She thought about how much better this would be without the wretched flavor of the condom. Going down on him without it made her want to get monogamous with him. The intrusive thought was wrenched from her head when his fingertips sank into her creamy ass, and his tongue found her clit again.

It took every last shred of concentration to focus on pleasuring him, rather than creaming his face. As another orgasm built, Rhea pulled away from Surfer Boy. She turned to face him again.

"*Please*," he moaned, "put me out of my misery already!"

Rhea slid against his member, rotating her hips in circles over his lap. It wasn't long before he grabbed those hips, thrusting into her with a hard shudder. She thought he'd come then, but he made that motion—with the same reaction—again. And again. So she followed his lead, sliding up and down him.

His right hand slid from her hip to cover her clit—he pressed it, rubbed it, and circled it with the pad of his thumb.

"Oh jeez—" she gasped, her climax rebuilding at break-neck speed.

"Come again?" he moaned.

And she did.

The ripples caressing his erection with her orgasm beckoned his, and he came hard. "*Fuck*—" Surfer Boy gasped through his.

They both fell quiet, catching their breath.

Rhea exhaled as Surfer Boy pulled her down to rest chest-to-chest.

"You're amazing," he remarked.

She closed her eyes, reveling in the feel of his muscles beneath her breasts. "Yeah well that's neither here nor there." If she concentrated, she thought she felt his heart pounding. Or perhaps what she felt was the clicking and clacking of train over track.

They were on a train; how easy it was to forget that in

the throes of passion. Rhea pushed herself to her knees again, and Surfer Boy moaned.

"It's so sensitive..."

She smiled, reaching around to gently manipulate his balls some more.

"Oh—God—yes—"

As his moan dangled there for want of a proper noun to attribute her amazing massage skills, Rhea regretted not giving her name to him. She was regretting a lot of things now, not the least of which was they'd used the last condom he bought.

And they would be arriving in Chicago soon.

She blinked, opening the window curtains enough to peer outside; she was expecting open plains but what she got was suburbs.

"When are we supposed to be in Chicago?" asked Rhea, gingerly dismounting Surfer Boy. For all her care, she knocked her head against the bottom of the upper bunk, which they failed to close.

"Oh! Are you all right?" gasped Surfer Boy, reaching out for her head.

She rubbed the back of her head, laughing despite the throbbing pain. "Clearance is lower than advertised." She kissed his forehead for his compassion; after all, he could have laughed at her for her clumsiness. "Yeah, I'm fine."

Surfer Boy snapped the condom off himself, wrapping the used rubber in a few tissues and dropping it into the trash. At the sound of the train approaching a railroad crossing, he peered out through the slit between the curtain panels. He announced flatly, "We're in Chicago."

"What?" she snapped.

"*We're in Chicago.*"

Rhea felt an unexpected panic rise in her chest, clamping around her throat with a merciless squeeze. She had to dress. She had to gather her things. She had to make a decision about Surfer Boy. "Damn. Shit. Oh hell, fuck!" She rushed to get back into her clothing.

Once dressed, she combed out her short hair with her fingers, shaking her head—as if that had any affect. "I've gotta go to my seat . . . Get my stuff . . ." It was miraculous she could think straight.

Surfer Boy zipped his pants and slid open the cabin door. Rhea swept her few articles from the bunk.

"Would you—" He cleared his throat.

She glanced at him, taking a steadying breath. If her expression read as even a smidgen the amount of conflicted she was, he could see it.

He finished, "—meet me on the platform for a proper goodbye?"

Rhea swallowed. Why couldn't she say 'no' to this guy? He was derailing all her plans! Or, rather, her lack of them. "How will I find you there?" She had no experience of Chicago's Union Station but assumed it was similar to any large city transportation hub: busy as all get out.

"I'll stand beside the train until we're the last two passengers left on the platform, if I need to."

Son of a bitch! Could he be any more romantic? "Anyone ever tell you you're too good to be true?"

"You'd be the first. If . . . you're telling me that."

"I'll be out on the platform," Rhea told him, turning into the stairwell. "I hope to see you there."

Two-hundred-some dollars, she mused as she returned to her seat and pulled her backpack from the overhead compartment. *For a seat I spent so little time in. But . . . I had amazing sex for the first time in my life.* On balance, she decided, it was all worthwhile. The laptop went into the bag; Rhea thinking she would have to chronicle her trip—in explicit detail—once she got to her hotel room.

The train jerked several times as it slowed in its approach to the station.

It stopped. With it, Rhea's heart.

Yes, she was going to meet Surfer Boy on the platform for a hearty handshake and a thanks-for-the-orgasms. But she was still undecided about keeping in touch with him.

Rhea watched as the other passengers gathered their belongings and one-by-one filtered down the aisle to the stairwell. And one-by-one, their heads bobbed and disappeared down the stairs until she was alone in the car.

Still without a decision on the sexy stranger.

"Ma'am?" An attendant cleared her throat from behind Rhea. "We've arrived in Chicago. I must ask you to detrain now."

"Oh. Oh, yes, of course." Rhea nodded absently. "Thank you." She slung the backpack over her shoulder, and slid the purse handles up her arm.

"The attendant downstairs will help you with your luggage."

"Thanks."

"Thanks for choosing Amtrak and have a nice day."

"You too." And, as every passenger had before her, Rhea descended the narrow staircase to the first level of the Superliner.

While the attendant pulled her tagged suitcase from the luggage storage compartment, Rhea rooted through her purse, pulling out the single piece of paper she'd torn from her little notebook. She was sorely tempted to crumple it in a fist and ask the attendant to throw it out for her. But the way her heart wrenched at the thought gave clear indication her mind was indeed made up about keeping in contact with Surfer Boy. Better yet, keeping in touch with him. *Direct touch. Literally.*

The attendant handed her suitcase over and with an unexpected lazy southern drawl, he told Rhea, "Ya have a nice day now, y'hear?"

"Thanks. You too."

By the time Rhea stepped off the Southwest Chief into the whole new world of Chicago, there were but a few people left milling about on the train platform. Some of them hugging fiercely; reunions, Rhea guessed. One was gazing at the station building—either lost or struck by awe. And, under an Amtrak sign: Surfer Boy by himself, a single suitcase by his feet and his large black portfolio tucked beneath his right arm.

With a steadying breath, Rhea approached. "Hey." It felt like greeting an old friend rather than a one-night-stand whose name she still didn't know. And maybe she *did* want to know it after all. But only if he volunteered it; she wasn't about to ask.

"Hi." His salutation was filled with the same familiarity as hers.

"You, uh . . . You owe me a self-portrait as I recall."

To Rhea's surprise, he pulled a piece of paper from his portfolio and handed it to her. "Don't be hard on me, I'm really *not* the kind of artist who does portraits."

Rhea's mouth fell open in a quiet gasp. She didn't know on what to comment first: his amazing likeness, or the sketch in the upper right-hand corner of a chibi-style Surfer Boy and Sunshine—each labeled as such—in profile and kissing, a single heart drawn between the two. It was painful in its innocence, especially considering the *not* innocent things they'd done together. "You have *me* fooled," she whispered. "It's perfect, thank you!"

"I agonized over it."

"Your hard work shows." Rhea considered her statement. "Your *talent* shows." She reconsidered her compliment again: "You have skilled hands." Let him interpret that as he would.

Surfer Boy laughed in hearty appreciation. "So do *you*."

"I suppose . . ." *Do it, do it now*! ". . . I should give you this." Rhea gave him the note she'd written him last night and held her breath.

He scanned it, then broke into even more laughter. "No wonder you liked me calling you Sunshine!" After a pause, he added, "*Rhea*."

God, it sounds sexy on his voice. And he pronounced it right: ray. Not the way the vast majority of her teachers did, like a truncated version of a popular word for the trots.

"Turn the portrait over," Surfer Boy told her.

Rhea did, finding his email address written on the back. "*Adam arts on the beach*," she read, nodding with a wide smile spreading across her face. *I guess I really do know him from Adam*! "Email me sometime. Okay?"

He nodded. "I will. My offer still stands, by-the-way, to take you around the Art Institute."

Rhea made a counter-proposal: "Only if a meal's included."

"You got it."

"*Dinner*, though. And maybe . . . Drinks afterward?"

"As long as there's a nice long night of screwing in a hotel room, after." Adam countered her counter-proposal.

"There'd better be shower sex like you described or I'm calling the whole thing off."

"Oh you drive a hard bargain. But . . . It's a deal if you promise to scream my name now that you know it."

Rhea was smiling so hard, her cheeks hurt. "Only if you leave me no other choice."

"Don't worry about *that*. I'll rise to the occasion." He was smiling every bit as big as Rhea now.

"I have no doubt you *will*."

"I've . . . I've got a gallery to get to," said Adam reluctantly. "I'll send you an email tonight."

"Best of luck to you."

"Thanks. Get some rest and enjoy your stay here."

"I will."

Adam leaned in, leaving Rhea with a lingering kiss.

She allowed herself time to recover before turning toward the train station building. Casting a purposeful glance at Adam, she made another decision; this one about the story she'd started writing on the train.

"It'll have a happy ending," Rhea told herself.

He was preoccupied with his cellphone by then. She hollered after him, "See you around, Artist Boy!"

He blew her a kiss in return.

Rays of Sunshine

PART 2

SMILES BY TRIALS

"Rather than allow ourselves to be burdened by regret for
our past misdeeds, we must strive to develop the inherent
goodness which lies hidden in our souls,
beneath layers of tarnish left by our sins."

—Rabbi Joseph Stern

Chapter One

Rhea Josse plopped down in front of her laptop while Skype sang her the song of its people. She clicked on the video call icon and Adam L'amoreaux's smiling face greeted her.

"Hey," she said, "how's the New Year's resolution coming along?"

He replied, "Proud to say I already broke it."

"Two days in? I'm impressed."

"Well I was striving to break last year's record of a week." Adam laughed. "Anyway, it's foggy and stupidly humid out so I've resorted to painting in my kitchen. Not the worst thing ever, I know, but . . ." The view in his chat window changed as he repositioned his laptop to show what was going on outside his apartment.

Orange County was visibly dreary even over the Skype connection.

He then shifted his laptop again to reveal the canvas on which he'd painted a muted interpretation of the Pacific Ocean—with the current weather used as depressing inspiration. With one last move, the camera was back on

Adam. He pouted. "Miss you."

"Last night's date didn't go well?" Rhea assumed, resting her elbows on her desk.

"She was pretty," replied Adam. "And nice. Majoring in physics at UCI."

"Oh." The pang of jealousy in Rhea's gut was unwelcome and she knew she didn't hide her feelings well by how his pout morphed into a frown.

Why did he always have to date pretty women? Why couldn't he pick someone who wasn't a threat to her? Regardless of his choice in partners, this arrangement had been mutually agreed upon and she wasn't ready to renege five months in—not if he wasn't.

In seven months, however? In seven months all bets were off.

"Yeah, she was great. But . . . she wasn't you."

Rhea forced her voice down an octave into the so-called 'cool' range. "Did you sleep with her?"

"She sure wanted to. I took a pass. Told her I had an early . . . art . . . exhibit."

She cocked her head and folded her arms across her chest. "That's weak."

He sighed. "I know. I'm not proud but I'd had a couple beers and wasn't thinking clearly."

"Oh come on, that's the ideal time to sleep with someone. I *told* you, it's okay. It's not as if we're on a break or doing the long-distance relationship thing. We're just two friends. Besties. Who . . . you know . . . Did it when we first met." They'd done it a lot, as memory served.

"I *will* sleep with someone else," swore Adam, "but not until you do it, first."

"This whole thing isn't gonna work if neither of us is even trying to get laid."

"Hey—" He stuck out his tongue at her. "I'm trying. I'm not convinced you are."

Rhea took a deep breath. Two thousand miles away and still he could call her on her bullshit. Not preferring to discuss it, she opted to change the subject to something else he probably wouldn't be thrilled to hear: "So . . . You'll never guess who friended me on Facebook yesterday."

"I haven't checked it since Monday. Who?"

"Brianna Huntington."

Adam was static so long Rhea wondered if Skype froze as it was wont to do from time to time, particularly during bad weather which it appeared Southern California was experiencing. It was what they considered bad, anyway. A few months living where bad weather meant more than overcast skies and intermittent spitting drizzle and Rhea had the wisdom to see how spoiled Southern Californians were.

". . . Adam?"

"Is she your high school crush?"

Rhea nodded. In case her side of the connection was the one failing, she also said, "Yeah. I think she added a bunch of us from band. I thought she sent me a request as one of the bunch or maybe by accident or whatever, until she sent me a DM saying she wanted to reconnect. Which is funny, you know, because to *re*connect, you have to have ever been connected to *begin* with."

"Yeah . . ." said Adam.

"Okay," she huffed. "What."

Adam glanced off to the left, where Rhea knew his kitchen window was located. "I just . . ." He exhaled. "I don't want you getting hurt. Remember, I read your blog. I know what she did to you."

"To be fair, it's what I did to myself. And anyway, things are different now. I'm . . . secure in who I am. And . . . I have the best friend a girl could ask for." She nodded at the camera in her laptop. "I won't let her hurt me."

Adam looked back at his camera. "Promise?"

Rhea cleared her throat. "Turns out, she . . . lives in Chicago now."

He frowned. "Small world."

"We actually spent most of yesterday chatting on Messenger."

Still, Adam was stoic. Or maybe Skype froze for real that time.

Rhea's phone buzzed with a notification from Messenger and she discreetly swiped the screen on to check it.

Hey Rhea, Brianna had sent. *Could use a friend in the area. U available to get drinks tonite?*

"Well I'm happy as long as you are," said Adam.

"Oh I'm very happy. I thought it'd be nice to have a friend in the area. But you know what? Nothing makes me happier than knowing I'll see you again in six months or so." Rhea smiled, casually closing the Messenger app on her phone without responding to Brianna.

"Um . . . about that."

Her smile faded, hands dropping to her lap. "What about it?"

He took stock of his surroundings.

"Adam." she prompted.

". . . Gary says nothing's moved in an age."

Her head dropped, too. "Oh." She didn't know for what to feel worse: that no one was buying his art or the lack of sales would impede his next visit.

"This happens sometimes," Adam assured her. "I'm not too worried. I've been watching videos of these amazing chalk artists on YouTube . . . thinking of branching out into other mediums . . . Sometimes that gets stuff going, you know? Oh and Gary suggested I paint a few pieces for an upcoming charity auction."

"Have . . . you already got the materials for it?"

He nodded. "He wants to pay my way to Catalina, thinks I'll do well with that for inspiration."

Rhea forced a smile. She would have loved taking the trip with him. "I'll bet he's right though. You should take him up on the offer."

"I will. Thanks for your encouragement." Adam smiled at her, though his looked far less forced than hers.

"Maybe things will turn around before next July."

Adam's smile turned impish.

"What's that smile for?"

"I was thinking about what I'll do to you when we *do* see each other again."

Rhea's eyebrows jumped. "Oh? You sound like you had something in mind."

"Well . . . The titty-fucking thing you keep describing to me in explicit detail sure as hell sounds fun."

She smirked; perusing Cosmopolitan's website and Tumblr's sex blogs was paying off at long last. "Getting a pearl necklace from you is one of my sex goals."

"Oh, Rhea," he sighed. "I dreamt of you last night."

"It took you this damn long to tell me? That's the kind of thing you open conversations with."

"Duly noted." Adam laughed, sobering quickly. "I'd gotten off the train and you were standing there in this . . . skimpy yellow dress with these thin strappy things which tied in a little bow on each shoulder. You were . . . it was . . ." He sighed. "It was sexy as hell."

She made mental note to find such a dress before he returned to Illinois. "Then what happened?"

"We went back to your car in the parking structure. No one else was around; we didn't question it. I was ready to go to your place and fool around in the shower, you know, like we did that one time—but without the incident which almost sent you to the ER."

"Yeah . . ." She bit her lip. "That would've been a hell of a thing to explain if you hadn't caught me. On an unrelated note, I've been working on my flexibility to keep it from almost happening again."

Adam's eyes went wide, his face alight. "A-ny-way . . . you told me you couldn't wait. And by then I really couldn't either. So much as seeing your smile made me rock hard. I got in the passenger side, you got in behind the wheel and started massaging me through my shorts."

Rhea cocked her head with a guilty little smile. "Sounds like something I'd do."

"You climbed to my side, flashed me in the process. You had this white G-string that was lacy on top and had pearls between your cheeks and up your slit. So innocent but so naughty at the same time. I reached around to caress you with those pearls while you gave me a lap dance. It was driving you crazy . . . Which drove me crazy.

"I don't know how you got me out of my pants—dream logic I guess, I won't question it—but the next thing I knew,

I was inside you right there in the passenger seat of your car. And the parking structure which was previously empty? It wasn't anymore and people were watching but neither of us cared—"

"How much do you miss me?" Rhea panted.

He moaned, "So much I've gotta fight the urge to get train tickets more and more every day. God, do you know what I'd do to you if we were together?"

"The same thing I'm doing to me right now?" Her hand was down her lounge pants, circling her wet pussy and clit.

"Yeah that's right," Adam's voice cracked.

There was nothing more in the world than his voice and the sizzling of her mounting climax.

"Come, gorgeous lady . . ."

"Oh, God, ohhh—"

Rhea's phone started ringing.

"*Ohh*—son of a *bitch*!" Her orgasm ran into hiding at the distraction. "I was almost there."

He sounded sheepish: "I came."

She glanced at her phone to see who had the audacity to interrupt her jilling off. "Shit. It's the chiropractor. I'd better answer it."

"Miss you, love you, text later. Bye, sexy."

"Love you too. Bye."

"Hello?" Rhea answered her phone with her left hand as Adam's video feed blinked from the computer screen.

"*Hi, Rhea? It's Lee-Ann.*"

Calls from the office manager seldom worked in her favor—there was a certain aptness that it was she who'd interrupted Rhea's masturbating. She put on a smile, however, hoping it masked her annoyance over the phone. "Hey Lee-Ann, what's up?"

"*Sheldon had a family emergency and needed to reschedule with someone. He'll need coverage for Saturday night in exchange for a shift tonight.*"

There was no apparent reason for Rhea to say no. She had nobody to hang out with in Aurora. No dates for the foreseeable future. And Saturday night patients were always so grateful to be seen that they were more pleasant than weekday patients, even those in significant pain. Especially those in significant pain. "I can trade."

Rhea hoisted herself from her chair and retreated into her bedroom well aware of the squishiness of her underwear. She scratched out her shift information on the desk calendar. "When do you need me?"

"*Saturday nine to six.*"

"Okay. I'll be there." Rhea jotted down the times.

"*Thanks so much. Your flexibility is duly noted. Doctor Kasick doesn't forget stuff like this and your probation period's ending soon.*"

She smiled crookedly at her calendar. "Good to hear."

"*Enjoy your evening off, Rhea.*"

"Thanks, Lee-Ann, you too. Bye."

Lee-Ann ended the call and Rhea exhaled, looking at her phone's home screen. She opened Brianna's conversation in Messenger and typed, *Can you meet me at Hoppy Endings in Lombard? Don't know how far that is from you.*

She then sent a text to Adam. *I miss you. 7 months will go by in a wink. Keep busy w Gary & Catalina & chalk. When you get here? All the titty fucking you can handle.*

He responded: *I love you. You're the best.* Followed immediately by another text: *Please get plowed by some guy in the meantime. Have fun. Sow oats you never got the chance to.*

Rhea sighed, closing his text conversation.

A message from Brianna came in. *I can be there by 7. That work for u?*

Yep, Rhea typed. *See you there.*

———smile———

Rhea paced out in front of a brick building with floor-to-ceiling windows, its patio filled with vacant round tables covered in a thin layer of snow and illuminated only by indoor lights. A metal fence with elaborate scroll-work separated the patio from the sidewalk and it was lined with closed umbrellas, each one capped with a fine dusting of white powder.

She pulled her hands from her parka pockets long enough to check her phone—it was ten minutes until seven and the butterflies in her stomach called in reinforcements, and they, reinforcements of their own.

What the hell am I going to talk about with the prom queen?

Okay, so she wasn't the prom queen but she may as well have been.

She took a single step toward her car and stopped herself. How many times had she almost bailed on something she was ultimately grateful for seeing through?

Adam.

The indoor skydiving guy. What was his name again? Ricky? Jonas? It had been a fun evening even though it didn't lead to sex.

Maybe this will be a fun evening, too.

Of course it'll be. Because fun is defined as meeting with the girl who deliberately shut me out of her cliques six years ago. The same girl I was more attracted to than the man I married. The girl I could obviously never have for any number of reasons. Yeah. Sounds fun.

Okay. Okay! This was a supremely dumb idea but maybe it'll be good for me. I can forgive her for being such a raging bitch when we were younger and then go home feeling like the better person for it. If, of course, she didn't make plans to purposefully stand me up because she hasn't fucked me over emotionally quite enough for one life—

"Rhea? Oh my Lord, is that you?"

Rhea's eyes lifted from the concrete to see Brianna approaching a few yards away.

Brianna was gorgeous as ever; her Facebook selfies were doing her no favors. Her blonde hair was tucked into a sloppy ponytail, blue strands popping out against the field of silken gold. She wore a pair of fluffy white earmuffs; the light bouncing off them from inside the restaurant gave her the appearance of having a faint halo. Her cognac brown eyes were rimmed with maroon dust and fringed with what had to be falsies.

Rhea remembered the holier-than-thou sway in Brianna's strut even the floor-length coat she wore couldn't hide.

Regardless of the bitter cold, she dressed as though she were a damned goddess, as if she expected Mother Nature to kowtow to her sense of fashion.

Long story short: The lousy bitch was luscious.

"Yeah, it's me," Rhea grumbled, retreating into her thick cowl, acutely aware of the tiny blemish she had in front of her right earlobe. It was in reality a pinprick of red; in her mind's eye it was the Mount Everest of zits and must have been all Brianna saw when she looked at her. "Hi." Rhea swallowed. "Brianna."

The rhythmic clicking of Brianna's stiletto boots against the pavement stopped. Rhea wondered how she walked with them, especially on the slippery sidewalk. "Bri. It's *Bri*."

Rhea cleared her throat and grumbled, "'K. Bri." To use Brianna's nickname felt uncomfortable, bordering on painful, the way it felt to rest her bare back against a cold bathtub filled with hot water. *Or . . . Maybe I don't use her name at all. Problem solved.*

"You . . . look . . . Unrecognizable," said Brianna. "Amazing. Actually."

"Thanks. I guess?" Rhea laughed stiffly.

"No, seriously. I love your hair. Wish I could pull off a cute little cut like that." Brianna opened her arms for a hug and Rhea in turn crossed hers over her chest, rubbing her biceps brusquely through the parka as she took a giant step backward. Her foot slid on a tiny patch of ice and she recovered quickly enough Brianna didn't appear to notice.

"We should probably get inside," said Rhea, gesturing with a stiff jerk toward the building. "It's frostbite weather."

Brianna pursed her lips. "Oh. Ye—yeah. Totally."

Rhea led her into the restaurant and they settled on the leather sofa near the fireplace after shedding their coats. Brianna wore skin-tight pants and a low-cut blouse beneath her trench coat. And she was cold. Very cold. Rhea didn't need to go by the goosebumps on Brianna's arms to know it.

It was surprisingly quiet inside despite how busy it was. Rather than talking with Brianna or staring at her high-beams, Rhea studied the décor: a strange reddish rug sprawled atop rich wood flooring; there were dark wood chairs with similar coloring to the sofa on which they sat, and paler wood tables complementing the frames on skinny rectangular mirrors which hung vertically on one wall. The place oozed opulence and Rhea assumed she couldn't afford to breathe the air there.

Brianna ordered a glass of the Malbec and Rhea selected a chocolate martini from the *hoppily ever after* portion of the menu.

While they waited for their drinks, Brianna squeezed her knees together, tapping the toes of her stilettos on the floor. She dropped her head. "I . . . really appreciate you meeting with me tonight. I needed a friend so bad."

Rhea didn't know how she qualified as a friend all of a sudden but she couldn't bring herself to inquiring about it in the midst of Brianna's misery. She considered asking why her local friends had hung her out to, well, hanging out with the high school riffraff. She exhaled. "What's going on?"

"I went home for lunch today and my boyfriend was gone. Completely moved out. Left his key with the leasing office after leaving." Brianna wrung her hands together. "He's gone. *Gone*-gone."

"Oh. Damn. I'm so sorry."

"I didn't want to be by myself and I couldn't exactly go back to work. You're the only one I know in the area. Jeez, I'm so glad you're here."

Rhea shook her head. "How on Earth are you—" Maybe calling Brianna alone at this point wasn't tactful. "How the hell am I the only one you know here? Did you move to Chicago just this afternoon?"

Brianna laughed, although she brushed a tear from her right eye with the side of her thumb.

"Seriously. You were the queen of the cool kids in high school. I'm sure you were head of your sorority in college—"

"I wasn't in a sorority. I focused on getting my degree in communication. By the time commencement rolled around, I had a relatively useless diploma, mountains of debt, sixteen hundred Facebook friends, a boyfriend . . . and no social life to speak of."

Poor unloved hot girl. Rhea rolled her eyes. *Those sixteen hundred friends must leave you feeling real lonely.* After a quick mental calculation, she realized Brianna had something around twelve times the number of friends on the social media network she did. That was probably an underestimation, too.

"Okay," Brianna sighed. "What."

Rhea blanched. "I . . . Look, I didn't come here for a confrontation. I'm just baffled by—well . . . why me? You don't know me now and you sure as hell didn't in high school. You had your cool kids group and I had . . ." She squeaked, *"mine."* Where 'mine' in reality meant virtually no one.

"Oh give me a break," Brianna scoffed. "Cool cliques are useless. I only ever happened to wear the right things. If I'd gone to school in boys' clothing, they'd have kicked me out of the group without a second thought and none of them would've missed me."

Rhea bristled, accepting the martini from the waitress with a grimace. She waited until after the waitress gave Brianna her wine and went to serve other patrons before replying, "Wear boys' clothing to school . . . You mean same as I did?"

"What?" Brianna yelped, gaping at Rhea. "I thought you were doing the grunge thing." She faltered. "Some ten years after it was cool . . ."

Grunge was never cool—wasn't that the whole point?

"No," Rhea said through her teeth and tossed back her martini. "Excuse me, I need another." She swept out of her seat to find the waitress. The idea of walking out without another word to Brianna was sorely tempting. She glanced toward the sofas by the fireplace. Brianna was hunched over, cradling her forehead in her palm. "God dammit," she sighed. Without a replacement drink, she returned to her seat.

"I'm sorry," said Rhea. "Look . . . I'm still working through some things."

"I really didn't mean it as an insult." Brianna lifted her head, catching Rhea's eyes and smiling briefly.

Rhea glanced away. "Was meeting me here part of some twelve-step thing?"

"No," scoffed Brianna. "Hey, if I came across as a bitch

when we were younger, I'm . . . sorry. I honestly believe if things had been different, we would've been BFF's. Could we at least try to be friends now? From what I knew of you in high school, I'd have been better off with you as my only friend than with all the friends I supposedly had." She muttered, "Some, especially, more than others."

"That's a consolation." Rhea took interest in the hearth, tapping the empty martini glass with her fingernails. *Jeez. When did I get to be such a liar?*

"I've got an older sister who's fashion-conscious and used me as her personal dress-up doll. I went along with it because it got me into the cool clique. And come on, you can't hold that against me. Being included in the cool kids' group is all any of us ever want."

Rhea supposed that had to suck—the part regarding her sister, anyway. "I . . . was raised in the wealthy white-trash family of our neighborhood. My parents were more interested in saving for retirement than they were for buying things like, y'know, clothing for their daughter."

"Yeah? My dad made big bucks," Brianna countered, "but he was away on business for most of my childhood."

"Oh." Rhea hoped she was lying for sympathy. "I'm sorry."

"Don't be. When he came home? He got drunk because he couldn't handle the stress of his job . . . and he'd beat the ever-lovin' shit out of my mom for screwing up the meatloaf. For letting the weeds grow too much in the front yard. For not pressing perfect creases into his stupid ugly slacks. Or sometimes for no reason at all. At least, none that I could tell. God only knows how bad things were in the bedroom. Maybe he beat her because she wouldn't put out for him enough." Brianna shrugged. "I dunno."

Rhea fumbled with her martini glass. "Oh my God!"

"The sperm donor had a heart attack and died my freshman year in college. I didn't attend his funeral and Mom got so mad at me she hasn't spoken to me since." Brianna finished her red wine, casting her empty glass an accusatory look. "I'm totally gonna need more of that tonight."

Brianna stood and Rhea stopped her with a hand to her

arm. "No. You don't. You . . . need to talk to someone who'll listen."

After standing in silence for what felt like a year, Brianna sunk back to the sofa, staring at the spot on her arm Rhea touched.

"See . . . This is the kind of friendship I needed when I hid in the closet holding my breath as my parents fought in the room next to mine. This is what I needed while I waited for the wail of sirens to drown out my mother's . . . To have one person who gave a rat's ass— just *one*! —about something other than my hairstyle, or . . . my dumb shoes." She looked Rhea in the eyes. "You're the first I've ever told. Lucy's never told anyone."

Rhea had vague recollections of Brianna's older sister: A blank piece of elaborate stationery came to mind. That is, beautiful but lacking any substantial content. "What's Lucy doing these days?"

"Off-Broadway musicals. And . . . any man who isn't totally gay." Brianna gazed off into the distance. "Although I think she did a couple of them, too, just so they could be sure they were. She claimed she 'changed' one. I let her believe it."

"Ah." Rhea nodded. "Well. Good for her about the Broadway thing."

"So. Um." Brianna gazed into her empty wine glass. "I have a little confession to make."

I'm on Candid Camera?

"You're my hero."

"What?" gasped Rhea. "Why?"

"I . . . actually found you on Facebook a couple weeks ago. And the day before I sent you a friend request, I read through your blog start to finish. The things you've done for yourself? Holy shit. I mean . . . My boyfriend of six months dumped me and I can hardly function. You waltzed out of your marriage and into your own life like it was nothing."

Rhea waved off her praise. "It wasn't like that at all. You must've actually been in love with *your* boyfriend. I waltzed away from a . . . a corpse."

"Lovely." Brianna sneered. "Anyway, I wasn't exactly

super into Travis. I was a teensy bit dependent on him. Okay . . . Honestly? I was definitely dependent on him." She cast what looked like a guilty smile at Rhea. "Hey, uh, there was this month-long gap in your updates after you shared details of your train trip on the blog. What happened with Surfer Boy?"

Rhea exhaled, tilting her face toward the ceiling.

"Oh, I—I thought that story ended well. I'm so sorry, I didn't mean to open old wounds."

"I ran into him in my hotel lobby after we left the train station. He was desperately trying to find a place to stay because his reservations somehow got botched. There was the *huge* Home and Garden show going on that weekend and he wasn't having any luck, so . . ." Rhea lifted her right shoulder.

"Are you two together? Oh my God it's a literal fucking fairy tale!"

"He's . . . in California. We're . . ." She sighed. "It's complicated. We're kinda long-distance fuck-buddies?"

Brianna straightened in her seat, eyebrows arched. "How exactly does that work?"

"Skype. I think you can fill in the details."

"So there's no commitment to him?"

Rhea shook her head. "He's actually been trying to get me laid by someone else."

"Oh. *Oh.*"

Rhea leaned toward Brianna with a smirk and lowered her voice. "I don't think it's gonna happen. The guys I've met here? Meh."

"Their loss, for sure."

"Huh?"

"You're . . . I mean . . ." Brianna rubbed at her right cheek. "You don't post many selfies anywhere and your user icon for Facebook is only half your face. Frankly, I didn't know what to expect when I pictured you during the drive over. I remembered you as this kinda geeky girl in the oversized grunge-style clothing and the thick-rimmed glasses. Not—" She flailed at Rhea. "Not *you*. You look absolutely amazing, girl."

What was it with the ass-backward compliments people always gave her? Nonetheless Rhea smiled. Hot bitch called her amazing.

Twice.

But she wasn't keeping track. Obsessively. "Well thanks." Rhea cleared her throat. "Funny what a woman can do with herself once she's able to figure out who the hell she is."

"I could use some pointers."

"Being on your own will help real quick."

"Yay," said Brianna weakly.

Rhea smiled. "Consider it a silver lining."

"I consider it a silver lining that we're talking. Can we be friends? Please?"

All sorts of red flags were flapping in Rhea's face. *I hope I don't regret this.* "S-sure. Yeah. Of course we can."

Brianna smiled and stood with dumbfounding grace. How the hell was she so fleet-footed while balanced on heels the shoe equivalent of porcupine quills?

"I'm getting us refills," she announced. "This calls for a toast."

*————*smile*————*

On Sunday afternoon, Rhea called Adam on Skype.

On his end of the video chat, things looked brighter—from the sunlight illuminating Adam's kitchen to his posture and the brilliant smile which only grew at the sight of Rhea's face. "How's my girl?"

"It's horrible outside. Like . . . *Hoth* horrible. Windy as hell, sub-zero temps, and blowing snow. But I'm indoors, so whatever. How about you?" she replied.

"I'm going to Catalina tomorrow."

"You are? That's fantastic. How long will you be there?"

"Gary got me reservations at the Pavilion Hotel through Friday. I expect I'll have my fill of inspiration in a week."

Rhea grinned. "This sounds like it'll be so good for you. Will you have time to check in with me?"

"The hotel's supposed to have Wi-Fi. If it does, we'll

Skype when we always do. If not . . . Phone sex? You know, like how they did it in prehistoric times?"

"Okay," Rhea laughed. "Will you get lots of photos for me? I always wanted to go to Catalina. Never got the chance."

"I'll tell you all about it, Sunshine, I promise. So. Tell *me* how things went with your Mean Girl."

"*Well* . . ." Rhea took stock of her living room: she had a multi-colored shag rug positioned beneath her small, oval, walnut coffee table; the little flat-screen television sat on a TV stand because she was too chicken to wall-mount it and was missing her tools, besides; and on her kitchen counter was the empty red vase from the flowers Adam sent upon his return to California.

In an instant, five months felt like an eternity. "Things started rough," she replied. "But I got some stuff off my chest. She apologized for things which—really—weren't her fault. We decided to be friends. Since I'm alone out here and apparently she is, too . . . It made sense to be friends."

"Are you so sure this isn't a mistake?"

"She opened up to me about things she's never told anyone." *Unless they were all lies.* And try as she might, she couldn't shake the feeling as though Brianna had been dishonest. "I've . . . gotta learn to trust. You know that. Especially when it comes to other women. The only one I've ever gotten close to is Cass and I keep even *her* at arm's distance."

"I know," replied Adam. "You know I want nothing but the best or you. It's just . . . I remember what you've told me about this girl—"

"And I told you, things are different now."

"Okay, okay." Adam took a deep breath. "I trust your judgment."

"Thank you, that's all I wanted to hear."

"So. Have you found another guy to bone you yet?"

"No. I'm going out with Brianna soon though, so maybe we'll find a pair of hot guys . . ." She glanced at the clock in the lower right corner of her laptop screen. "Actually, I've gotta go get ready. I'm sorry to cut things short here."

"It's okay, I should be packing anyway. Keep your wits about you, drive safely, and remember I love you."

"I will." Rhea blew him a kiss. "I love you, too. Have a wonderful trip, okay? Let me know you got there safe?"

"I will. Stay out of mischief, Rhea. Bye."

"But if I stay out of mischief, how will I get boned by someone else?"

Adam laughed. "Bye, Rhea."

"Bye," she said, logging out of Skype.

*————*smile*————*

The jukebox in the corner of the restaurant played the only song from The Monkees Rhea was even remotely familiar with thanks to *Shrek*. It was one she'd ordinarily sing along with but she was far too embarrassed by the possibility Brianna might hear her.

"Let's do something *stupid*," Brianna proposed during the lull in their conversation, dipping a fried mozzarella stick in honey poppy seed dressing.

Rhea coughed around her bite of cheeseburger and took a swig of strawberry lemonade to dislodge the chunk of beef. Probably the piece of pickle relish would be stuck in her tonsil forever. It'd join allegiance with the piece of French fry from the band trip to Disneyland in 2006. God only knows what they'd do once banned together.

As it was, Rhea was having a terrible time focusing; Brianna's thin shirt left few details to her imagination. *Seriously, it's as if she wants her nipples to catch frost bite. Is frost bite something you catch? Or get?* This was her first winter living someplace where such things were a distinct possibility and she didn't know. Maybe she'd investigate that at home. *Rhea! Concentrate!* "Uh—what did you have in mind?"

"Oh, I dunno . . ."

"Says someone who obviously knows exactly what she's thinking." Rhea's eyes narrowed in suspicion. *Can those get any pointier? Oh my God, stare at her face, weirdo.*

Brianna laughed. "I thought we could bond over ink."

Holy shit, don't stare at her face, it's creeping her out. Look at the food. "I sure as hell hope you mean books. Or art."

"Tattoos, silly," Brianna giggled. "They're . . . a *type* of art."

"Yeah, no, I don't think so." If she were to bond over a tattoo, it would be with someone she was closer to. Much closer to. Perhaps Adam.

Nudging Rhea's foot beneath the table, Brianna said, "C'mon, don't be chicken."

Rhea imagined the pain of getting a tattoo would be somewhere in the neighborhood of how her assorted body piercings felt while getting them: Mostly anxiety beforehand, mild discomfort during—but for however much longer it took to complete the art.

If she got it someplace inconspicuous, work wouldn't even know—although Doctor Kasick was lenient on such things anyway. Lee-Ann had paw prints all along her right arm. Sheldon had large-gauge plugs in his ears and often wore ones with marijuana leaves on them.

Rhea wondered on many occasions if the doctor even realized what those were. Maybe he mistook them for maple leaves like she did as a young teenager. The naivety caused significant embarrassment the first time she chatted online about the Canadian flag with a patriotic Canucks fan.

"You're considering it," Brianna sang, twirling some hair around her finger.

Rhea sighed. "Fine. I mean hey. It'll give me something to blog about." Her voice was shaking. Was why her voice shaking? "It's been kinda hard to be as isolated as I am and with a career most people don't actually consider a real career . . . and my friends are all making their dreams come true left and right and, *ugh*. I haven't even realized mine. I'm over here like . . . add reminder in my phone memo app to buy more fish oil. That's my normal day." *Oh shut up already, I sound like such a loser.*

"I'm sure something amazing will happen for you. You're so sweet. And super pretty. I'm a firm believer good things happen to good people."

Since when could Rhea be classified as 'good people?' Or 'super pretty,' for that matter?

"When did you want to go to the tattoo place?" Rhea asked, turning her attention to her French fries.

"Oh, I dunno . . . How 'bout after we're done here?"

"Then I'm gonna need something with way more *oomph* than this Freckled Lemonade."

"You go do that and I'll make an appointment for us. I know a great place but they get busy as hell. Do you mind going to Chicago for it? We can take my car," Brianna offered.

"Why the hell not?" Rhea sighed. "If you think you can get us in."

Brianna smirked. "I'm tight with the owner. I can get us in."

*———— *smile* ————*

An hour after they left Rockin' Robin, Brianna led Rhea to a pair of glass double-doors. They were covered in crosshatch on black paper and the business information printed in white on the glass: Tet-Nis with the requisite reversed *N*.

Brianna tossed a glance over her shoulder. "Not what you expected?" she said through chattering teeth. "Just wait." She pulled open the door and ushered Rhea inside.

"Oh," gasped Rhea. "Holy shit."

"I know, right? It's amazing."

The parlor was expansive and open with only a couple pillars strategically placed down the center of the room, the ceiling lined with tin tiles which reflected the rich amber-colored hardwood flooring opposite them.

Small, elaborate crystal chandeliers hung above each of the six artist's stations, each with a plush seat for customers to attempt to relax in during their procedures.

Its waiting area—occupied by several people poring over photo albums filled with flash—was situated in the center of the room between those pillars and around an old, black, wood-burning stove currently adding to the heat of a thermostat already set to oven. The girls shed their outer layers. Still, in jeans and a long-sleeved turtleneck, Rhea was hot.

The cashier's counter in the front quarter of the shop looked like a beautifully restored and repurposed bar which sported a selection of body jewelry, shirts and mugs with the store's logo emblazoned on them, and framed paintings for sale.

Large black ducts snaked overhead and several stations were partitioned off by lush, heavy velvet curtains. A couple were drawn closed, the constant buzzing of tattoo machines permeating the fabric.

The shop was both eclectic and opulent.

"The place I got my piercings was a hole compared to this," Rhea remarked as she absorbed her surroundings. "This is a freaking palace."

Brianna laughed, bumping against Rhea with her shoulder. "You got your piercings at a hole. Very funny!"

Rhea smiled; the pun hadn't been intentional but for saving face she wouldn't admit it. "Thanks."

"Oh, Serenity's in the back. Let's go say 'hi.'" Brianna grabbed Rhea's hand and tugged until she followed.

She's not letting go. Why isn't she letting go, I'm already following her? Rhea wracked her brain for memories from high school. She recalled a few girls in band were more affectionate than what she deemed normal; she couldn't remember if Brianna had been among them. She hung out with other girls—to the best of Rhea's recollections—but always draped herself around some guy.

A drummer.

The drum major.

The prom king.

Rhea snapped out of her reflections once Brianna dropped her hand in favor of hugging Serenity, following that with a peck on the lips.

Rhea's mouth dropped open. *Well now what the hell does that mean?*

"Rhea? This is Serenity. Serenity? Meet Rhea."

Serenity was an absolute dumpling and Rhea couldn't fault Brianna for greeting her with a kiss. She was petite but curvy and Rhea found a new understanding of the 'bag of bobcats' phrase her father often used on women with similar builds.

Serenity's black onyx hair was done up into a magnificent bouffant. There were multiple industrial piercings decorating her ears, a tiny crystal stud catching light from the right side of her nose, and tribal tattoos covering both arms. She'd gone easy on the makeup around her stunning toffee-colored eyes in favor of a thick fuchsia lip sparkling with glitter whenever she smiled. She paired cut-off jeans with a long-line bustier in a bold floral print.

Rhea figured she would look like a nut, herself, for dressing that way—especially in the throes of winter—but Serenity rocked it. "It's nice to meet you."

"Welcome to my shop," replied Serenity, shaking Rhea's hand. It was a strange blend of a tight grip with a non-existent shake. They were just holding hands.

Serenity smiled at Brianna. *Sparkle, sparkle.* "Huvie will be here soon. Me and him will work on you two tonight, 'k?"

"Sounds good," said Brianna.

"Go ahead and hang out. Look through the flash and albums if you need help with ideas."

Brianna nodded. "Can't wait, can we, Rhea?"

"Uh huh," was Rhea's weak reply.

Brianna looped her arm with Rhea's and escorted her to the waiting area. "I'm thinking of getting a cluster of stars behind my right ear. What do you think?" She plopped into the only unoccupied seat—a wide lounge chair—and snatched an album from the coffee table.

"That'd be cute," replied Rhea, shifting from one foot to the other. *Guess I'll just stand and pray I don't pass out while waiting.*

Brianna looked at her. "The hell are you doing? Sit."

"Um—"

She scooted over as far as she could and patted the upholstery. "Join me, girlfriend. I'm current on all my shots, right hand to God."

Rhea didn't want to appear stand-offish or be mistaken for a prude by declining so she wedged herself between Brianna and the arm of the chair. She couldn't decide if she was grateful for wearing jeans or annoyed by it; Brianna's thigh pressed against hers, her skirt short enough it was unsurprising the guy across from her wouldn't stop staring.

Rhea hoped Brianna wasn't going commando, although she hadn't noticed any panty lines from behind. *Maybe a thong?* Not as if she'd been paying such close attention; though how could she not look at Brianna's rear end as it sashayed in front of her the whole walk to the waiting area? Rhea considered pointing out the gawker before Brianna crossed her legs with a sly smirk at her.

How very Basic Instinct of her.

"I think you should get something sexy. I dunno, maybe a really colorful sweepy floral design that follows the arch of your hipbone," suggested Brianna.

"That sounds excruciating." *And expensive.* "Maybe later if this one goes well."

Brianna flipped through flash in the studio's album. In the back half, crude black-and-white drawings were replaced by photographs of previous clients' ink. "Butterflies?" She pointed. "Like these?"

"Y'know, I actually think I've got an idea." It was something she'd bounced around in her head ever since she and Adam parted ways; she'd never had the guts to get to a parlor for it. Now she hadn't the guts to leave one.

"Is it involved? 'Cause what I'm thinking of getting might take some time."

Rhea scratched at her collarbone through her shirt. Goddamn it was hot in there. "Probably not? But don't worry, I can keep myself occupied." She had her phone, a fully charged battery, and that morning downloaded a new puzzle game she hadn't yet gotten sick of.

"If you finish before me, keep me company. We'll talk." Her eyes lifted from the photo album and her face lit up. "Handsome Huvie's here!"

Rhea followed Brianna's gaze to the front of the shop where she saw who she assumed was Huvie: a man of average height with a tall, kinky, high-top fade which was mostly black with caramel highlights; rich, clear skin matching those highlights, chocolate brown eyes and a neatly groomed Van Dyke so thin it almost wasn't there at all. He had industrial piercings in his ears and large-gauge black plugs in his ear lobes. He wasn't Rhea's type yet she didn't doubt he had his choice of women.

Serenity hustled out to greet Huvie with a long hug before leading him to Brianna and Rhea. He and Brianna fist-bumped. "It's been *way* too long, lady. How's Travis?"

"Fuck if I know. He moved out without warning a week ago."

"Oh shiiit," Huvie groaned. He addressed the ceiling: "The *fuck*, Travis. Seriously? Leaving the best girl in the world? The fuck are you smoking?" Back to Brianna: "So sorry, babe. You'll be okay."

Brianna pressed her shoulder to Rhea's. "I know I will. I got me a homegirl, here."

Rhea somehow doubted she'd ever used 'homegirl' in conversation previously—ironically or otherwise.

Huvie reached out to Rhea for a handshake.

"I'm Rhea," she introduced herself.

"—Of sunshine?" replied Huvie.

Rhea's breath hitched. *Is it a sign? Is he my qualifying plow? As if it'd be so easy.* "Ye-yeah. That's me." *He's not Adam but . . .*

Huvie smiled. "It's a pleasure." To Serenity he asked, "Can I take this one? Please? I want this one."

"Fine by me." Serenity nodded. "It sounds like Bri and me need to talk through this Travis bullshit."

"Eh. It's fine, honest." Brianna shrugged.

Huvie held out his hand to help Rhea to her feet. "You've gotta sign a couple forms 'n' then we'll be good to go."

So apparently this is happening. Rhea drew in a steadying breath. *Okay.* She followed Huvie to the front of the store where he pulled out a couple pieces of paper from a file cabinet at one end of the bar. She glanced back to see Brianna talking with Serenity, motioning with one hand across her ribcage. *That's nowhere near behind your ear, Brianna. And do you even have the money for it? Oh so not my place.*

"Here you go, Rhea." Huvie put a pen atop the forms and slid them across to her. "Top form is shop policies, waiver of liability, you know, legal bull. The other is care instructions. Follow them and your artwork is golden."

"'K." Rhea skimmed the forms without actually reading them and signed the waiver.

"Shop minimum is ninety." He rested his elbows on the countertop and folded one forearm over the other. "Whatcha got in mind."

Rhea flinched. *Holy shit, ninety.* She assumed the amount was exorbitant though she had no frame of reference. Nonetheless it was roughly the cost of groceries for two weeks; three when being especially frugal.

But she was already there and knew if she walked away, she'd never go through with this. Besides which, walking away wasn't so easily done knowing Brianna was committed to getting her own ink, and she'd driven Rhea a good forty miles from her home. "Well, uh, I wanted the word 'smile.' Here." She bunched her sleeve back to her elbow and drew a line with her index finger across the top of her left wrist. "I know, it's totally lame huh?"

Huvie smiled, catching Rhea's eyes. "Not at all. That's an awful small tat for the shop minimum, though." He glanced toward where Serenity and Brianna were engrossed in conversation before dropping his voice and leaning forward. "Tell ya what. Let's haggle a bit. You let me turn your smile into a little bracelet—" He took her hand and ran his middle finger the whole way around her wrist. "And I drop the ninety to fifty if you let me take you out for drinks this weekend."

Free drinks, cheaper tattoo and potentially qualifying plow? I'm not seeing a downside to this. "'K," she squeaked.

Huvie grinned and clapped once. "Let's get this party started." He filed away her form in a drawer beneath the counter and gestured for Rhea to follow him into one of the two open stations at the rear of the store.

She settled into the chair and he leaned against his tall red tool chest. "What colors were you thinking?"

"Oh. Uh . . . Just black, I guess." Rhea forced an awkward smile at him, hoping he wouldn't somehow be offended. "If that's okay."

"Of course it is. Give me a sec to get everything prepared."

While Huvie prepared his tools, Rhea looked around at the artwork in his station. He was good—to say the least—and seemed to have a penchant for the clean lines of tribal designs. Rhea wondered if he'd done Serenity's arms. Whatever the case, she lucked out. And the more she considered it, the more she realized she indisputably had a type: artists.

"Did you want any particular font? Simple? Fancy?"

"*Actually* . . ." Rhea dipped into her purse and pulled out her little notebook. She flipped through it until she found the page in question, on which Adam had left her several notes of varying importance. "Could you copy this?" She held it out to Huvie.

He glanced at it. "Oh yeah, sure. Let me get it transferred and we'll get started."

Rhea handed him the notebook and he stepped out of his station. In the neighboring one, Brianna was settling down. She gave Rhea a wide smile and small wave before pulling her top off over her head. Rhea looked away, blinking furiously. The flash of Brianna's chest would be seared into Rhea's memory until the end of time. She was wearing an unlined lace bra in a flesh-tone a hint paler than her actual skin. *I saw nipple.*

Two. Actually.

"You okay there?" asked Huvie, pulling over a wheeled stool with his foot and plopping down on it. "You're a little flushed."

"I'm fine," Rhea chirped, well aware she was sweating and he could see the telltale stains forming on her clothes if he glanced beneath her arms. "Just anxious. This is my first tattoo."

With a suggestive smirk, Huvie replied, "I'm a big guy but I know how to be gentle." He grabbed her arm and rubbed it brusquely with an ice-cold alcohol towelette. Catching the abject horror on her face, he apologized. "It's a rite of passage. It's fun to put the fear of God in people before they discover the needles themselves aren't so bad."

"*Needles?*" yelped Rhea.

Huvie looked at her, his eyes popping open and jaw falling the same.

"I thought tattoos were licked on by kittens."

He exhaled and shook his head. "Oh God, you got me. Fair 'nuff, I deserved it. *Friends* fan, huh?"

"You *did* deserve it. And yeah . . . I've been known to watch it on occasion." *Or all the damn time.* Rhea could own any opponent in *Friends* trivia but it wasn't something she broadcasted. Even Adam had no idea she was obsessed with the show and he was the best bestie she'd ever had.

Shaking his head, Huvie smiled and turned his attention to positioning the copy of Adam's handwritten '*smile*' on Rhea's wrist. "No one ever tries to freak me out. You're feisty." His gaze met hers long enough for him to say, "I like that."

She'd never been accused of being feisty; rather, she was Routine Rhea, predictable, and boring as brown grass. What next? Someone would call her sassy? "Thanks." *But I'm really just trying to keep from shitting my pants, here.*

"How's this look?"

Rhea scrutinized the positioning of the copy. "I think it looks good." If it were crooked or off-center, she didn't know and wouldn't be able to tell him how to adjust it to her liking. *Looks good* was more than good enough.

"Okay, then. Get comfy. Take five deep breaths." He switched on his tattoo machine and with her fifth exhalation, pressed it to her skin on the top of her wrist.

It wasn't at all as painful as she anticipated.

She studied the tin tiles of the ceiling above her and bit by bit, fell into a trance. Conversations around her dimmed to white noise and the buzzing of Huvie's tattoo machine immediately followed. Rhea was vaguely aware of his gentle touch manipulating her arm, repositioning her hand while he worked. And there was the occasional sharp but brief sting that brought her back to reality.

He paused to wipe off the excess ink— or blood? — before continuing to work and Rhea found herself wondering how his touch felt without the nitrile gloves between them.

He was being gentle, she had little doubt, and the whole experience with him was surreal, even Zen-like. Rhea saw how getting inked could become addictive—if not for the steep studio minimum. *Not as if I'm hurting for money.*

She glanced at Huvie and he met her gaze as he wiped her arm again.

"You're a superstar," he told her. With a smile, he repositioned her wrist and continued along its underside.

Rhea found this area considerably more unpleasant and she turned her face away so he wouldn't see her grimacing. The idea of being regarded as a superstar for her pain tolerance pleased her.

His voice low, he assured her, "Almost done, baby. Hang in there."

Oh thank God. It wasn't the worst pain ever but the less meaty areas stung so much she felt it tingling in her teeth. Her next tattoo would be on a thigh or maybe an upper arm.

Sometime later—it was probably a few minutes although it felt like several hours—the buzzing stopped and he wiped her wrist a final time.

"Whaddaya think?"

Rhea scrutinized it and fended off tears, swallowing around the lump in her throat. "It's *perfect*. Thank you so much."

With more of the same gentle touch, Huvie applied some colorless salve and enough cling wrap to cover it. He taped it down before snapping the lavender-colored nitrile gloves off his hands like a satisfied proctologist.

"Leave that on 'til you get home. Wash with Dial several times daily—*pat* dry with a clean paper towel, apply A & D after for the first couple weeks." He ticked off with his fingers: "No sun, no pools—indoor or otherwise—no hot tubs, no lotions while it heals. Try to keep your clothing off it. Treat it like an open wound because—y'know—that's what it is. It'll scab like a sunburn. Pinky promise me you won't pick at the scab." He held out his little finger.

Rhea smiled, hooking her pinky around his. "I promise."

"Expect it to itch like a mofo. That's perfectly normal.

Anything weird, you give the studio a call for help. Everything's great? Give the studio a call for more ink. And also? I'll need your number to make our date."

She gave Huvie her phone number on the back of one of his business cards and he led her toward the cash register to pay for his services.

"Can't wait to see you again this weekend," he said.

"Me too." For once, she figured it might be difficult to decline sex if he pursued it. "So, um . . . I gotta join Brianna. She's my ride."

"Cool. Cool. You take care of her for me, okay? She's a good girl."

"I will." Rhea headed to Serenity and Brianna, keeping her gaze trained to the floor. From outside Serenity's curtain she asked, "Brianna? Can I join you?"

"Of course," replied Brianna. "Get yer ass in here!" As Rhea stepped inside, Brianna asked her, "How's it look so far?"

"You're—you realize you're kinda exposed there and I can sorta see—"

"Yup," she chirped, tossing a saucy smile at Rhea. "So what do you think?"

Rhea swallowed hard, shifting her gaze to Brianna. *Those are pretty damn amazing.*

She's asking about the tattoo, dork.

Are you so sure?

Oh shut the fuck up and look at her tattoo before this gets weird . . .er.

Serenity was nearly three-quarters finished outlining a floral design that—once colored—Rhea guessed would be cherry blossoms.

"They're—it's—lovely." *You're sexy and it's killing me. Happy now?*

Brianna glanced at Rhea with a frown. "*Lovely*? See now you're scaring me—"

"I don't mean to," Rhea yelped. "Serenity's doing an amazing job, I swear. 'Lovely' is a good thing."

Serenity smiled, still hard at work tracing the transferred guidelines with her tattoo machine. "We're gonna stop with the outlines tonight and I'll add the color in a couple weeks. Gimme, oh—" She paused to check her watch, its face placed against the inside of her wrist. "—twenty more minutes."

"That's—fine—" Rhea faltered. "I'm in no rush."

"*So . . .*" Serenity cleared her throat. "How do you two know each other?"

"We're both reformed band geeks," replied Brianna.

Serenity leaned back, wide-eyed. She glanced between Rhea and Brianna. "*You*, Bri? Really? Color guard, right?"

"No." Brianna chuckled. "Flute and trumpet."

Rhea wondered if she should have been offended over Serenity's shock that Brianna was a 'band geek' when she clearly had 'band geek' tattooed on her forehead.

"You two go way back, huh?"

Brianna flinched and whimpered as Serenity continued to work. "Yep."

"Hey . . . on all those overnight competition trips, did you ever . . . *you know* . . . ?"

Rhea glanced at Brianna who slowly smiled. "I dunno about her," said Brianna, "but the thought's crossed *my* mind." Her smile faded. "She's obvs not into me though. My loss for sure."

If there was any further conversation that night, Rhea didn't remember it.

*———— *smile* ————*

"So. How are things in Illinois?" asked Adam.

"They're . . ." Rhea hesitated. "*Interesting.*"

His smile soured. "I don't think I like the sound of that 'interesting.'"

"Everything's fine, Adam."

"So . . . Have you slept with anyone yet?"

She smiled and shook her head. "Nope. But I've got a date on Saturday so who knows?"

"*I* do." Adam snorted. "I know how it'll go."

Rhea's smile faltered. "How about you?"

"I'm gonna give the physics major another chance."

"Oh, good." Her voice pitched upward. "Good! At least try 'n' screw her this time if she's willing to put out again?"

He exhaled loudly. "We'll see."

"Y'know . . . I might just sleep with my date if I'm reasonably assured you're doing the same."

Adam groaned. "You're asking me to make myself aroused."

"You're asking me to do the same."

"This arrangement isn't working, is it?" He pinched the bridge of his nose. "I'll try this time. I *promise*."

"Just . . ." She forced a smile. "Close your eyes and think of me."

He chuckled. "So how's what's-her-name? Brianna?"

"She's fine." *Hell yeah, she's fine.* Rhea dropped her gaze to her new tattoo. It was still inflamed. *Do I show him? No, I'll surprise him with it in person. Do I tell him what Brianna said about me last night?* She looked at his chat window.

Adam cocked his head and raised an eyebrow.

Nope. I don't want him worrying needlessly and this will worry him. Needlessly.

"I'm really glad she reached out to me. She needed a friend and she's totally not the girl I thought she was in high school." Rhea added with a wink, "You know. School politics and all."

"On a scale of Charmed to Cass, how close are you two?"

Rhea laughed at how he chose to phrase his question. "Your scale would be more accurate spanning Charmed to you. But that's beside the point. We're getting to know each other. But I imagine someday—if things continue going the way they are—we could be tight."

Brianna's voice echoed in her head: *The thought's crossed my mind.*

She wondered if Adam considered another woman a qualifying lay.

"Really?"

She nodded absently. *Yeah. Because that's happening. I'd have better luck winning the Powerball jackpot.* She perked up. *Ooooh, maybe I should play. Oh, no. Never mind. That would involve going outside*. Rhea glanced at her apartment window. The sun set hours ago already and with the wind chill, it was well below zero degrees Fahrenheit. *Ew, never mind.*

"So then should I send her a friend request?"

Rhea shrugged. "If you wanna. She's a fun girl, I'm sure you'd like her." *Just hopefully not too much.*

Speaking of liking a girl too much: His second date with the physics major was scary beyond all reason. "All right, okay," Rhea said. "Enough about my petty crap. How's Catalina?"

"It's a whole other world. The ferry ride here was chilly. Not New York-in-winter-chilly, but definitely a marked difference from inland Orange County. I'm glad Gary warned me to take a sweatshirt. I wouldn't have otherwise and probably my nipples would've sliced right through my shirt on the trip over."

"Have you gotten to do anything touristy yet?"

Adam nodded. "I went to Wrigley Mansion, checked out the botanic gardens. I walked the pier and found a chalk artist. She mostly drew flowers and butterflies but they were gorgeous. I asked her for some pointers and she was nice enough to let me practice a little with her supplies."

"She sounds nice."

"Yep. I'm gonna visit with Janelle again before I leave."

She has a name. "Janelle—" Rhea furrowed her brows. "Is that the same Janelle you added on Facebook?"

He smiled. "The same. Look through her galleries sometime."

"I will." *Don't be jealous, Rhea.*

"Tomorrow I'm snorkeling in Lover's Cove. I feel like it won't be the same without you."

Rhea folded her arms across her chest. "Enjoy yourself anyway."

"I'll try." He sighed.

"Have you gotten any actual painting done?" *Wasn't that the whole point of this exercise?*

"Not yet. But I'm taking a crap-ton of photos and I'm getting *real* inspired." Adam smirked.

Rhea frowned. "What's that look for?"

"What look?"

"You look guilty as hell. You do know I can see you, right? Video call? 2014?"

"No, yeah, I—I know—"

Rhea asked, "Did you already sleep with someone? Because if you did, good. Was it Janelle?" *Although that would probably be less good if they friended each other on Facebook.* Her breath hitched.

"No, no—*no*!" Adam shook his head. "It's nothing like that, I promise. First of all, if I slept with someone, you'll be the first I tell how disappointing it was and I'll volunteer the news. And second, Janelle—she's—" He puckered his lips. "She's not my type."

Rhea made a mental note to look at Janelle's photo to see what didn't qualify as Adam's 'type.' It was insignificant, of course, but her curiosity was piqued.

"I've gotta get going. I love you, Sunshine."

"I love you too, Surfer Boy. Enjoy your trip."

"I am. We'll talk again in a few days?" he confirmed.

"I look forward to it. Bye, sweetie."

"Stay warm now. Bye."

Chapter Two

That Saturday after arguing briefly in regard to transportation, Huvie retrieved Rhea from her apartment and drove them to the Roadhouse Grill. Conversation focused as good conversation should: on inane topics such as the weather and celebrity babies.

Roadhouse had just opened for lunch service and Huvie and Rhea were among only a handful of patrons when they were seated in a booth by the bar and provided menus by the host.

"Someone will be with you shortly to take your order."

"Thanks," said Huvie, watching as the host—playing the convincing role of country bumpkin—swaggered back to his podium. Huvie cleared his throat, turning his attention to Rhea. "May I say you look incredible?"

Rhea smiled and ducked her head; it took her over an hour to look the kind of incredible as though she hadn't taken an hour to do it. "I wouldn't dare stop you. Thanks."

"I should be straight with you though. I respect you and don't want to string you along. I'm not looking for a relationship out of this." His gaze was sincere though apologetic.

She exhaled. "Oh that's great!"

"It is?" He blinked.

"It's perfect. All I really need is a one-night-stand."

"Awesome. Wait, what?"

"*Yeah*. It's a . . . a long story. Don't ask."

"So." Huvie hesitated. "I could've just taken you to my place?"

"You still *could*, frankly." Laughing, she added, "Hell, we could've stayed at mine for all I needed you."

"Oh." He swallowed. "I had something pretty cool planned to lure you into bed, though."

"Did you?" The corners of Rhea's lips lifted. "How sweet. What was it?"

"I signed us up for an Iron Man challenge at the laser tag place down the street."

Did Adam and she agree they couldn't also have some fun in the pursuit of an alternate lay?

No.

"I could probably get a refund—"

"Don't. Let's do it." Rhea patted his hand. "It sounds like fun."

"And now that I know it's just postponing sex, it'll make the challenge even more challenging."

"I appreciate your honesty," said Rhea with a little laugh. "Thanks."

"This is looking real good," Huvie remarked, admiring his tattoo around her wrist. "You must be treating it well."

"It was an investment." She tucked some errant strands of hair behind her ear. "Hey . . . I know I'm looking for a one-night-stand but I still wanna get to know you since you're friends with Brianna."

A plump woman with thick glasses cleared her throat as she approached their table. "My name's Franny. Can I get you something to drink? Get some appetizers started?"

"Oh yeah. Um . . ." Huvie chuckled. "Didn't really get a chance to look at the menu. Sorry."

Franny tapped her pen against her notepad and Rhea couldn't decide if Huvie's cheeks were going pink.

"What do you think, Rhea? Appetizer sampler?"

"Sure."

"Mozzarella sticks, mac 'n' cheese bites . . . sweet potato fries?" he asked.

"Sounds good to me." Rhea waited while Franny took notes. When she paused and glanced over expectantly, Rhea said, "I'll have a lemonade, please."

"Sweet tea for me," Huvie added.

"All right. I'll have your drinks out shortly and I'll take your order then."

Rhea lowered her voice even after Franny was well out of ear-shot. "How much of our food do you suppose she's gonna spit in?"

"Well if she does," Huvie replied, "she's a bitch. We didn't do anything to deserve it."

They fell quiet to study their menus.

After Rhea decided what she'd order, she muttered, "*Sneeze muffins.*"

"*Friends* fan." Huvie laughed. "I remember. I binged a few seasons this week."

"Aw, for me?"

"Don't flatter yourself." He raised his face from the menu long enough to wink at her. "A couple of my buddies were talking about its racist undertones. It never bothered *me* any so I re-watched it with that in mind, thinking maybe, you know, I missed something."

Her heart stopped. The type who always shied away from discussing such topics, Rhea feared she might inadvertently offend Huvie with an innocent remark. "A—and what did you think?"

He shrugged. "If I had to complain, yeah, it'd have been nice to see another person of color besides the woman who played Charlie."

Rhea straightened. "What about Gabrielle Union? I mean I know she was basically an over-glorified extra but she was on the show, too."

"Oh. Yeah. I guess."

"And I can't remember the actress's name but what about the girl who played Julie? She was on the show for several episodes and she isn't white."

"*True* . . ." Huvie's handsome smile was amazingly crooked.

"Then again, the show was putting out new episodes for ten years, took place in like one of the most diverse cities on the planet and the number of non-white speaking roles can be counted on one hand. *And* they kept forgetting one-third of the main characters were Jewish in the December episodes, which, frankly, always pissed me off. They had, what, one holiday episode where they actually acknowledged it in ten years?"

Huvie's handsome but amazingly crooked smile turned compassionate. "You a Jewess?"

Rhea faltered; she didn't care for the term but didn't dare say so. On the scale of things to get offended about, she supposed he'd been called far more offensive things in his lifetime than she had in hers. *Not that any of it's okay just because some is less bad than others.* She chose her reply with care: "Technically, yes, I'm Jewish. Is that a problem?"

"Oh of course not. I was just surprised. You don't seem—I mean you don't look—"

"I don't broadcast it. My parents always told me to keep it secret. For my safety." She'd surprised others in the past, Adam among them. There'd been several heartbeats she feared his stunned silence when she told him. That *had* been a case where Skype froze during their call; Adam later told her he was excited to learn about a culture she, herself, knew little of.

Huvie frowned. "Okay. Well. You don't have to get all riled up about race issues on my account. But I appreciate it. I admit I've been real lucky I haven't encountered the type racism and violence others with my skin color do. My dad though? He could tell you stories that'd curl your hair." He smirked. "Well, maybe not *your* hair. Aren't Jews supposed to have curls?"

"Yeah. We're also supposed to have horns." She laughed despite herself and this conversation, running her hand over her sadly straight hairdo. "But you're right. My hair holds a curl the way a sieve holds water."

"So . . . What I ultimately wondered was why people were so obsessed with the monochromatic cast of *Friends* when *Will & Grace*, *Seinfeld*, and *Sex and the City*—all of them shows set in New York around the same time—were every bit as bad?"

"Huh." Rhea drummed on the table with her fingertips. "Maybe . . . Because *Friends* was the most mainstream accessible one? *Will & Grace* focused on stereotypical LGBT characters—in my opinion, anyway, the closet-case and the sassy friend are total clichés—that homophobes would never watch. The lead character of *Seinfeld* was in a minority nobody considers to actually be one, and *Sex and the City*'s audience was limited to people who subscribed to HBO. *Friends* was the obvious whipping bo—" She slapped her hand against her mouth so hard it stung and she gaped from behind it. "Oh my God—*oh my God*! I didn't mean that—"

"I knew what you meant. And anyway, I remember from History class that *that* was more about the sixteenth century educated elite than it was slavery in America." Huvie exhaled, gesturing with both hands for her to calm down. "Fuck, Rhea. *Relax*. You're not gonna offend me. We're out on a date in public. If you were racist, would you be out with me? Would you have let me tattoo you for shit's sake?"

"If I said *no*," Rhea slowly mused out loud, "then it would serve to follow I know what racists think . . . because I *am* one?"

He looked unconvinced. "Fine. You can be a racist if I'm a shallow prick who just wants to bone a white girl. Screwing white chicks always makes me feel like I'm a *big man* if ya know what I mean." Huvie gave her an exaggerated wink.

Rhea exhaled. Her hands shook as the waitress set down their drinks.

"Apps will be out shortly. Whaddya having?" Franny's disposition seemed to have soured considerably.

Of course, with the things she'd overheard from their table, Rhea couldn't blame her.

"The ham and Swiss chicken sandwich," Huvie ordered.

"I'll have the Outlaw Burger. Please. Um—without the

onion rings, though. If . . . that's okay?" She was going to get extra onion rings; she just knew it.

"How rare do you want your burger?" asked Franny.

"Well done, dead as it gets. Charred. Please." *It's gonna come so raw there'll be blood on the bun.*

"Got it." Franny swiped their menus from the table and hustled off without another word.

"Think we could make her any more uncomfortable?" Huvie asked with a wicked glint in his eye. He took a long sip from his glass.

"We could always invite her to your place with us," Rhea teased.

Huvie covered his mouth in what looked like an attempt to keep from spitting out his sweet tea. He coughed. "Would you?"

"Oh God no, not her. She's not my type."

He leaned against the cushions of the booth seat, crossing his arms over his chest. "Indulge me."

"Artists, apparently."

"Does that . . . go for women, too?" Huvie's voice lifted hopefully. "Because—not gonna lie here—a three-way with you and Serenity? Goddamn."

As far as Rhea knew, Brianna's artistic talents were in following sheet music and little else. They still didn't know each other well. "No."

"So then if you *were* to get with another woman—"

"Brianna," Rhea whispered.

He bobbed his head slowly. "No shit."

"But she's way out of my league. Basically, my type is unattainable. And you cannot tell her any of this. You promise me this doesn't leave our table."

"I won't." He grinned viciously.

"Seriously, Huvie!"

His impish smirk faded. "I promise. I swear I won't tell her."

"You know what, actually? The more I think about it, promise me you won't tell anybody."

Huvie frowned. "Are you not . . ." He circled his hand in the air in a gesture Rhea couldn't decipher. "Are you not out?"

"I'm—" Rhea sighed. "Neither here nor there." She'd never cared for labels of any type, nor did she fit neatly into the labels people insisted on thrusting upon her. To call herself bi-curious felt more ill-fitting than being called straight or otherwise. What was with everyone's infatuation with labels, anyway? And why was it anyone else's business?

Rhea's attraction to and arousal by other women was not curiosity. No one called straight virgins curious because they hadn't gotten a person of the opposite sex to consent to intercourse with them yet. *No, those people are falsely called losers. Or sad.* She knew both of those things from firsthand experience.

The question remained: Why were her feelings about women any different from a straight virgin's? Maybe Rhea would revisit the topic on her blog later.

She cleared her throat. "And anyway, look: it's not a big deal, *whatever* I am. I'm me. Nothing more. Nothing less."

"Didn't you say you used to be married?"

"Yeah. So?"

"Is that 'neither here nor there' business why you divorced?"

She snorted. "Mark didn't know. What's it say about me if I didn't trust my husband enough to tell him, and yet I've alluded to it any number of times by now on my public blog?" *Alluded to it, flat-out said it. Is there a difference?*

Huvie studied Rhea in silence prior to answering. "Well, it's easy to do such things on the internet because there's this feeling of anonymity, especially if you use a pen name and don't show your face."

"I use my real name and . . . well, the lack of pictures has nothing to do with wanting to hide." She pointed at herself. "This mug breaks cameras."

"Bullshit. That only serves to perpetuate my belief you're a sweet girl who's too hard on herself."

Rhea glanced at her lap, swallowing around the fiery lump in her throat. That hit her a little hard for some reason; people saying kind things to her usually had that effect.

"I see a lot of similarities between you and Bri. She has a

lot of guilt for things which weren't her fault. She'd probably kill me for telling you it's why she journals."

Rhea looked at him, cocking her head with a frown.

"Her therapist suggested it."

"Seems the older I get, the more troubles I find in the people around me."

Huvie huffed. "Ain't that the truth. Y'know, Bri was real lonely without a girlfriend like you. She used to drag me shopping because she didn't have a chick to go with. And that, by-the-way, included trips to Victoria's Secret. Which is totally fine by me but it was weird she kept asking for my opinions on her sex clothes."

How weird. Rhea rubbed her eyebrow in thought. It almost sounded like awkward flirting. "I don't understand. She didn't have any problems making friends in high school. Why is she alone now?"

"Time changes people. Softens some, hardens others." Huvie sighed. "I didn't mean—well, shit, if this isn't the most depressing date ever."

Slowly, Rhea smiled. "I think you're a sweet guy who's being too hard on himself."

He deflated a little with a half-smile.

"Look, I'm gonna be *real* blunt here: if you wanna screw me on this date, I'm more than willing to put out. You don't need to stress about impressing me, 'k? My decision's already made." She prayed she could stick to it.

Franny cleared her throat and plopped the plate of appetizers on their table.

Laughing despite himself, Huvie told Franny, "Y'know, you have piss-poor timing."

She made a noise that was a combined groan and sigh. "I regret my timing more than you do. Your food should be out soon."

Rhea's eyes widened and she watched as Franny went to a neighboring table with an exaggerated shiver. "I kiiiinda feel like I don't wanna tip her very well."

"I kinda want to suggest on the receipt that she remove her anal plug before her next shift." Huvie's gaze fell on Rhea with a wicked smile. "Maybe it'll go viral."

"Maybe then we pay with cash."

"Smart idea." Huvie picked several of each appetizer to move to his plate. "Except *I'm* paying and don't bother arguing it."

This was problematic for Rhea; ordinarily she would counter, 'then I'll pay next time.' But there would be no next time. The promise of sex regardless, she didn't want to feel indebted to others over anything. Ever. It was an obnoxious trait she'd been criticized for on many a previous occasion.

Rhea perked up. "Fair 'nuff." She plucked some appetizers for herself from the joint plates.

"That was easy," Huvie said, perplexed. "I'm used to getting *some* argument at least. Even thinly veiled insincere argument."

She replied, "No arguments here. I'll just have to come by Tet-Nis for more ink soon. For shop minimum at least."

"You're a cool girl. How the hell are you still single?"

Rhea shrugged. She'd spent the last five months asking herself similar questions. On nights when loneliness and doubt took advantage of her, Rhea wondered if Adam's insistence she sleep with another man was his way of avoiding commitment with her.

No.

She knew him by now; Adam wasn't the type. And besides, if he wanted distance from her, there was plenty of it with some two thousand miles between them. They'd discussed it more than once: he wasn't leaving California unless he had damn good reason, and she had no intention of returning unless she had the same.

Conveniently, what qualified as 'damn good reason' had never actually been brought up in conversation. *Maybe I ask him the next time we chat.* She was racking up quite the list of mental notes today.

"Out of curiosity—and you don't have to answer this if it makes you uncomfortable—does your family know you're . . . the way you are?"

"Actually? My father does. But he's the only one. It didn't help that it took me a real long time to realize what my deal even was."

"Yeah, denial's a bitch," Huvie replied.

"It wasn't denial," said Rhea, baffled by his assumption. "I honestly didn't know. It's the same as before I learned I'm nearsighted—isn't everyone's vision blurry like mine is? I know better now, of course, but when you're young you don't *assume* you're different. At least I never did. As things came together for me, I was more confused than anything else. Because it was like . . . 'this is wrong.' But at the same time it wasn't. And the older I get, the luckier I feel in being able to find both men and women arousing. I think it's nice to see what both sexes find attractive about the other."

"So you're pansexual?"

"No," she snapped. Then she said, "I'm sorry. I just . . . I really don't understand the need for labels." And frankly, she didn't even know what the difference was between bisexual and pansexual. Maybe she was pansexual. She was certain, however, it didn't matter to her in the slightest. Calling it one thing as opposed to another didn't at all change her disposition.

"I'm Rhea. I'm a massage therapist who's helped people from virtually every walk of life. I was born with and still have girl body parts that flip over figurative tables every month I don't get knocked up. I like dresses as much as I like pants. I love to shop, I love to write, I love kicking a ball around on a grassy field. I'd play hockey if I knew how to ice skate and felt confident I wouldn't break my neck.

"I want to learn how to knit someday. I hold doors open for anyone who follows me and I love men who pull out my chair for me—I'll fight to the death anyone who tells me chivalry is anti-feminist. I like glittery nail polish and digging around in the dirt to find hidden treasure."

Huvie chuckled.

"Hey don't laugh, people really do that. I'm not even talking about geocaching. Anyway. I loved The Legend of Kyrandia—do you remember that game? I was around ten I think when I discovered it and had to play it on my father's ancient computer, but I loved it! At the end of the day, long story short . . . Being labeled pisses me right the hell off."

"You are so fun." Huvie smiled with what appeared to

be untold affection.

Rhea's phone buzzed in her purse. She acknowledged it with a single, brief glance.

"You can check it you know," he said. "I won't be put off."

"No. That's rude. I don't roll like that."

"What if it's important?" he asked.

"I'm nobody's emergency contact." Rhea savored a couple sweet potato fries. "*Trust me*. Whoever it is can wait until after we have sex. And let me guess: Franny's here with our food?" Rhea gestured dramatically toward the side of their table before turning to look for her. No poor-attitude waitress. "Huh. I guess that wasn't nearly offensive enough for her bad timing."

Huvie snorted.

For the sake of not wanting conversation to peter into uncomfortable silence, Rhea cleared her throat and asked, "How does a guy end up with a name like yours? You're the first Huvie I've ever met."

"It's short for Huveane." He extended his hand to her above the table. "After everything you told me—and since I'm planning on fucking you senseless soon—the least I can do is give you my full name."

Despite herself, Rhea smirked. "You'd probably be surprised how little such things matter to me."

"Huveane Duvalier."

"You're French?"

"No need for the shock. I'm not the first black Frenchman there was."

She blurted, "That's not what I meant—" and she didn't want to explain how the only other man she'd ever been attracted to was also French.

"Lighten up." Huvie winked. "If you can, I mean."

"You should see how light I am by the time spring rolls around." Rhea cleared her throat and took a long sip of lemonade. "Have you, um . . . *been with* other . . . white girls?"

"A couple."

"Oh." She exhaled. "I'm equally disappointed and relieved."

He smirked.

"Ham and Swiss?" muttered Franny, setting Huvie's plate down beside his appetizers. "Outlaw Burger, extra onion rings." She set the plate beside Rhea's. "I'll be back with drink refills. Plan your conversation accordingly."

Huvie watched her go while Rhea verified there were, in fact, no onions on her hamburger. *I hate those jokes. They're never funny.*

"So how about you?" he asked.

"'How about me' what? Have I been with other white girls? No."

Huvie laughed; it was nothing short of adorable. "*No. Am I your first black guy?*"

"Let's just say I was raised in a super vanilla neighborhood and if my parents knew I'm with you right now and planning on being fucked senseless by you later—"

Franny reached across the table to refill her glass. *Of course.*

"—they'd lose their shit," Rhea concluded. "Just so we're clear, I'm not doing this as a defiant daughter thing. I couldn't care less about their racial hang-ups. I want this because I think you're hot. And, also, I'm horny."

"To be perfectly fair, my mom would haul my ass around by my ears for the same reason." As Franny reached to refill his glass, he added, "*Momma don't want no mix-race grandbaby.*"

Franny made a guttural noise and left.

"She doesn't know about any of the white girls. No reason to give Momma a stroke for nothing that's not a serious relationship."

"Have you ever considered getting serious with one—"

"I'm not down for commitment with anyone regardless of color. The one exception being Tyra." He gazed at the restaurant ceiling with a wide smile and sighed. "Oh, Tyra."

"Yeah, I don't come close to meeting that standard." Which was fine because Huvie was no Adam and even if he was the best lover in the history of sex, *he was still no Adam.* Rhea sighed. *Shit. I am so in love with him.* And that was the very last thought she needed before climbing into the sack with another man. It wasn't news to her she was in love with Adam, but the reminder right just now was unwelcome. *Back to the date, Rhea. Damn.*

"You okay? That shouldn't bother you if you weren't lying about the one-night-stand thing. Most girls *do*."

"Oh—no—" Rhea waved it off. "I was thinking. I am definitely, absolutely, irreversibly only in this for one night of sex. And for what it's worth? I am not 'most girls.'"

"What if I'm the best you ever have?"

Rhea picked up her hamburger, studying it carefully. It didn't leave a bloody bun-print on her plate. *Shocking.* "That's a risk I guess I'm just gonna have to take."

"Thanks for taking care with my ego." He tucked into his Ham & Swiss.

"No worries."

*———*smile*———*

Huvie and Rhea didn't win the Iron Man challenge at the laser tag place, not by a long-shot, but in the end they were breathless, sweaty, smiling ear-to-ear and riding magnificent waves of adrenaline. Stepping out into near-freezing temperatures was refreshing after such exertion, though it became unpleasant prior to reaching Huvie's car.

"Well," Rhea exhaled as she collapsed into the passenger seat of his red Impala. "That was *way* more fun than I imagined it could be."

"Yeah it was." Huvie slid into the driver's seat casting a smile at her. "No offense but you make a great human shield."

She gave him a crooked smile. "That's good to know."

He made a motion for her to smile. "A real one, though. Yours is beautiful when it's genuine."

That did the trick. "Thanks. So, um . . ."

"Let's go to my place? We can put on the radio, then ignore it?"

Rhea faltered. "I got super sweaty, though."

"You can use my shower if you really want." He started his car.

"Oh. Okay." She cast a sly smile at Huvie. "Let's do it."
And hurry the hell up before I backpedal.

The drive to Huvie's place was short, conversation light and filled with plenty of laughter.

Rhea found it strange they intended to have sex but nothing either of them said was the least bit sensual and getting aroused by a fun, otherwise attractive man was going to be the strangest chore ever.

It was an even stranger thing to pray maybe she would climax quickly when the time came—and then he would, too. Sex wasn't something to 'get over with, already.' Well, it had been that way with Mark and she knew now just how much was wrong with that mentality.

That fucking didn't even appear to be on Huvie's radar made Rhea a little jealous of how easy these things must've been for men. All they needed were willing partners. And a guy as good looking as Huvie couldn't have had much difficulty in that department.

I'm doing this to move things with Adam along. I can do this. Huvie's hot, focus on that.

Rhea was going to have to accept the peculiarity of the situation and with luck, sex would be enjoyable but over soon. God forbid he had the kind of stamina Adam did.

Huvie pulled into a parking spot at the base of a tall building. "I've got a loft here. Fantastic views. Well," he said as he unbuckled his seat belt with a laugh, "you'll see for yourself."

She grimaced, unbuckling her belt. "Can't wait."

They got out of his car and he extended his hand. Rhea took a quiet, deep breath before taking it. He had a firm grip and soft, warm skin. However this went, Huvie was a vast improvement on Mark. *At least there's that.*

The challenge would be in forgetting Adam.

Huvie led her into the building where they waited for an elevator.

"So. You originally from here?" Rhea asked.

He squeezed her hand. "I was born in New Orleans. Family moved here after Hurricane Danny. I was—jeez—like nine or ten by that point, I think?"

"Oh. My God. Is it really scary? Being in a hurricane, I mean."

"I don't really remember much of it." He shrugged. "My parents decided not to evacuate—I don't know if evacs were ordered and they ignored it—whatever the case, we hunkered down. Shit, I was ten, what the hell did I care? I buried my face in a Game Boy through the worst of it."

Under her breath, Rhea replied, "Wish I'd had that option through earthquakes."

"Are those really so bad?"

The elevator pinged, its doors sliding open a few moments later, and a small family stepped out. The ghostly pale matriarch cast a conspicuous disparaging glance at Huvie and Rhea's clasped hands; her disapproval must have been more for their benefit than it was for her desire to express her opinion.

They stepped into the elevator and Rhea hissed, "Did you see that look she gave us?"

"It's her problem." He pressed the button for the eighth floor. "Not yours. Or mine." Huvie kissed her cheek. It felt entirely platonic. "Or *ours*. So. Earthquakes really so bad?"

"Most of my early childhood is a big blank." Rhea had little doubt her memories lacked for good reasons. "I was four when Northridge hit. I cried and cried, just *knew* it was the end of the world. Can you imagine a four-year-old girl fearing the apocalypse? I did. To this day, I can still taste my fear as if it were fresh." She swallowed; the mere thought of it made her terror palpable.

The shuddering of the elevator car as it stopped at the eighth floor gave Rhea an unwelcome start.

"This elevator does that," Huvie reassured her. "Don't worry, though. The inspection papers are expired by only a few months."

Rhea attempted to verify if he was teasing, but Huvie pulled her out of the car and into the hallway.

His complex was on the older side and although the building was kept clean, the carpet, wallpaper, and occasional decorations were dated.

There was a musk in the drafty air that made Rhea

wonder how badly the place leaked during storms.

Huvie's apartment was at the end of the hall, his door plain dark wood with a brass-colored knob and matching brass-colored numbers 807 nailed to it.

He unlocked the door with a key that had to be older than she was, any design on its handle worn clean away.

"Come on in." Huvie dropped his keys and wallet into a small ceramic bowl on the far end of his kitchen counter.

Rhea took careful stock of the studio apartment.

The walls were covered in artwork—mostly monochromatic abstracts she guessed were his pieces. Then followed the sick musing she should introduce Huvie to Adam. She swept that idea from her head, noticing a set of bowls on the floor in one corner of the kitchenette and a scratching post right outside the bathroom door left ajar. Otherwise, there was no sign of any cat.

It was probably hiding out under his bed and she hoped it had plans to relocate soon.

Huvie's studio was clean but the man was a collector, with a tall and skinny bare wood curio cabinet in a corner behind his two-chair, round kitchen table.

The cabinet was full of sculptures and Rhea drew near to get a better look. There was Cyborg from *Teen Titans*, Poison Ivy from *Batman*; a miniature gold football helmet with a black Fleur-De-Lis on its side and an ice-hockey figurine in a uniform Rhea was unfamiliar with. There was a tall piece of colorless quartz. She straightened when her eyes fell upon the item propped against it. "Is that a voodoo doll?"

"Yeah. It was a gag gift from Serenity. Joke's on her because the thing is damn cool," he replied.

"And—and this . . . this isn't a *real* shrunken head—" Rhea motioned to the third shelf.

"Come check out my view." Huvie opened his drapes, allowing the Illinois sunset to flood his studio apartment.

"Oh," Rhea sighed, pressing her hand to her chest. "It's beautiful." She joined him by the window, trying to admire his view despite how it made her queasy how far away the ground was.

"Chicago River at dusk. Few things beat this sight." He

glanced at her. "Except maybe a pretty girl's smile."

She smiled despite her best efforts against a corny line. "I'm not so sure about that."

Huvie wrapped his arms around her waist; Rhea wanted so badly to enjoy the embrace. *He's not Adam.*

"Just take the compliment," he said, kissing her on the side of her neck.

Rhea was keenly aware of his tongue on her skin. "I—was gonna shower—" Her voice went as weak as her knees. Damned if kisses on her neck weren't an Achilles' heel. *Thank God vampires aren't real.*

"The more I think about it, the more I realize I'd much rather taste your endorphins than my man-soap."

"O—kay—" she breathed. "If you insist."

Huvie squeezed Rhea. "You done admiring the scenery? 'Cause I really wanna admire yours."

"Oh, um, yeah." Rhea didn't see what was so objectionable with leaving the drapes open but she guessed it must have bothered him. Willing to bed a stranger? Sure. Willing to screw where there was minimal chance someone might see? No.

Funny what peoples' hang-ups were.

He switched on the bedside lamp and closed his drapes, turning to her. "Ladies first."

Rhea considered quipping she was no lady—what kind of lady screwed a man on the first date despite being in love with someone else?

Now she was just prolonging the main event. She removed her coat and lifted her long-sleeved shirt over her head, draping it on the back of one of the kitchen chairs before stepping out of her jeans and folding those atop her shirt. Rhea turned to Huvie. "Well?"

He ogled her in her petal pink underwear set. "Yeah, I can totes work with that." Huvie followed suit, though he stripped all his clothes off.

Shrugging under her intense stare, he remarked, "There's a morsel of truth in some stereotypes, I suppose. I'm fine perpetuating this one."

Rhea never obsessed about cock size but this one left

her with a few things to consider.

Among those things: the abject horror of *where the hell is that going to fit?*

"Well," she squeaked, "I, myself, am a stereotype: a white girl who wears yoga pants, has a Starbucks gold card, and pursues all things pumpkin spice."

Huvie pursed his lips before he smiled at her. "That's good to know. I've seen memes about how to summon you so now I know how to find you when I want a booty call."

"Uh huh." That would be problematic; Rhea Josse was no man's booty call. "Um, I've got a . . . a weird request."

He inhaled, puffing out his chest and replying, "Okaaaay."

"Can I touch your hair?"

Huvie exhaled, relief washing across his features. "Yeah, sure, of course. I love when girls touch it."

"What did you think I was gonna ask?"

"Does it really matter?"

"Might be good for a laugh." She shrugged. "But I suppose not."

He cleared his throat. "You're nervous. There's no reason to be. Here, lemme help." Huvie stepped close to her, guiding her hands into his hair. He embraced her, dropping kisses on her neck.

Rhea tangled her fingers amid his kinky coils, finding it increasingly difficult to concentrate on what she was touching while he kissed her. His hair was soft and lush. She'd have to ask him what his secret was; her hair felt like straw lately even though she hadn't dyed it in forever.

"You know," Huvie remarked between his kisses, "this is how I trap women."

Amid her laughter, Huvie guided her to his bed. His lips were warm, his kisses teasing her skin into goosebumps as he explored her body with his mouth.

Rhea's hands fell away from Huvie's hair and onto the mattress where he entwined his fingers with hers.

Bit by bit, kiss by kiss, caress by caress, Rhea's reluctance washed away in a sea of delight.

There was even a point at which Huvie's hand warming

between her thighs brought her such pleasure she convinced herself she'd be able to relax and enjoy the ride.

When he sneaked his hand into her underwear, Rhea became intensely focused on his palm cupping her ass. She stiffened, panting breaths catching in her throat. God forbid he sneak a finger between her cheeks for a drive down the ol' dirt road; for her, that had always been an exit-only deal. Do not back up, severe time damage, that sort of thing.

"No?" Huvie asked, pulling away.

"I—" Rhea shook her head. She was wet and horny as hell and no amount of her own caresses or vibrating rabbit was going to replace the feeling of a man pressing her into the mattress and making her body come alive with its assorted sexual cheat codes. *Now or never.* And she was so aroused, it might as well have been now. To cover for her hesitation, she yelped, "—condom—!"

Huvie laughed. "Oh, yeah, duh. I wouldn't dream of screwing you over that way. I may be a devilishly handsome rake with a dick that won't quit but I'm no asshole."

Rhea rolled onto her stomach to reach for her purse—pretty much everything was within reaching distance of the bed in a studio apartment—and Huvie drew circles around her pussy through her underwear. She bit her lip to swallow a gasp as she retrieved a condom from her bag. A single syllabic word came with great struggle while he continued to fondle her: "*Here.*"

Huvie laughed as he dragged her panties off her and tossed them to the floor. "Yeah, no. Those don't fit me."

They were Adam's preferred type—for both fit and ribbing. Rhea's eyes widened and she was stunned into silence. *Condoms aren't one-size-fits-all?* That was a lesson she didn't especially want to learn the way she was learning it.

He drew a couple of fingers along her slit. "Don't worry, baby." He shifted until he could reach his bedside table, popping open its drawer. "I have plenty that *do* fit me. I have to special-order them from Lucky Bloke."

Rhea tried to decide if he was joking as she watched him roll one of his condoms down the ample length of his erection. He wasn't necessarily any thicker than the other men she'd been with—all two of them—but his willy looked as long as they came. While she hadn't slept with many men to know it, her frequent visitation of Tumblr was nothing if not educational.

Huvie applied some additional lubricant to himself.

"How do you—" Rhea's voice trailed off as Huvie mounted her where she lay, squeezing her thighs together with his knees and maneuvering his cock against her ass. He slapped her right cheek with it a few times. *Yeah. Yeah, that's hard.* For a few terrifying moments, she feared he expected anal with it and visions of the resulting ER visit flooded her imagination. It wouldn't be too much unlike sending the shaft of a canon through a Krispy Kreme donut.

Then the tip of Huvie's member spread her lips and sank down.

Horror shifted to relief before it became bliss—the position in combination with her ample rear kept him from plunging too deeply, defending her cervix from certain impalement. She still got all the weight and friction she craved, from his member to his bed sheets.

Huvie started slow, resting his hands on her shoulders as he thrust and retreated.

Rhea closed her eyes, giving herself permission to envision Adam in Huvie's place.

Adam's knees against the outside of her thighs.

Adam's hands pressing her shoulders into the bed with each thrust.

Adam filling her up without mercy, her clit rubbing against the bedsheets in time with his strokes.

"*Oh God*—" Rhea gasped, her climax building by surprise.

Adam grabbing the hair at Rhea's crown, yanking her head back from the mattress.

"Louder," Huvie demanded.

She would've been louder then, anyway, as she came—crying out the single word she'd been keeping at bay the whole time.

A few more thrusts, the sensation of a dam bursting between them, and Huvie finished, groaning and plunging his full length into her.

RAYS OF SUNSHINE

Rhea yelled at the flash of pain it brought, resisting the urge to fight against him while he recovered still inside her. She thought the position had been a good one for his endowment when it was, instead, his restraint keeping her from injury. That was, until the final thrust; it sure as hell felt as if he speared her cervix and went halfway into her womb. Was it possible to dislodge an intrauterine device that way? She prayed not.

A couple minutes masquerading as a half hour later, Huvie retreated, resting on his back beside Rhea with a satisfied sigh. His hand remained wrapped around his dick, the same length but now limp.

She exhaled and put her face down against his mattress, trying to process what the hell happened.

I had sex with a guy who's not Adam. Or Mark. I somehow came and it was the least satisfying thing ever. That's what the hell happened. She hadn't just come; she'd become a human geyser. Rhea didn't know she was even capable of such things.

Oh who cares it wasn't Mark?

It was Adam who mattered. Sure, he insisted he wanted her to sleep with another guy and she had, herself, agreed to it but now she regretted the whole damn thing. And she had no clue how to leave Huvie's place with any shred of dignity left intact.

Oh my God. How am I going to tell Adam I actually went through with this?

Rhea lifted her head from the mattress. *Maybe I don't. Maybe I insist I don't need to sleep with another guy to know I want to be exclusive with him. That's all he needs to know, that's all that matters.*

"Rhea?"

She nodded. "Mmm-hmm?"

"Who's Adam?"

Rhea glanced at Huvie with a frown. Sure, her mind wandered to Adam more than once while she was with Huvie today but she didn't recall his name coming up in conversation; she'd been exceedingly careful not to mention it.

"He's—um—" She cleared her throat. "—just some guy I know."

"He must be some guy if you screamed his name in the height of passion. Frankly, I thought you'd already come until you did that."

She glanced at him sheepishly. "Oh."

"You're the first white chick I've gotten to squirt. First time I've ever had a girl yell another guy's name, too. I've gotta admit," he exhaled, "it's . . . humbling."

"Oh—God—I am so sorry for all of that! It's nothing against you, I swear—"

"I'm sure." Huvie smiled. "And it's not you, either, baby. Don't feel bad. But—" He cleared his throat. "*Do* send my regards to whoever this 'just some guy' Adam is. Now if you'll excuse me, I'm gonna use the bathroom. You can go when I'm done."

"Uh—yeah, okay."

Huvie excused himself as she sat up with a sigh and adjusted her bra until it was comfortable again. Literally, The Deed was done and she could move on. So where was the sense of freedom, the relief she'd been longing for since she and Adam devised this ridiculous plan?

The toilet flushed and the faucet kicked on and back off before Huvie emerged. "Go on now." He nodded toward the bathroom. "It's all yours."

Rhea stood from the bed, her much-abused pussy making certain she knew it had no interest in entertaining future foot-longs. She slipped into the bathroom, sparing a glance at Huvie's flaccid junk on the way.

Okay, so maybe it's only seven or eight inches long. But still. Fuckin' ow.

She took her time cleaning herself—thankfully the litterbox near the door was recently scooped so she didn't have to contend with any objectionable smell.

"Hey," Huvie greeted her when she came out. "Your phone's been buzzing non-stop. I think someone's desperately trying to reach you."

"Yeah, I'll check." Rhea glanced around the apartment, her eyes lingering on the sizable wet spot she'd left in her wake. "Hey, where'd my underwear go?"

Huvie leaned over the edge of his bed. "I dropped them right here—" he glanced around, his eyes settling on something in the kitchen. He leaped to his feet.

On the kitchen floor was a cat that looked more like an unsheared white sheep than a feline. It was writhing all over her underwear.

"*Chat!*" Huvie hissed, shooing him away and snatching the garment from the floor. "I'm so sorry," he sighed as he handed them to Rhea. "I really need to have Voodoo neutered one of these days. He's a horny little fuck."

Rhea gave him a stiff smile. "Thanks." She retrieved her shirt and jeans to dress herself in the bathroom.

The damp crotch of her petal pink panties had a fine coat of tiny white hairs which were definitely not hers. Rhea didn't relish the idea of having cat fur in her lady-business so she folded her underwear and tucked them into a pants pocket after dressing. Having denim in her lady-business was only marginally better; she'd have to change pants as soon as she got home. Rhea took a deep, steadying breath. *Walk out. Thank him for a good time, use the old 'I've got work early' line.* It was more believable than Adam's excuse of having an early art exhibit, anyway.

"Rhea?" Huvie asked. "Seriously, if you don't answer your damn phone, *I'm* gonna."

"Yeah, yeah—" She stepped out of the bathroom, dodging his face in favor of her smartphone's.

There were four calls and ten texts from Brianna of increasing urgency. The last came in while she was looking through the earlier ones: *SOS 911 IDK where U R but pls call me now!*

"Excuse me, I'd better—"

Huvie waved it off. "No worries."

Rhea selected Brianna's number from her contacts.

Brianna answered on the first buzz. "*Rhea, where the hell have you been?*"

"What's the matter?" asked Rhea.

"*I need help, I'm gonna get evicted!*"

"What—how—" Rhea shook her head. "Can I . . . do

something to help?"

"*Do you think you can come now?*"

"I—really don't see—"

"*Please, Rhea? I'm desperate!*"

Rhea sighed. "Hang on." She muted her phone. Perpetually suspicious of technology, she whispered to Huvie, "I need to go. Can you take me to Brianna's place rather than mine?"

Huvie nodded. "Yeah, of course, sure thing. Is she okay?"

"I'm sure she *will* be." Rhea unmuted her phone. "Brianna? I'll be there as soon as I can."

She could hear sniffles over the line. "*Thanks, Rhea.*"

———— smile ————

Huvie's Impala idled on the street in front of Brianna's complex as Rhea unbuckled her seatbelt.

"Are you sure you don't want me coming in with you?" he asked.

"Yeah, yeah. I've got this. Thanks for everything, Huvie."

"You're welcome, it was fun." Huvie stole a kiss on her cheek. "Let's do this again sometime, okay?"

Though Rhea had no intention of doing so—outside of getting more ink—she replied, "I'll call you soon." She let herself out of his car. "See ya."

"Bye."

Rhea huddled into her coat and trekked into the community, equally touched and annoyed when Huvie waited for Brianna to let her inside. As Brianna shut the door, Rhea breathed a sigh of relief she'd been withholding for much of the day. It was done. *Thank God.* She could resume normal Rhea boring-as-brown-grass programming.

Brianna's apartment was the polar opposite of Huvie's in that it had few decorations and was sparsely furnished. Nor had she dressed for company, in grey cut-off sweat shorts and a thin, stained, white tank top. Rhea saw Brianna's tattoo and more than the vague outline of her breasts through it.

Was she deliberately doing this sort of stuff to drive her out of her mind?

"What's going on?" Rhea asked.

Brianna turned to her with puffy, blood-shot eyes, mussed hair and ruddy, blotched cheeks. She was still attractive as hell but Rhea didn't realize until then how much makeup she wore in her pictures and on outings.

The proud, confident goddess Rhea knew was devastated.

At Rhea's double-take, Brianna dropped her head and retreated for her couch, flipping the throw cover onto the top of the cushions. "I look like shit. I'm plenty aware of that, thank you very much." She swiped a piece of paper from the coffee table and held it out to Rhea, plopping onto the couch with an *oomph*.

Rhea took it and Brianna covered her face with both hands.

After a quick assessment of the letter, Rhea said, "Bri . . . This isn't an eviction notice. This is an extension of your leasing contract. And they gave it to you almost two months ahead of time. You don't have to renew until the end of March. Why are you freaking out?"

"Because it might as well be an eviction notice." Brianna smacked her hands down on her bare thighs. "They're raising my rent a hundred dollars a month. Travis used to pay half. Without a roommate I'll be out of savings *and* checking in two months." Tears streamed anew down her red cheeks. "I'm fucked."

"No," Rhea said slowly. "You're not." She shrugged her purse onto the floor and sat on the couch beside Brianna. "Calm down. Things always seem *far* scarier in the heat of the moment. If you're worked up, you're not thinking straight and either you'll make a bad decision or you'll overlook a totally obvious solution, huh? Come on. Take a deep breath."

"Okay, I—I can do that." She took a shaky breath.

Rhea patted her on the shoulder. "Okay. Have you thought about finding a place you can maybe afford?"

"Of *course* I have. Give me a little credit, I'm pretty, not dumb. I don't have enough for security deposits. Travis covered ours for this place."

If she has enough to cover rent for a couple months, why can't she cover a security deposit with cheaper rent from there, on out? Despite her internal monologue, Rhea nodded as though what Brianna told her made sense. "Okay then. What if you found a new roommate?"

"I'm too scared to. I don't trust strangers." Brianna heaved a shuddery sigh, digging her knuckles into her eyelids. "I am such an *idiot*. All that time I should have saved my money and pfft, *no*, I had to repay my goddamn student loans like a fucking dumbass."

Rhea looked at the letter again. Brianna's rent would be 300 dollars higher than hers. It must have been a stellar location when the apartment itself was no nicer than hers and maybe even a little smaller from what she saw of it.

If they split Brianna's rent in half, Rhea would spend less than she was on her current place. She glanced around the apartment, her stomach knotting in warning. *I offered to help. And if I'm in the position to, what kind of awful friend would I be to stand idly by?* "What if . . . What if I moved in?"

Brianna's head snapped up. "Don't tease me, Rhea."

"I'm not. Look." Rhea took a deep breath; she felt nauseated. "My lease ends in a few weeks. I'm lonely and I could always benefit from paying less on where I live, y'know? I mean *sure*, the commute will be shitty on a good day, but you know, whatever." She shrugged.

Brianna lifted a shaking hand to her lips.

"We could essentially have the same arrangement you and Travis did. Say I move in for six months with a definitive end-date. That should be plenty of time for you to save up enough for a security deposit and then I'd help you move into a place you can afford on your own."

"So . . . when you say same arrangement as me and Travis had, like . . . does that include sexual favors?" Brianna chuckled weakly.

"If you don't judge me for having never been with a girl before." Rhea's lips pulled taut in an uncomfortable smile. "I mean, besides myself."

Brianna's tentative smile fell. "Okay now you *are* teasing me. Quit it."

Rhea put the letter on the coffee table, sitting back into the couch cushions and white-knuckling her hands in her lap. "I . . . had—okay, promise me you won't freak out—the *biggest* crush on you when we were in high school."

"Oh—my—God." Brianna straightened, casting her a hard stare. "Wait. *No*! You talked about the girl you had a crush on in your blog once. I thought you were just blowing smoke for attention." She gasped, putting a lithe hand over her heart. In a tiny voice, she asked, "Was that me?"

Rhea nodded once. Well if nothing else, this confession might get her out of the ridiculous promise to move in with Brianna she was already regretting.

"Well . . . How's that crush doing now?"

Rhea licked her lips and bit down, refusing to make eye-contact. "How couldn't I still have a crush on you? You've been so fun and so sweet and you're hotter now than you were in high school if it's even possible." She blinked. "And oh my God what the hell did I just do, now I'm babbling and freaking out—" Rhea jumped to her feet, hands shaking. "I'm so sorry, this was a *huge* mistake—" She raced to the front of the apartment.

"No, wait—" Brianna caught her at the door by her shoulder and turned her around.

With her eyes locked to the floor, Rhea blurted, "I don't know what I was thinking telling you any of that, I'm so embarrassed!"

"Don't be." Brianna's voice softened. "It's always nice to hear someone thinks so kind of you. I mean . . . How would it feel if I'd prattled off a list like that about *you*?"

Rhea swallowed, hesitantly lifting her gaze, her cheeks aflame. "Why would you do that?"

"What if someone had a similar list but could add things like . . . You're brave. And smart. And talented. And jeez Christ, generous to a fault, don't even get me started."

"Well—" Rhea chuckled despite herself. "I'd think she was nuts—"

Brianna shoved Rhea against the door, pressing their

mouths together.

After several heartbeats of deafening silence, Brianna retreated. "Oh. Shit. Oh God. I'm so sorry! I shouldn't have done that—"

Rhea put a couple fingers to her own lips in a daze. "No. Don't. Don't apologize."

"Really?"

"Sure. I mean, *yeah*. You're single. *I'm* . . . single—" —*ish*. "It probably wouldn't be wise to pursue an actual relationship or whatever if we're gonna be roommates," *and apparently that's happening*, "but who's to say we couldn't maybe screw around sometimes?" *At least once. Tonight, while I'm on a roll?*

"Oh my God," Brianna whispered, a giddy smile spreading across her beautiful, flushed face. "Do you even know how long I've dreamt of doing something like this?"

She shrugged coyly. "Can't be for as long as I have. I was gross in high school; you didn't give me a passing thought."

"Well I'm giving you more than a passing thought now. Holy shit, I've dreamt about doing stuff to you since I found your blog and those amazingly hot stories with Surfer Boy. Only I may have put myself in his shoes a teeny, tiny bit. And that, by-the-way, was back when I envisioned you still looking like you did in high school. Where there's a woman behind glasses and beneath a bun, there's a sexual goddess in hiding." She grinned. "Librarian porn taught me that."

Boring-as-brown-grass Rhea would have left a Rhea-shaped dust cloud in her wake after Brianna kissed her. Train-riding, anonymous-sex and one-night-stand having, so-called New Rhea was more concerned with taking advantage of fulfilling a long-standing fantasy before making any long-term commitment to Adam.

Because she was sure as hell going to demand a relationship the next time she got him on Skype after what she'd done with Huvie.

"Okay, you're not saying anything. Um. I owe you *big* time for coming to my rescue tonight," Brianna continued. She lowered her head and stepped closer to Rhea, entwining their fingers. "Now I should warn you: I've never done this before, 'cept for in my dreams, so . . . I don't know how good I'll be at it."

Rhea's heart fluttered. "I've never done this before either so I have no frame of reference. You could be the worst in your inexperience and I won't care. I'm just excited for the opportunity." She knew she sounded desperate and cringed. "Oh my God I sound like a job applicant."

Brianna laughed. "Okay, let's agree we're both awkward and inexperienced. So why don't you lead?"

"What?" Nerves shoved Rhea's voice upward half an octave. "Me? Hell if I know what to do. Why don't you . . . start by kissing me again." She hesitated, deciding to quote something she read in a romance novel. "Kiss me slow. Sweet. Just how I always dreamed you'd kiss me."

Brianna's beautiful mouth curled into a wicked smile. "I read that book too!" She tilted her head and leaned in, touching her lips to Rhea's. Brianna's were dewy, plump and warm, her pout gentle and relaxed.

Rhea reeled as she tried to memorize every last thing about the moment: Brianna's soft lips tasted salty, the faintest hint of bubblegum on her breath. She applied the perfect pressure, her body moving in closer, her shaking hands grasping Rhea's and squeezing. It had been an eternity since she'd been kissed *just so*.

How can that be? I left Huvie's place less than two hours ago.

Huvie hadn't kissed her on the lips, and maybe that was what accounted for the overall lack of intimacy in the encounter. The same lack of intimacy being compensated for—and *then* some—by the simple, gentle touch of a woman who clearly longed for the same things Rhea did.

Brianna pulled away. Her voice low, she asked, "How's that for starters?"

Rhea smiled, pulling her right hand from Brianna's grasp and putting a couple fingertips to Brianna's lower lip. "Good enough that I want more."

"Really?" Her face lit up.

"Oh yeah, much more." Rhea gave a small nod, her smile turning sly. She wrapped her arms around Brianna's shoulders and pulled her close, seeking her luscious mouth for more.

Brianna sighed in her embrace, sneaking her tongue out against Rhea's lips.

Rhea's first impulse was that it was so wrong she should have pushed away. Instead, she invited her in with coy flicks of her tongue.

"Oh my God," Brianna whispered, "this feels so naughty!"

What followed were words Rhea had never spoken for as many times as she'd written them: "I know, right?"

"So kiss me like you mean it."

Rhea lifted her eyebrows and smirked. She teased, "What if I did and you fell in love with me?"

"Well, then . . . I guess I'd be grateful same-sex marriage was just legalized here."

Rhea's eyebrows jumped another several feet and she leaned back, knocking her head against the door. "Ow."

"I—" Brianna cleared her throat. "I didn't mean it that way." She cringed, caressing the back of Rhea's head. "You okay?"

"I'm . . . really not in this for a relationship." Because it could never be good enough with anyone else to replace Adam, not even with Brianna. No matter how sexy she was.

No matter how long I fantasized about this.

Rhea was in love with Adam, and she flat-out refused to be tangled in a love triangle. Not even for the sake of making her dumb old blog a little more interesting. Not even if it meant having fodder for the second book she longed to write but for which she lacked inspiration.

Brianna nodded. "I was just saying—"

"Stop. Don't. *I* was just saying I'm looking for affection. Companionship. But it's so nice to know someone actually might actually someday actually care enough about me to actually want a commitment. You know?"

"Actually?" Brianna teased with a wink, "I'd be happy to be your bestie 'til the end of time. Say the word and I'll go full barnacle on your ass. How's *that* for commitment? Actually."

". . . Ignoring how you mocked me?"

"Hey, hey. Don't be pouty. We mock 'cause we love."

Rhea snorted. "The barnacle part sounded real sexy."

"We could even be besties with benefits. Bestiefits? Breastifits!" Brianna tittered, leaning in for another kiss. Rhea met her halfway, wondering how much alcohol Brianna drank prior to her arrival. There wasn't a hint of booze on her breath; was it possible she was just a closet geek?

Focus on the moment, dumbass!

They explored each other's mouths, toyed with each other's tongues. Encouragement came in the form of little giggles and sighs, Brianna sliding her hands down Rhea's back all the way to her ass.

"You really know what you're doing with those buns," she said.

Rhea laughed, her cheeks aflame; gin blossoms had nothing on the upshot of kissing another woman. "Thanks. So do you. Hey, um . . . How's your tattoo doing?"

"You don't have to play games to get me to take off my top."

"I'm not playing games. I was just asking for a friend—" *who fucked me about two hours ago.* Rhea's smile faltered. *Why? Why did I have to think of that? Immeasurable moron.*

If Brianna noticed it, she didn't pursue it. "Come on." She pulled Rhea into the living room, nudging the coffee table away from the couch with her knee.

"Um . . . Whatcha doin'?" Rhea squeaked.

"Don't be nervous."

"I'm not—"

"—says someone who sounds super nervous," Brianna laughed.

Rhea couldn't help laughing at her own expense. "I'm not nervous. This is how I sound when I'm aroused."

"To answer your question about my tattoo, see it for yourself." Brianna pulled off her tank top, tossing it onto the kitchen table.

Her breasts were as full and perky as advertised; she apparently didn't wear padded bras and Rhea didn't think she needed to. She didn't need any bra at all and opted not to wear them in the comfort of her own home. Or at least she chose to forgo wearing the undergarment on nights she planned to seduce a friend. *God only knows what she does on a normal night.*

"Wow," Rhea breathed. She couldn't even bring herself to drop her gaze the couple inches to see the tattoo in question. "Those are . . . *Wow.*"

Brianna smirked. "Shut up baby, I know it. You wanna touch 'em?"

"Uh huh." It wasn't eloquent, not by a long shot, but the whimper of desire was a tiny gesture that screamed volumes.

So why the hell were her arms pinned to either side of her?

"Here." Brianna took Rhea's hand, guiding it to her left breast.

"This is so weird," Rhea squeaked.

Brianna sang, "But you're smiling. You like it."

I love it. It was wonderful, in addition to being weird. It was silken, soft, and heavy like her own, but infinitely better because it wasn't. Rhea asked, "Can I kiss them?"

"Frankly, I'd be offended if you didn't."

"Oh. Well. I wouldn't want to offend." She took a deep breath before bowing her head and pressing her mouth to Brianna's breast; it was everything she imagined it would be and then some.

"Could I maybe do this to you?"

Rhea pulled back. Though she'd have been happy to fondle Brianna's chest more, she replied, "Uh, yes please."

With a wide smile, Brianna removed Rhea's shirt, dropping it on the coffee table. "Oh that's pretty. Maidenform?"

In disbelief, Rhea replied, "Seriously? That's what you're concerned with, the brand of bra I'm wearing?"

Brianna smirked. "You could say I have a little bit of a bra obsession." She unhooked Rhea's and pulled it off. "Oh yes, yes, very nice. I love what you've done with them."

"Ha! Do you suppose this is how the 'first time' goes for other girls?"

After musing a moment, Brianna answered, "Probably

not." She glanced at the tag of Rhea's bra and set it atop her shirt. "Maidenform. I love being right." She used her fingertips to circle Rhea's nipple around its barbell adornment. "Did it hurt?"

"The piercing?" Rhea shrugged. "It wasn't so bad."

"Got any others like it?"

"Only one way to find out . . ."

"No!" gasped Brianna. "Your clit? Your hood? Oh my God, both?"

"Oh no, no. But the thought's crossed my mind . . . a few times." *At least.* Rhea put her hands on the button of her jeans. "Are we *doing* this, doing this? Whole hog? Or just making out?"

"I'd personally prefer not to call it 'whole hog' when talking about doing it. But if you're in, I'm totally down for going down."

"Oh," breathed Rhea. "I'm all in."

"Okay." Brianna pushed Rhea's hands away from her pants. "Let's both stop being so shy, huh?"

"I'm not shy." Rhea lied as she watched Brianna unbutton her jeans on her behalf and drag them down. "*You're* shy."

"You go commando. And Brazilian."

Rhea was going to correct her about the commando remark but decided against it. She didn't want to explain why she wasn't wearing her underwear and there was nothing inherently wrong in Brianna's belief she was that sexy and cool. So she chirped, "*Yep.*"

"Christ. The kids in high school had you figured all wrong."

"You have no idea." She reached for Brianna's shorts, bunching them down her legs along with her disappointingly conservative underwear.

"Well it's their loss, that's for damn sure." Brianna stepped out of her shorts and leaned in to Rhea, pressing their chests together, rubbing their breasts against each other.

Rhea was captivated by the sight.

"You've got the most gorgeous rack," Brianna

commented.

Rather than saying thanks, Rhea kissed her, reaching around to cup her perky little ass with both hands.

Brianna moaned against her lips: "You're getting me so wet."

"What—really?" That was a little too easy. She was lying. "No—"

"Really," insisted Brianna. "Hey, can I tell you a secret?"

"Of course."

"Just being near you is so exciting that by the time I get home after we've hung out, I have to get fresh underwear."

Rhea looked at her in utter disbelief, thinking she'd been the only one to have that problem all this time. "You liar."

"I swear on the sperm donor's grave. Don't believe me?" She reached around and pulled Rhea's left hand from her ass cheek, guiding it between her legs.

"Oh holy sh—" Rhea lifted her glistening fingers. There was nowhere she could dry them. After letting the implications of Brianna's confession sink in, Rhea caught her gaze, and brought those fingertips to her lips.

"Oh my God Rhea—" Brianna gasped.

She suckled tentatively, her eyebrows quirking at the flavor. Rhea didn't know what to expect but she was sure she was imagining fruity undertones. Maybe that was to preemptively stave off any gagging at the thought of what she was doing.

She ultimately decided it wasn't objectionable. *Far from it, actually. Hell, it could become addictive. An upshot of heavy caffeine consumption maybe? Focus, Rhea, focus!*

Brianna pushed Rhea down to the couch, kissing her on the mouth before traveling her body with lips and hands.

Rhea's fingers curled around the edge of the couch cushions and she moaned as Brianna's mouth settled against her clit. She had no earthly clue what Brianna was doing down there, but it was sublime. Brianna even had something over Adam: not a hint of five o'clock shadow to scratch against her delicate, sensitive skin. Just smoothness, softness and oh, so wonderfulness.

Brianna coaxed out Rhea's climax like satin bedsheets

being drawn down her body, except at the end, she felt electrified, as though all her cells wanted to go every direction at once.

Brianna came up for air, brushing her chin against her shoulder.

Rhea took several moments to catch her breath. "Holy—oh, my God. I wanna try that on you."

"I hoped you would," said Brianna, her voice high and giddy.

They switched places, Rhea still trembling as she knelt beside the couch. Brianna settled in and spread her legs, dew glistening on her smooth lips. They looked like the petals of a flower after a spring sunrise, her clit a peach pearl Rhea found at their apex. She brushed by it with her thumb, watching Brianna's smile grow.

"You tease—"

It took a bit of steeling her nerves before Rhea had the courage to kiss her mound.

Brianna gasped, her glorious chest rising and falling in exaggerated spasm. *Damn. I should have played with those more.* She tickled Brianna's clit with the tip of her tongue. *Maybe later. Or next time. Later next time. Seriously? 'Next time?'*

Hey, dummy. Pay attention to her!

Rhea closed her eyes, continuing to kiss and suck on her pussy, feeling Brianna gyrate against her mouth, listening to her gasps and moans. It was surreal. When she was confident her knees would support her, Rhea shifted in her spot, sneaking a couple fingers inside her.

"*Rhea—*" moaned Brianna.

"*Mmhmm?*" Rhea slid her fingers in and out a few times, pleased with the relative lack of friction.

"*I—I can't—*"

Rhea tried not to smile, switching to a come-hither motion she enjoyed, herself, easily locating a more textured patch with her fingertips. *Is that her g-spot?*

"*Shit, I'm coming—*"

Yep.

Brianna cried out, grabbing Rhea's hair a few moments later to push her away. Rhea landed on her butt, watching

Brianna's breasts heave while she panted.

Whoa, Rhea thought, pleased with herself. *How very romance novel!*

It was silent until Brianna caught her breath and looked down at Rhea. "Wow."

"Really?" Rhea smiled.

"Oh take a fucking compliment already." Brianna reclined on the couch, beckoning for Rhea to join her.

She wrapped her arms around Rhea's chest, her silken legs resting atop Rhea's. She sighed, nuzzling and kissing her on the neck. "I never imagined it could be like that."

Rhea smiled, staring at Brianna's ceiling. The ceiling which, in a few weeks, would also be hers.

Things were going to be okay.

Brianna cupped Rhea's breast, teasing her nipple.

No. Things are gonna be great.

It was a crying shame she couldn't write about this on her blog. No one could know; they'd think she was a two-timing skank.

Actually, the secret thing makes it even hotter. Holy shit.

"Whatcha thinking about?" Brianna asked.

"Oh . . . Nothing . . ." Rhea slid her fingertips down Brianna's arm. "Just wondering who turned who."

"Wait—what?"

"You know, as far as everyone's concerned we were both straight. So did I turn you gay or did you turn me?"

"Oh honey, isn't it obvious?" Brianna laughed. "I turned you."

Rhea craned her neck to look at Brianna. "How the hell do you figure?"

"Because I instigated?"

"But I've crushed on you for forever. That's gotta be worth at least something." Rhea exhaled. "I really wish I'd had the guts to pursue this fantasy earlier."

"You 'n' me, both."

"I was thinking for next time I kinda want to get you off while pleasuring myself."

"Oh my God no way." Brianna smiled. "I had that thought, too. It's good to have goals."

RAYS OF SUNSHINE

Rhea frowned. "Stuff like this makes it *really* difficult to want to get exclusive with Adam."

"So maybe don't. Stay single, move in with me and let's see how nasty we can get together."

"But I want to be exclusive with him. I love him. I'm in love with him."

Brianna gasped. "Wait a minute. Adam. Is that Surfer Boy's real name?"

Rhea nodded.

"And . . . you're in love with him?"

Again, Rhea nodded.

"Why did you have sex with me then? I mean, I'm not complaining or anything but it seems counterintuitive to sleep with me when you're balls deep in love with him."

"Well . . ." Rhea took a deep breath. "Because of how and when we met, Adam was afraid of being my rebound. We agreed to sleep with other people before we committed to each other. To be more exact, he wanted me to sleep with someone else and I flat-out refused unless he was doing the same thing. I wanted it to be fair."

"Makes sense?" Brianna gave a half-hearted smile.

"Do you think this will count as sex for those purposes?" Rhea shook her head at herself, wriggled out of Brianna's embrace, and picked up her pants. "Never mind, it doesn't matter." Her underwear fell from the pocket and landed on the floor.

"What's that?"

"Nothing." Rhea pulled on her pants and stuffed her underwear back into the pocket. "It's nothing." Now the crotch of her jeans were wet and uncomfortable. Damn Huvie's cat.

Brianna frowned. "Rhea . . . what's going on? Why did you have panties in your pocket?"

"I may have sorta . . . been with a guy before coming here."

"What."

"If I'd known you and I were gonna happen, I wouldn't have gone out with him. I just used him for sex so I could tell Adam." *Well. I sound awful.* She cringed. "In retrospect, I could've just lied about it. Wish I had."

"Who was it?" asked Brianna. "Somebody I know?"

Rhea focused on dressing, slipping on the bra and adjusting herself in it. "It was Huvie. Really it's no big deal. I'm never seeing him again unless I decide on another tattoo." *And maybe not even then.*

"Huvie?" she whispered, her voice trembling.

"Yeah." Rhea glanced at her. "It wasn't all it was cracked up to be, trust me."

"Rhea," she cried, yanking the throw cover down over her nakedness. "How could you!"

A chill washed down Rhea's body, her stomach tumbling toward the floor. "How—how could I what?"

"I've been crushing on that asshole for forever. And you just fucked him?"

"I'm sorry," Rhea yelped. "I didn't know you had feelings for him. I'd never have slept with him if you'd told me."

Brianna's voice wavered with the threat of tears as she said, "I can't stand the sight of your face anymore. You need to go."

Stooping to grab her shirt, Rhea was certain she would puke. She straightened and pulled the shirt on. "I can't leave. Huvie drove me here."

"Oh my God. *Oh my God!* Get out, Rhea!" A steady stream of tears shimmered against Brianna's flushed cheeks. "I don't give a rat's ass how you get home. Take a cab, a bus, for shit's sake walk. Just get the fuck away from me!"

"You have got to be kidding. Do you even know how cold it is outside?"

"Get out, get out, get out!"

Without another word, Rhea grabbed her coat and purse, fleeing Brianna's apartment. She barely cleared the threshold before Brianna slammed the door behind her.

Rhea was in a fog as she hustled through the community, yanking her coat on.

She had no idea how she got to be standing in the dim, yellow spot of light from a street lamp in front of the complex; shivering and disoriented as her heart throbbed in her throat, her juices probably freezing to her girl bits through the crotch of her jeans. It was probably best if they froze off so she couldn't ever enjoy them again.

She figured she deserved to be spayed for what she'd done that day alone.

Here I am. Thousands of miles from family, no one here to come to my rescue, thirty miles from home. And I'm freezing my dumb fat ass off.

Calling anybody from work to help her was out of the question.

Maybe I could try Uber. Will someone get me this late? Rhea checked the time on her phone. 10:55.

Do they even cater to losers? Idiot whores? A sorry sack of human shit like me?

Stop it.

Stop it!

Brianna's the only one who hates me. Plenty of others around who don't. Like—

"Huvie," Rhea whispered in realization. He had, after all, told her to call him. With shaking hands and numb fingers, she scrolled through her call log for a number she hadn't yet added to her contacts: the incoming 'unsaved number' from that morning.

She took a steadying breath and placed the call.

After two rings: *"Hello?"*

Judging by his salutation, Rhea guessed he hadn't added her to his contacts, either. That hurt more than it had any right to.

"Huvie?" she greeted him through chattering teeth. "Hey. It's Rhea." When he didn't say anything immediately she added, "Rhea Josse?"

"Oh hey, baby. I wasn't expecting a booty call so soon. I haven't even gotten my sheets back from laundry—"

"It's no booty call. I kinda . . ." She inhaled and blurted, "I need a lift."

"What?"

"I'm stranded at Brianna's, I'm outside, it's fucking freezing, and I need a ride back to my place."

"Yeah, sure, okay. I'll be right there, hang tight."

LEONARD 71

*————*smile*————*

Rhea collapsed into the passenger seat of Huvie's car with a relieved sigh. The heater was blasting and she'd never been more grateful for the warmth. "Thank you so much."

She closed the door and shed her coat, sparing a quick glance at her crotch; she'd soaked right through her jeans. And Huvie noticed, his gaze trained nowhere near her face. Or even her chest. Rhea buckled her seatbelt and said, "You're a real life-saver. I owe you one."

"Oh you know I'm gonna ask what happened—"

"Don't." Rhea held up her hand to him. He was probably curious why she looked as though she'd pissed herself, and he likely feared she'd leave urine stains on his car seat. "Don't." She draped her coat across her lap and tried not to think of how uncomfortable she was. "It's nothing."

Huvie cocked his head. "You gonna be okay?"

"I don't know." A moment later, she came to her senses. She'd had a fight—if it even counted as one—with a girl she hadn't considered a friend until less than two weeks ago. "Yes, of course. I will. Be okay, I mean."

Huvie pulled away from the curb and into traffic. "And Bri?"

Who gives a shit? Rhea sighed. "You'll want to check on her as soon as you can. She won't talk to me." *The girl who promised she'd be my friend forever kicked me out of her apartment an hour later.* Brianna had a strange concept of *'until the end of time.'*

"Seriously, what happened?"

Rhea had no doubt Brianna would tell him everything. She had no doubt she'd be vilified. And maybe she even deserved to be. Nonetheless, Rhea didn't feel at liberty to share any of it. "I'm sure she'll tell you all about it."

"Mmm."

"I owe you big-time for rescuing me."

"Just pay it forward, y'know? Be there for someone when they need you."

Doing that is how I got into this situation in the first place.

Against her better judgment, Rhea promised, "I will."

———— smile ————

Rhea didn't hear from Adam until after work the following Monday. When his video feed turned on, he wasn't smiling.

"Hi sweetie," Rhea greeted him. "What's the matter?"

"I did it."

Her stomach clenched. "Huh?"

"I slept with her, it was awful, I hope you're happy now."

I've course I'm not happy. Rhea struggled to swallow around the lump in her throat. "You *did.*"

Adam nodded.

Her chest hurt. That was maybe the last thing she needed to hear from him.

He asked, "How was your date?"

No. That was. "I . . . slept with him."

Adam jerked his gaze away from the webcam. "Good. Great. *Fantastic.*"

They were silent for several excruciating heartbeats.

"Was he good? Better than me?"

No. *That* was the last thing she needed to hear from him. "What the hell kind of question is that?" She hadn't interrogated him when she very well could have. After all, the whole sleeping with other people thing had been his stupid idea.

"And yet you're not answering me."

"It was—" Rhea had to pick just the right word. When she couldn't find it on the tip of her tongue, she sighed, "—distant. He never kissed me on the lips. It was painful. He's a nice enough guy but . . . he hurt me."

"Was he bigger than me?"

"Adam!"

"So he was."

"What the fuck is your problem? Bigger isn't better. *Trust me.* Yes, size matters, I'm not gonna lie." Rhea furrowed her brows. "Consider it like pizza. Too little is gonna leave you unsatisfied and too much is gonna give you a stomachache." That would probably go into the annals of worst-analogy-ever but it was what popped into her head on the fly.

"Well." Adam sneered. "I don't think I'll ever be able to eat pizza again."

"Honey, come on. You have absolutely nothing to worry about. You are well more than enough for me. I know that now for sure."

"Mmm." He bit his lip and looked around his kitchen before glancing at his laptop. "So how's Brianna?"

Rhea's eyes narrowed. "Why do you ask?"

"She vaguebooked this morning. You didn't see it?"

"No." Rhea looked at the Facebook app on her phone, scrolling through its feed. "No, nothing here." She visited Brianna's profile. The last update was two days old and in no way vague: a complaint regarding the wait times at ALDI's checkout counters. "She must've deleted it." *Thank God.*

"No . . . I just refreshed the page. It's still there—" Adam's voice trailed off.

"She left me out of a filter." *God dammit that hurts.* Rhea pressed her fingertips to her forehead. "Huvie and I decided to stay friends. Brianna and I . . . did not."

"*Huvie.* So it has a name. And you're *friends*?"

"Of course he has a name. Seriously, don't be this way. I really don't need this kind of shit right now."

"Yeah. Fine." Adam exhaled. "Are you okay?"

Rhea looked away, putting her hand to her lips. "Not really—"

"See, this was what I was afraid of—"

"Adam please! Don't. I don't need *this* kind of shit, either."

"I'm sorry. I'm sorry. What do you need?"

Rhea took a few moments to compose her reply. Surely this would help: "I might feel better if I had some sort of actual commitment from you now. We've both slept with other people. We both know we didn't want to and don't want to again. C'mon, let's make this official. I'm so ready, without a doubt. You're the one I want, please be my boyfriend."

Adam sighed.

Her insides turned to ice. "What?"

"The thing is . . . I . . . don't want a girlfriend right now."

His words sank in like a lead vest dropped on her shoulders. "You told me you were a nice guy," she said, the last of her coolness evaporating. Rhea jumped from her seat, smacking the laptop shut. "You're a bastard!"

She squeezed her hands into shaking fists, cold fingertips pressing into her palms, fingernails gouging her skin. Without further consideration, she grabbed her parka and left her apartment to try clearing her head.

It was bitterly cold out, the wind tearing right through her parka.

Everything looked bleak to Rhea as nighttime gloom blanketed her community. She lapped the complex twice, settling on a bench at the small park in the middle of the apartment buildings.

She snuggled into her parka, her hands tucked into its pockets and her head bowed to the strong gusts of wind.

The playground was vacant and dark, every bit the same as her soul.

Stop it, stop it. Rhea squeezed her eyes shut. *This isn't what I moved to Aurora for.*

I came here to find myself and I got wrapped up emotionally with Adam even after I promised myself I wouldn't. I got invested in and then conned by Brianna. And with all my dates, I never really gave any of them a chance. My fault, my fault, my fault. All my fucking fault.

Okay. Damage control: I can fix this.

I'll start by renewing my lease here. Actually try dating for real if this thing with Adam isn't gonna go anywhere, which apparently it isn't. Nice of him to finally admit it. I never took him for the type to string a girl along but, well, here I am.

The lack of friends thing, however, she had no clue how to fix. *Shame there's no Tinder for friends.*

Maybe I'll create a friendship app. I'll call it the Frapp. And consequently get my dumb fat ass sued off by Starbucks.

Any other time, Rhea might have cracked a smile at her self-deprecating humor. Instead, she stood. *Time for booze.*

*————— *smile* —————*

Drink and Be Merry was walking distance from Rhea's apartment—a decided perk to city living. She went there on the odd Saturday if for no other reason than to get adequately soused; their bartender mixed a mean cocktail.

Of ten stools at the bar proper, only two were unoccupied and she took the one furthest from everyone else. She wasn't there to be hit on, to make friends or even to drown her sorrows; she just didn't want to feel so much anymore.

Bartender Barry—which, she assumed, was not his given name—worked his way down to her.

"You okay?" he asked. "You look depressed."

Bitch, you don't even know my depressed face. "I'm fine. Can I get a Rum 'n' Cola?"

"Sure." Bartender Barry backed away to mix her drink and Rhea sighed.

Yeah, step away from the loser. Better I push people away than to let them in so they can hurt me.

The bartender set her drink down. Rhea nodded an acknowledgment, turning her gaze into the dark amber liquid.

It was a while before Rhea had strength enough to lift the drink to her lips; she sipped it steadily.

Someone sat on the stool beside hers. "Hi."

Rhea's impulse was to snap *leave me alone*. Or *what the hell do you want?* She spared a quick glance at the dark-skinned, raven-haired woman. "Hey." *Now leave me alone.*

"You look like you could use a friend."

"Friends suck." *Holy shit. I actually said that out loud.*

"Yeah, you could definitely use a friend." She held out a lithe hand angled downward, her fingers dressed in a variety of turquoise and silver rings. One had an owl incorporated into the design, its eyes made of dark faceted crystals. Another ring was a serpent snaking several times around her middle digit. "I'm Coraline."

She supplied a name. Guess this one's not gonna leave me alone. Damn. It. So I have sex with one girl and now I'm appearing on other people's gaydar? Suddenly I have that so-called quality? Rhea looked her over.

Well at least this one was an improvement on the last person who hit on her here: the used car salesman with the lame secret agent story and a sorry excuse for a toupee. At least Rhea had moved on to a higher class of weirdo.

Coraline was a stunner in an eccentric mix of Asian and Native American motifs. Her cheekbones were to die for, beautiful chocolate crème eyes surrounded by thick plum eyeliner and a liberal application of golden yellow eyeshadow.

"You don't want to mess with me," muttered Rhea. "I'm nothing but trouble."

"My favorite people always were troublemakers." Coraline replied, her thick mauve-tinted lips lifting into a broad smile. "What's your name, beautiful?"

She sighed. "Rhea."

"That's pretty."

"Thanks."

"C'mon now. Tell me what's going on."

I attract such freaks. "You *really* want to know?"

"I wouldn't have pried, otherwise."

"Okay. Fine." Rhea finished her drink. "I was in a sorta long-distance relationship with this guy but apparently I was more invested in it than he was. We both agreed to sleep with other people, right? He did and it absolutely killed me inside but I didn't flip out about it because that was our agreement. I sleep with another guy and he loses his fucking mind about it. And of course the guy I slept with was someone the closest thing I had to a best friend here actually had feelings for so she lost her shit over it. So . . ."

She itemized her complaints, ticking them off with her fingers. "I have no boyfriend, I lost my best-friend, and the sex I had to even get to this point? So not worth it." She exhaled.

If she'd slept with only Brianna, maybe she wouldn't have felt that way. If she'd not climaxed—and squirted—with Huvie maybe she would have felt less betrayed by her body. *The whole thing sucked, start to finish, and I still came the way a good, obedient little slut should. God I hate myself.*

"When I met Adam, I'd just gotten divorced. I didn't want anything at all from him but we hit it off and, oh, it was impossible not to fall in love with him."

"*Mm-hmm.*" Coraline nodded, taking a dainty sip of her drink after Bartender Barry dropped it off, airborne pinkie and all.

"And the thing with Brianna was my own dumbassery."

"Oh?"

"All I'm saying is maybe there was a damn good reason I wasn't her friend in high school. All those times she had opportunities to include me in her group? Or to at least be cordial in passing . . . would it have killed her?" Rhea kicked the wall of the bar. "I'm such an idiot! 'Let's be besties, Rhea!'" She muttered, "Like people actually change?"

"I think you're being too hard on yourself."

"I blindly took her side when Travis left her. Maybe he dodged a bullet. I was gonna move in with her. Maybe *I* dodged a bullet, too." She shook her head. "I'm an awful friend, an awful person, and God knows I deserve to be alone."

"I think you're a sweet, trusting person who's been hurt."

"Hate to break it to you, sister, but you're an awful judge of character."

"No," Coraline replied, shaking her head slowly. "I'm not."

Rhea rolled her eyes, calling for Barry. "Can I get a refill here?"

He nodded, waving at her. "Yeah, just a sec."

"Everything will be okay," said Coraline.

Rhea looked at her with impressive deadpan. "How the hell do you figure?"

"You've been touched by love."

Rhea didn't think it was possible to roll her eyes hard enough. She put on a fake smile instead, hoping to end this nonsensical conversation.

"I can see it in your eyes, you know. Even when you roll them like that. Trust me, I know these things."

"What are you, some kind of sexologist?"

Coraline giggled. "Something along those lines, yes. Why don't you go on home, get some rest? You'll see, tomorrow is a whole new day."

"I'll go after I finish this drink."

"Have you got a ride? I can take you—"

"I walked," Rhea blurted. "I'll be fine."

It turned out Rhea didn't consume enough alcohol to sufficiently numb her feelings by the time she returned to her apartment. She did however feel beaten down enough to compensate for the lack of drunkenness. She dropped her purse by her front door and dragged herself to bed. Instead of snuggling underneath the covers, she fell to her knees, pressing her forehead into the side of her mattress.

She sorted through her jumbled thoughts, searching for the appropriate prayer. Her parents only ever taught her one, and thanking God for food wasn't going to fix anything here.

Rhea opened her mouth, two tiny words slipping out as she dissolved into tears: "Help me."

Chapter Three

The next morning, Rhea woke on the floor like someone recovering from a good drunkenness, not as though she'd experienced anything close to being good and drunk last night. She'd scarcely qualified for good and buzzed. Unfortunately, nobody in her liquor-tolerance department notified her head she had been well within her limits. Her temples throbbed uncontrollably, giving her pathetic excuse for a hangover at least a few symptoms of the genuine article.

She'd never made it into her bed; only decent people deserved to sleep on a mattress. Rhea, on the other hand, deserved this damn near debilitating cramp at the base of her neck from having slept crumpled on the floor like dirty laundry.

Her shift started in an hour and a half which afforded a dose of ibuprofen plenty of time to kick in; she swallowed two blue gel caps before sitting at her kitchen table and cracking open her laptop. It was a surprise when the screen came on; she was certain she'd broken it after Skyping with Adam last night.

While Windows 8 loaded, Rhea checked her phone for messages.

No missed calls.

No texts.

No alerts from Messenger.

No one asking about her on Facebook.

In this case, unsurprisingly, 'no one' included Brianna. *Which is good.* And, unfortunately, 'no one' also included Adam. *Which is bad and scary.*

There were no comments on her blog, of course, though lack of replies was nothing out of the ordinary. To be fair, she hadn't updated in weeks.

For the most fleeting of moments, Rhea was inclined to update now but her post would be so venomous—primarily toward herself—and so full of bile it might dissolve her keyboard as she typed it. She opted to revisit her blog at another time when she wouldn't be reading her screen through tears.

Rhea put her hand on the top of her laptop screen to close it but stopped. She Googled what she felt she needed most at the moment, hoping maybe some undeserved compassion from a higher power would do her heart some good. On a page filled with prayers, one stood out as being especially pertinent:

When I feel tainted, God, remind me that I am holy
When I feel weak, teach me that I am strong.
When I am shattered, assure me that I can heal.
When I am weary, renew my spirit.
When I am lost, show me that You are near.
Amen.

Rhea stopped reading when her vision blurred with sadness.

She rubbed her burning eyes and caught sight of her tattoo.

Smile.

It did nothing but conjure memories of a physically painful one-night-stand, and the girl who'd pressured her into getting the ink in the first place.

Smile.

It was the reminder to smile she detested needing. And in Adam's cursive no less.

Smile.

She wanted to take a knife and see how much of the damned *smile* she could cut from her flesh.

And if she took too much, it would be Aftermath's problem. Did crime scene clean-up companies handle that sort of stuff?

Stop it, Rhea. Stop!

She closed the laptop and vacillated over going to work, getting dressed and then deciding to call in. On the second ring, Rhea canceled it; she couldn't remember the last time she took a sick day but despite the nausea, she didn't think being in the absolute depths of despair was a good enough excuse for missing work.

Probably the patients won't care if I cry through their appointments. Doubt they'll even notice. She took a cleansing breath. *I'll be fine.*

*———*smile*———*

Rhea made it in to work without incident and even managed to massage two people before catching the chiropractor between patients. "Dr. Kasick?"

His face firmly enshrouded by a patient's file, he said, "Rhea, good morning."

What's so good about it? She sniffled.

He glanced at her. "Oh. Is everything okay?"

Her breath came with a shudder, her voice high and tight. "No. I think—I think I need to go home."

"Okay . . ." He said hesitantly with a frown. "Can you get there safely?"

Rhea nodded. "I'm just . . . I'm not in a real good place right now. And um, can I take a few mental health days?"

Dr. Kasick sighed, setting down the patient file on his desk. "You know the rules here, you're still in your probationary period."

"I do, I know, but I really don't think I can stay . . ."

"It'll have to be unpaid."

She nodded again. "Yes, Doctor, I understand."

"And we'll really struggle without you. You know how important you are to us here. We're overwhelmed lately as is, you'll be putting us in a bind."

Bullshit, anyone with a set of hands can replace me. Rhea tilted her head to the ceiling, tears stinging her eyes. "I know— And really, I'm so sorry, I'd never ordinarily do something like this but—"

"You can have the time off, Rhea, of course. I understand."

"Oh God, thank you, Dr. Kasick."

"*But.*"

Rhea groaned inwardly.

"I insist you get a massage before you leave."

She glanced at him with a frown; that wasn't at all what she expected. "Oh. Okay."

Naturally, it was Clarence to have an opening when Rhea needed it. He was a nice enough guy; Rhea had nothing against him, except he had a penis—she could assume—and anything equipped with one of those was troublesome. *Tom cats. Male polar bears. Bull elephants going through musth . . .*

As she disrobed and got under the sheet on the massage table, Rhea recalled something random from her teenage years she hadn't thought of for nearly a decade. It was a key chain she'd purchased that—as memory served—humiliated her mother for whatever reason. A simple, rectangular plastic fob with a saying typed in a bold, no-nonsense font: *If it has tires or testicles, it's bound to give you grief.*

At the time, she was naïve to its candor.

"You ready, Rhea?" Clarence asked from outside the room.

"Yeah." She sniffled; her nose burned. "Come in."

He stepped inside the room and paused to turn the lights down. "So." He closed the door. "What do you need?"

Something kind and gentle. "Pulverize me."

"What? Are you sure?"

"I'm sure."

He asked, "Do you want to talk about it?"

"No. Thanks," she replied around the lump in her throat. Her voice shaking perilously, she clarified: "Please, just the massage. And quiet time."

"Oh. Um. Okay." He must have been confused; any time he'd given her a massage in the past, she'd been more than happy to talk his ear off. Clarence adjusted the iPod dock, the strains of New Age relaxation music filling the air. After taking a moment to warm some oil between his hands, he began his deep tissue massage at Rhea's feet.

Some forty-five minutes later, he worked down Rhea's left arm and couldn't resist a remark: "Awesome new ink."

Rhea, who'd been lost in the most self-deprecating thoughts, began to weep.

"Hey, uh . . . I know it's not my place or nothin', but I've got the name of a pretty amazing man you can talk to. He takes our insurance, helped me through some pretty rough times. You know, Dashonda and my brothers, and all?"

She pulled her arm from his slick hands. "I'll be *fine*," Rhea insisted; after all, her problems paled in comparison to his wife sleeping with his brother. Or two of them. And strictly speaking, one of the two was superfluous as his younger brothers were identical twins and probably did things pretty much the same way in the sack. "Thanks for your concern." And anyway, she had a doctor she liked. *In California. Aw damn.*

Clarence finished Rhea's massage, leaving her to dress and flee the office without further comment.

Rhea drove herself home through a torrent of tears. They ebbed as she shut the door to the outside world and all its ills.

Tears replaced by a welcome numbness, Rhea slithered into her flannel pajamas, curled up on her futon wrapped in her favorite chenille blanket and did what she always did at her absolute lowest points: she read a Debbie Macomber book. The most recent one she'd purchased was *The Shop on Blossom Street*.

It was a fast read that was easy to get lost in and what

she needed most to forget her troubles. The double-edged sword of books like those, however, was that they were quick reads for an already speedy reader; she finished this one by dinnertime.

She settled at her table with a bowl of Chex and reflected on the tale.

There was something simultaneously uplifting and aggravating about those types of stories. The neat, almost too easy resolution with ultra-happy endings for the characters who were, a few chapters prior, at absolute rock-bottom. Great for them. As a reader, it was what Rhea wanted. But as a human being at rock-bottom herself, it made her even more miserable; where was her ultra-happy ending?

Oh that's right.

I don't deserve one.

She choked down her cereal and as she went to clean the bowl and spoon she muttered, "God is good, God is great. I thank Him for the food I ate."

Not the sincerest *Birkat Hamazon* Rhea'd ever done, nor the proper Hebrew one by a longshot, but in her defense she'd fallen out of practice saying Grace after meals as a child; she supposed a grumpy English blessing was better than none at all. She also supposed her parents might disagree with her. Maybe God disagreed with her, too.

Probably God disagreed with her marrying the first man to show interest in her when she was barely old enough to sign the marriage contract, later divorcing him; sleeping with a stranger on an eastbound train repeatedly, having sex with said stranger in her hotel room, again repeatedly; sleeping with another man she barely knew just for the sake of having done it; sleeping with a girl less than a few hours later.

Probably all the masturbation and exhibitionist kinks were at least marginally disagreeable too.

What did Rhea know of it? She wasn't God. And if she were God, she wasn't a good one. *Rhea the Failgod.*

The exhibitionist kinks did make her wonder if she chose a life of massage therapy as an excuse to continually put her hands on strangers' bodies?

She didn't choose massage therapy to help people. She needed the skin-to-skin contact and it was better when it was people she didn't know. It always had been.

Sleeping with strangers and doing it in public—she'd discovered thanks to Adam—were huge turn-ons. Or at least the thought of such things were. The train had been semi-public.

Her mouth dropped open. *God has to be more disgusted with me than I am.*

Probably what she needed was to get in touch with a counselor.

Or a rabbi.

Rhea settled at the kitchen table to check her phone, expecting an email from Dr. Kasick's office telling her a box of her belongings was in the mail and she needn't return to work. Ever.

Now that two days had gone by since she last said a word to anyone in cyberspace, certainly someone had to have noticed her absence and checked on her.

No phone calls, second verse same as the first. Rhea cradled her forehead in her hand, fighting off her tears. Hadn't she cried over this crap enough already?

Maybe there was something good on Facebook. She scrolled through her feed.

Page update selling something.

Suggested post. Also selling something.

Friend liked a meme. Not just any meme; an offensive one.

Page update with a cat meme. *Okay, well at least that one's cute.*

Friend liked a meme with a glaring grammatical error in it.

Rhea continued scrolling through more of the same, wondering what was the point in checking Facebook anymore.

Suggested post selling something. *Really? Wasn't there one of those just a few posts back?*

An actual update. Rhea sighed. *By a friend complaining she couldn't sleep last night.*

Someone mentioned a trending topic on a celebrity she couldn't care less about.

Charmed Mooregood liked this.

"Oh." Rhea straightened. "Whose misery did she get a kick out of today?"

The post in question was the photograph of a woman's left hand with a spectacular engagement ring parked on it. The accompanying description read, *He asked and I said 'you betcha.'*

Rhea looked to see which 'he' was tagged in her former co-worker's engagement announcement: Mark Coleman.

"Whose misery? My misery!" Rhea smacked her palm on the table.

It was so tempting to pitch the phone into the wall across from her but this same frenemy cost her a couple hundred dollars in splintered-cell-replacement already.

Taking a deep breath instead, Rhea did what she should have done years ago: she pressed on Charmed's name beside the notification and unfriended her with a chipper, "Fuck you."

For a few blissful moments, Rhea let herself feel good about having done that before she realized the assorted implications of the post she'd seen.

Charmed had to be friends with Mark because she never knew Amanda, not even through Rhea—and *that* had to have happened after the divorce was finalized since Charmed and Mark hadn't been friends when she was still married to him. He disliked Charmed because of how she always treated Rhea.

Unless that was for show. God knows what he did behind my back. What they were doing behind my back. Not as if she'd given a damn.

Then: *It's been five months and he's engaged to the co-worker whose massages he always chose over mine. Kinda proves he was cheating on me with her.*

She huffed: "Figures."

That was more her speed of giving damns.

Rhea resorted to cleaning her kitchen and tried to put the news out of her head; even if she felt like maggot shit, her apartment needn't smell likewise. Two disinfected countertops into the task, her phone started buzzing.

Her first impulse was to let it go to voicemail. *Whoever it is, let them worry.* By the third buzz, vengeance was replaced by desperation and she rushed to answer it while drying her hands.

Her bestie was calling.

Why? Cass never calls.

Rhea answered just before voicemail took it. "Hello? Cass?"

"*Rhea, hi,*" Cass replied. "*God it's good to hear your voice.*"

Rhea wasn't so confident she could say the same. Cass sounded odd. "What's up?"

"*Oh—nothing—just, um . . . Calling to see what's going on in your neck of the woods.*"

"Well, I guess in the divorced-spouse-races, I just officially lost."

"*Huh?*"

"Mark's already getting remarried and the only thing I've successfully done is to ruin every good thing I had in twenty-four hours or less. I must be a remarkable kind of loser."

The line fell quiet for a while. Rhea pulled the phone from her ear to check if the call had been dropped.

No.

"—Hello?" said Rhea.

"*What about Adam?*" Cass asked.

"Oh yeah, no. It's . . . that's over."

"*It can't be.*"

Rhea rolled her eyes. "Why not?"

"*Because he loves you?*"

"Yeah well whatever." Rhea paced around her kitchen table. "It's over. Trust me, I made sure of it. I fucked everything up." Damn near literally.

"*Everything? Do you still have your job?*"

Rhea hoped she would when she returned from her time off. For the moment, as far as she knew: "Yeah."

"*And you still have a place to live, right?*"

"Yes." Unlike Brianna, soon.

"*Have some perspective, huh? Your problems could be so much worse.*" Cass's voice cracked through the last several words.

"Y'know, if I wanted this kind of so-called help, I'd have called my parents." Rhea gaped at herself for having the guts to say that and she braced herself against the table.

"*Rhea . . . Pika Tomes Orange County is closing.*"

She blinked. "I don't understand."

"*They're closing our whole office and laying everyone off.*"

"Oh shit," Rhea whispered, collapsing into her kitchen chair. "Everyone?" As she recalled, Cass's husband Jack worked in a different department within the same company.

"*Yeah. Now you're catching on.*"

"Oh my God—"

"*They called the entire staff of our office into a conference room a month ago. I was one of the first ones to get there and a bunch of people from upper-management filed in carrying stacks of tissue boxes. I knew it wasn't gonna be a good meeting.*"

Last month? *This happened a month ago and she didn't bother telling me?* That was far from the point of this exercise but Rhea's feelings were still hurt for being kept out of the loop regarding such significant news. "I thought they were grooming you for a move into management."

"*They were gonna promote me next month. Apparently international corporate doesn't give a rat's ass what we were doing here.*"

"What about the other corporate offices? Are those still open?"

"*Of course they are,*" Cass snapped. "*They're only screwing us over.*"

"Could you maybe put in for a transfer?"

"*That was the first thing I did the day they made the announcement. I was approved by the end of that week to move to King of Prussia.*"

"Where?" asked Rhea.

"*Pennsylvania. Anyway, we filled out an application for an apartment, put money down on it and then I saw the relocation package wouldn't cover even a fraction of a cross-country move. The money we put on that apartment is non-refundable and now we have a house we have to scramble to sell and somehow find an affordable apartment nearby—which I think you know doesn't exist in Southern*

California."

"Well . . ." She wracked her brain for a non-stupid-sounding response. "Did they give you severance packages?"

"Sure. But they're an absolute slap in the face. Oh and guess what I found out today?"

Rhea didn't want to know. She cringed, asking, "What?"

"EDD thinks I've already cashed out my benefits and said I'm not eligible for any."

"How the hell can that be?" cried Rhea. "You've never used unemployment."

"I know! Convincing EDD is a whole 'nother nightmare. They said if it wasn't me then my identity was stolen and that's something else I'm gonna have to deal with in addition to the staggering loss of income."

"Well . . . did they at least tell you how to fix it?"

"Of course not, it's a state agency, why the hell would they? And I dunno if it's because the person I talked to didn't know, herself, or because she didn't give a shit, but either way I'm gonna have to figure it out on my own. And I'm willing to bet it's neither simple or quick."

"I'm so sorry, I don't even know what to say. I wish I could help." There was the stupid-sounding response.

"Jack's off at an interview right now for a job that pays a fraction of what he got from Pika. Our office closes in a few weeks but they've stopped funneling work to us so I was sent home early today because there was literally nothing for me to do there. Would you stay on the phone with me? Don't say anything about my issues. Just . . . keep me company, please? I really can't be alone right now."

Rhea thought what Cass needed was to be spending every waking moment looking for a new job. She kept her opinion to herself.

They spent the next hour and a half talking: about the weather—as polite company did when trying to ignore the elephant in the room—but only for so long until conversation turned to ruminations on why Pika Tomes was closing and what Rhea should do to fix her missteps. Neither resolved anything except to waste time until Jack returned.

They ended the call.

Though it had been a dreadful thing for Cass, Rhea was reminded she was important to at least one person.

RAYS OF SUNSHINE

She drew herself a bubble bath and soaked in it, giving herself some time to think—maybe even clearly. Some of Cass's suggestions had merit; they were things Rhea could have figured out herself if she hadn't been in a state of panic. She didn't suppose there was any apology that would make Brianna willing to talk to her again. And maybe that was for the best.

But God . . . Her lips. Her body. Her skin. She hadn't gotten enough of Brianna and the longing for more of something she never should have done was painful.

Rhea exhaled a long, shaky sigh. *And Adam.* She traced the word *smile* on her wrist. She was a fool for getting romantically involved with him and it probably wasn't wise to try to salvage their friendship; then she'd never get over him. Who had she been kidding when she let him stay in her hotel room after they parted ways upon arriving at the train station in Chicago?

Oh but his touch, his chest, his smile. His hard-on. His boner wasn't his best physical quality of course, but it remained one of her favorites.

Sure, maybe with enough time she could get over Brianna. Their tryst had been the fulfillment of long-standing fantasies.

But Adam.
I'm in love with him.
I love him.

She sunk into the soapy water, closing her eyes against the sting of unshed tears.

Well, here I am. Back at square. Fucking. One.

*———*smile*———*

Rhea's first full day off work was uneventful. She took a brief walk around her community and sat on the vacant swings until she couldn't take the bitter cold any longer. She did some grocery shopping: a loaf of bread, a half-gallon of nonfat milk, sticks of what she referred to as not-butter, a brownie mix, and a single serving package of devil's food cake for dessert.

She was complimented on her tattoo.

She visited the nearest bookstore and added *The Cat Who Walks Through Walls* to her book collection and received two more compliments on her tattoo. By the time she got home, Rhea was contemplating researching the cost of tattoo removal.

For dinner, she indulged in a full tray of Betty Crocker brownies. For dessert? Devil's food cake. While finishing off a glass of milk, Rhea texted Cass: *Officially a sad single woman. Had chocolate for dinner. Followed by chocolate dessert. Tomorrow I'll be an awesome single woman: join a yoga class & rescue a kitty from the nearest shelter. How are you doing?*

Cass replied: *Been better. I applied to a temp agency today from a job posting I found on Monster but it was already filled. Nothing else open I qualify for atm.*

Rhea heaved a deep sigh and typed, *What about Walmart cashier?* She corrected that to *I'm so sorry* before sending.

Moments later, the message came in: *Jack got a second interview.*

That's promising right? Rhea sent and took her dishes to the sink. Her phone buzzed.

Trying to work out logistics. It's a long commute for less money. We'd still lose our house.

Rhea texted back: *Can he negotiate a higher starting wage?*

IDK, Cass replied. It was ten minutes before another text came through. *Have you heard from Adam?*

Rhea rolled her eyes and snorted. *Lol no.*

Would you consider reaching out to him?

It was Rhea's turn to text *IDK*. She added, *What for?*

I think you should. I think he's your 1.

"My 'One?'" Rhea scoffed. "Oh please." To Cass, she texted, *Yeah? So did I.*

Cass sent, *I'm sorry.*

Me too. Check in tomorrow, OK?

Several minutes later, Cass replied, *I will.*

Rhea closed the app with a sigh. She did her social media rounds and still no one wondered to where she'd vanished. It was so tempting to send a 'btw guys I'm fine, thanks for asking' post but passive aggressiveness never solved anything; at least it never did for Rhea. And—besides—to say she was fine was also a load of steaming bullshit.

To avoid temptation, she put her phone in the bedroom and began her hunt for something to watch on television. Rhea wanted to make herself miserable with a good tragedy.

"Something like *John Carter*. *Phantom Menace*? Ooh, maybe *Fantastic Four*." She chuckled weakly at herself. A weak laugh was better than none. She decided on something uncharacteristic for Rhea-in-depression when she flipped by FXX: *Megamind*. A happy, *fun* movie.

She fell asleep before the title character got the girl.

———smile———

The next day, Rhea followed through with her threats by going to the local gym and signing up for not only a yoga class but for Zumba, as well. She'd gained a good fifteen pounds, easy, since moving to Aurora. Huvie had been nice to say he could 'work' with her fluffy physique and Brianna kinder yet to not shame her for being the decidedly chunkier of their girl-on-girl romp. Would Rhea's next sexual partner be so open-minded?

Adam, of course, never noticed it as their Skype sex only ever involved the showcasing of one body part at a time—which was universally her chest. If he noticed she gained a cup size and a little over, he'd never complained.

The yoga instructor was an extroverted waif who was as enthusiastic as Rhea was reluctant, and she made Rhea promise to return for her first class tomorrow.

Rhea grabbed some chicken rings at White Castle on the way to the animal shelter. She finished them off in a parking space with the car idling and heater on full-blast before going inside, assuming the lingering smell of chicken on her hands would make her a popular attraction among the kennel set.

To her disappointment, it appeared to be puppy season with fifteen homeless dogs awaiting adoption—her complex didn't allow for those—but only three cats. To her dismay, none of those cats gave her the time of day despite her poultry hands. She couldn't dismiss the obnoxious parallel between the felines and all her friends. Rhea returned to her apartment pet-less.

There was a note on her front door from the leasing office indicating they were holding a package for her so she walked down to pick it up, exchanging brief pleasantries with the manager.

Upon her return home, she set the box on her kitchen counter, the Amazon smile on its side greeting her.

Rhea wracked her brain—she hadn't ordered anything from them recently and to the best of her recollection had nothing on backorder.

Holding her breath, she opened the box. Inside was a bouquet featuring sunflowers, snapdragons, solidago, Peruvian lilies and pompoms, as well as a colorless glass vase.

Rhea squeezed her eyes shut to quell the burgeoning tears. She removed the flowers from the box, cut their stems and arranged them in the vase with some fresh water.

While preparing to toss the box, she found a notecard tucked into the packing material. On it was typed: *The Rays of Sunshine bouquet for my Rhea of Sunshine.*

Rhea smiled until she read the rest.

Please Skype me. We need to talk.

Her smile fell and her heart sank along with it. She snapped a photo with her phone and sent it to Cass with a brief comment: *See Cass? Over.*

She texted Adam. *You want to talk?*

Adam replied a couple minutes later: *Can you Skype tonight?*

"Ah. Gonna break up with me to my face. Ballsy."

She replied to him: *I've been off work. Available whenever you are.*

"Better get used to saying I'm available and actually meaning it."

He answered, *I'm with Gary now. We'll Skype 9 PM your time?*

Rhea sighed, realizing she was parched. *Ok. Give my regards to Gary pls.*

Adam didn't text her back.

*————— *smile* —————*

At ten minutes to nine, Rhea settled into her bed with her laptop figuring luck favored the prepared.

Adam would tell her he just wanted to stay friends, it was him and not her.

She would smile and say she totally understood, and that she was fine being just friends.

They'd make brief and uncomfortable small talk before closing Skype and all she'd have to do was roll onto her stomach to cry into her pillow until she fell asleep. Or suffocate herself, if she were lucky. Luck never favored her as far as she was concerned.

Soon after, he'd stop replying to her Facebook updates, and a few months down the road, he'd unceremoniously disappear from her friends list.

Then one-by-one, their few joint friends would tell her he was telling them what a crazy bitch she was.

"The anatomy of a modern break-up." Rhea opened her laptop and checked on Facebook. Her current relationship status was set to *It's complicated.* She switched it to *single* but didn't save her changes.

The Skype icon in the taskbar flashed with an incoming call accompanied by its characteristic melody: *Boo-BEE-boo, BEE-boo—*

Rhea drew in a steadying breath. *Single again in 3, 2, and 1* . . . She clicked on the video icon, adjusting the angle of her screen as she reclined on her side.

"Hey Rhea."

Rhea forced the most insincere smile in the history of faux smiles. "Hi."

"Um . . ." Adam rubbed the nape of his neck, ducking his head until he was off screen. "Listen. I'm so sorry for how things went during our last call."

She didn't want to apologize and wasn't too keen on accepting his. "Yeah."

"How are you?"

Small talk. Really, Adam? Oh hell no. "I got the flowers.

Why did you need to talk to me?"

Adam popped his head into the frame. "I wanted to apologize. And I was starting to worry you were never going to talk to me again!"

"Why didn't you reach out to me sooner?"

He frowned. "Oh shit. Rhea. Don't do this."

"Don't do what?"

"I've been busy as hell visiting galleries all day, every day, and painting at night 'til I can't see straight and my hand is seized in cramps. And besides, I was waiting for *you* to reach out to me. After all, you were the one who hung up on me. Between a brush stroke and dozing off to sleep I'd check my phone waiting for something—anything—from you, and nothing. Don't think my silence was me ignoring you. Remember why Sally dumped me? Please don't do that to me, too!"

Comparing me to an ex? Especially that ex? Okay, ouch. She closed her eyes, fending off tears. He couldn't have meant it as such a low blow. She rolled onto her back and took a deep breath, exhaling through burning nostrils.

"Doors are starting to open for me. It looks like I'll be taking my yearly trip early this year."

"What?" Rhea opened her eyes. "Really?" She turned onto her side. "How early?"

"At the end of March. But . . ." He dropped his gaze. "I'm not gonna go east."

It was well-known fact in Southern California that everywhere from there was east. "Excuse me?"

"Gary pulled some strings and got me a stall in the Spring Best of the Northwest Art and Fine Craft Show."

"Where exactly—?"

"Seattle."

Rhea blinked furiously. "You mean to tell me you're choosing to go to some art show over coming to visit your parents?" *I thought they were your priority. I'd hoped maybe I was.*

"I'll be out there again in a year or so. I promise. But I can't in good faith miss this opportunity. My parents wouldn't have wanted me to. And," he took a deep breath, "neither should you."

"That's not fair," whispered Rhea.

"If life was fair . . ." Adam turned his attention down to something below his camera. The keyboard or perhaps his lap. "The woman of my dreams wouldn't have chosen to move to Chicago rather than return to California once I found her."

She ran her hand through her hair. There was no good rebuttal so she opted for a semi-related topic: "Until we figure out some suitable living arrangement . . . Since we've both slept with other people, can I at least get a commitment from you?"

"Rhea, I love you so much. It's just—" He groaned and sighed. "I'm not ready yet, please don't push me. But I don't want you screwing other men." Adam flinched. "Does that make me the worst person ever?"

She thought to say she wouldn't forgo sex with other men without commitment. Maybe she'd sleep with other women and give him explicit details of those encounters until he couldn't take it anymore—either from jealousy or longing. "You're *not* the worst person ever but only if you afford me the same courtesy."

"Fair enough. Honest, Rhea. I will be ready someday. Just—"

"Not yet. I understand." *No I don't. Big fat fucking liar.*

"Please know I love you so much. And I miss you."

Sure you do. Whatever. Rhea muttered, "I miss you more."

"We're okay, right?"

"Yeah." *No.*

"Hey, um . . . Not to change the subject but Brianna sent me a message through Facebook this morning."

Rhea's heart stopped, her body experiencing the sensation of falling into a cold pool on a hot summer day. "Oh?" she squeaked.

"Seriously, what happened between you two?"

"Remember the guy I slept with?"

Adam's eyes darkened but he said nothing.

"So you do. Um. Apparently she has a crush on him." *And nothing else happened. The end.* "And I had no idea, she never said anything about it. Had I known—"

"*Oh . . .*" interrupted Adam with notes of recognition.

If that was explanation enough to satisfy his curiosity, maybe Brianna hadn't revealed much to him at all in either the vague Facebook update she'd made last Saturday or in the message she sent to him that morning.

"What do I tell her?" he asked.

Tell her to suck a giant bag of whale dicks? "She kicked me out of her apartment knowing I didn't have a safe ride home and she lives over thirty miles from here. It was at night, below freezing out—you know what? Tell her whatever the fuck you want, tell her nothing. I don't give a rat's ass."

As it were, Rhea did give a rat's ass. Many of them. She wanted Adam and Brianna to stop communicating with each other altogether but with how everything was going for her lately, she didn't dare make that request.

Adam frowned. "Rhea?"

Oh Lord what now? "Yeah?"

"Are you laying down?"

Shit. This can't be good. "Yeah."

"Why? Aren't you feeling good?"

She blew out a sharp puff of air. "No. I haven't been feeling real well. I stayed home from work the last few days, have a couple more mental health days off before I return."

Adam put his hand to his forehead, eyes going wide. "Oh. Hell."

"Yeah. I made mistakes and now I'm paying for them. Hope I won't pay for them with my job."

"Rhea, I need to go do something real quick here. Would you maybe close your eyes for a couple minutes?"

She sighed. "Sure." Rhea shut her eyes. *Well, it isn't the worst Skype ever. Not the best, either.* The sad thing was thinking what a relief it would be to end the call. It made her want to cry. Then again, everything did lately.

"Okay," said Adam. "You can look."

She opened her eyes. "Oh my God. Are you lying in bed, too?"

He nodded. "I am now."

And there were the tears for his sweet gesture. "Thank you." She propped herself on her elbow and reached to touch his face on the screen. No flesh, only the cold reality of cyber friendship.

Adam squinted at his screen. "Hey . . . What's that?"

"Oh—" she sniffled. "I finally got some ink." Rhea showed off the full thing as she slowly rotated her arm.

"Is—that—my handwriting?"

Rhea nodded.

He sighed, tears glistening in his eyes. "Next time we're together, Sunshine? I'm gonna hug you and never let you go."

Lord only knew when that would be.

Chapter Four

The morning Rhea returned to work was a busy one: First, the text from Cass with an update on her lack of unemployment benefits and the confession she and Jack got into an argument about the job offer he'd accepted.

Then came the text from Adam checking to make sure she was well enough to return to work.

And as she dressed, a notification came through Facebook Messenger from Brianna.

The texts, Rhea immediately replied to. The message from Brianna got deleted as she walked out the door. "Whoops," she muttered. "Finger slipped."

"Good morning, Rhea," the leasing office manager greeted her as he taped a notice to her next door neighbor's peephole. He appeared to have little dexterity while donning thick mittens.

"Hi, Steve, how are you?"

"Oh, missing spring an awful lot right now. You?"

"I'm good." It wasn't true of course, rather her habitual response to such inquiries. *I'm doing better* would have been far more accurate but she was sure the question was a pleasantry and nothing more.

"I didn't see you return to the office for renewing your lease. Please don't tell me we're losing you here."

"Oh. No you aren't. I'll come see you when I get back from work."

"Phew," Steve exhaled. "Good news for us! Thanks." He nodded at her. "I'll see you later?"

"Yep." Rhea waved to Steve as he stepped into his golf cart and drove on to deliver more unfortunate news to troublesome tenants. She paused at her neighbor's door to snoop on their notice. It was a reminder to vacate in thirty days.

She felt for them. They rarely spoke to her—she assumed they knew little English—but they always waved or said 'hello' in their thick middle-eastern accents whenever they crossed paths. They didn't smoke and were quiet older people who kept to themselves. *God only knows who will replace them.* Walking to her car, Rhea prayed they wouldn't be frat boys—especially if she wasn't sleeping with other men. She needn't the temptation of a single, hot neighbor—or more than one of them.

Her workday was pleasant, co-workers greeting her with warm receptions. Dr. Kasick ensured her workload was light and checked with her between his appointments. Although he'd made concessions for her, he quietly informed her that her time off may negatively impact her ninety-day review.

She texted with Adam on her breaks and with Cass at lunch. Right before the end of her shift, a bouquet of red roses arrived addressed to her. The accompanying note from Adam said, simply, *I love you.* She posted a photo of the bouquet on Facebook with the caption: *I love you too, Surfer Boy.* It was one of few posts she set to public instead of friends-only in the hopes it would find its way to Mark—not as though he'd care. *See?* She thought. *I'm not alone, either.*

Except I still kinda am.

Another notification came through Facebook Messenger from Brianna moments later. She deleted it without opening it.

Rhea returned home, signed a new lease agreement for a

twelve-month term and attended her first Zumba class. It left her feeling uncoordinated but energized, overall better for having tried it. She rewarded herself with a quick shower and a dissatisfying Southwestern-style salad for late dinner.

The bathroom scale reminded her of the weight she needed to lose despite the Zumba and salad; she and the scale were no longer on speaking terms until it changed its mind. The logical portion of Rhea's psyche knew that hinged on her not being as sedentary as she'd been nor eating at fast food restaurants every other meal and ordering some of the least healthy foods they offered.

It was high time she took care of herself even if her social life had effectively gone to hell.

She turned on the television and texted Adam as she plopped onto her sofa: *Signed a year-long lease agreement here.*

He promptly replied: *great*

No capitalization, nor punctuation. He wasn't happy.

Well tough shit; her choosing to remain in Aurora was all his fault.

Rhea sent to him, *Took my first Zumba class tonight. You'll be pleased to know I have the grace of a drunken 3 legged hippo.*

His text came a couple minutes later. *LOL! I'm sure that's not true. Show me moves next time we Skype.*

She laughed and replied, *Nope!*

You're no fun but I still love you.

Rhea forced a smile even though he couldn't see it; she had difficulty believing anyone could love her. *Love you 2 & appreciate it, thx.*

Hey Sweets? he sent.

Yes?

Brianna sent me a message today.

Rhea's eyes narrowed and she scowled. After staring at his text long enough for her eyes to start watering, she replied, *What's she want from you?*

She begged me to convince you to talk to her. He followed that with a screen capture of Brianna's message to him:

"*I need 2 talk 2 Rhea but she's not replying 2 me im desperate 2 reach her can u help*"

"Oh God dammit," groaned Rhea. She sent to Adam: *Give me 1 reason I should.*

His response was instant: *Because you're a wonderful woman.*

"No I'm not," she snapped at her phone—as if he could hear it?

And don't argue with me, he added.

Rhea gaped at her phone.

He sent another message without waiting for her to interject: *& I know if the shoe was on the other foot you would want the chance to apologize. You were so happy to have her as a friend & you're so miserable without her. You should at least see what she wants.*

She sighed. *Whatever*, Rhea replied. *Fine. But don't be upset when she screws me again & I let her do it.*

Several minutes later, he responded. *I love you Rhea. Gonna go paint. Reach out to Brianna & tell me all about it later. Bye!*

TTYL, Rhea replied. *Love you too.* She shoved her phone across her coffee table. "Screw you, stupid technology. You stay there and you *think* about what you've done." After a few moments, Rhea groaned and snatched it back. "Fuck me."

She opened a new message to Brianna in Messenger's app and typed *What the hell do you want from me.*

Rather than sending it, she back-spaced until the only word remaining was the first. Rhea stared at it until she deleted that, too. *Please leave Adam out of this, he doesn't deserve your drama llamas.* She groaned and cleared all the text again. *Against my better judgment I'm asking what you want from me.*

It would probably come across as having more animosity than intended. Nonetheless, it was the message Rhea sent.

She watched the telltale dots of Brianna preparing a response. They vanished for several minutes and reappeared. This happened multiple times before Rhea's phone buzzed with Brianna's incoming message.

I want the chance to apologize to u.

Go ahead, Rhea prompted.

Can u come to my place tomorrow nite?

Rhea burst out laughing; this was one of those infamous 'fool me once' scenarios. "Oh fuck no!" Nonetheless she answered with the far more tactful, *I'd rather not.*

Pls Rhea? I promise this isn't a trick.

"Oh well then that changes things." Rhea rolled her eyes. "Pfft." She sent: *If you absolutely insist on making amends there is no way in hell I'm going to your place to do it.*

There was a ten-minute lull in conversation. Rhea hoped maybe Brianna changed her mind.

No such luck: A message buzzed through.

R u inviting me to ur place? Cuz ill do it if that's what it takes.

"Um, I'm thinking *no* on this one. Unless I could return the favor. See how much you enjoy being kicked out when you've done nothing wrong. Of course it still won't be the same because you won't be stranded and left outside to freeze to death." She let her head fall back against the sofa cushions. "I am the biggest goddamn idiot on the face of the planet."

Fine, she told Brianna. *Come to my place tomorrow night. I'm home after 7.*

———— smile ————

A timid tap on the front door came at 6:59. She took a steadying breath. *The sooner I do this, the sooner it's over and I can move on.*

Rhea peered through her peephole.

Brianna stood with her head bowed and shoulders rolled forward. Well, she put on a convincing regretful posture if nothing else. Sighing in defeat, Rhea opened the door. "Brianna."

"Hey." Brianna's eyes remained locked on the ground, her hands kneading her purse handles.

"Come in. Leave your shoes by the door." Rhea stepped out of Brianna's way and closed the door after her. *God she has a cute little butt. Shut up, heart, you stay the hell out of this.* "Have a seat."

"At the kitchen table, or—?"

"Your choice, I guess." *What difference does it make? It'll be equally uncomfortable wherever we sit.*

"Well, um . . ." Brianna pulled a box of twelve Ferrero Rocher confections from her purse. "I brought these to share with you as a part of my apology. So then kitchen table?"

Rhea wasn't sure how interested she'd be in eating the chocolates now, or any time in the near future with how her stomach turned into a pretzel whenever thoughts strayed to this so-called apology. "Yeah."

Brianna took a seat and looked at Rhea expectantly. "I'm sorry."

On a scale of sincere to utter bullshit, survey says? Raging bullshit. Insincerity off the charts.

"Rhea?"

"What."

"Please sit. Talk to me? Maybe even go as far as accepting my apology?" Brianna pouted.

Rhea thought she deserved a Nobel Peace Prize for refraining from punching Brianna in the face for that remark. "Why the hell should I?"

"Because—I . . . I apologized."

"You didn't accept *my* apology."

Brianna reclined in her chair, her eyes wide. "When did you apologize?"

"I think it was one of the last things I said before you threw me out of your apartment."

"Oh." She flinched. "Oh, well, I accept your apology now so you can accept mine?"

Rhea gaped. "Are you even kidding me?" she cried. "Do you realize how I felt when you kicked me out? You know I came to your rescue and ended up feeling like the queen of all skanks because I went from Huvie's bed directly to yours?"

"Hey now in my defense we didn't technically ever get to my bed—"

"Oh my God." Rhea's jaw fell further. "That's not even my point! Did you know I was so humiliated by what I did in the name of comforting you that I can't even tell Adam and I don't keep any secrets from him? So now I get to feel even worse about the whole thing. And you. *You* want me to accept your apology on account of some token acceptance of mine well after I made it?" Rhea turned away from Brianna, flushed, shaking, breathless. This was so much unlike her, she feared she might have a coronary. "You've *got* to be kidding me."

As her pounding heart settled to normal, Rhea heard quiet sniffles. She turned around.

Brianna held a trembling hand to her lips, tears pooling in the area between her thumb and index finger. "You did that to comfort me? I thought—it was—because you wanted me—"

She was well aware she'd never be able to explain all the things that went through her head that night. It was comfort. It was desire. It was a challenge to make something fantastical happen for herself for once. Not as though Adam hadn't been remarkable—but this thing with Brianna was a whole different beast with two backs.

Rhea sighed the most aggrieved sigh of her lifetime. *God dammit, Rhea, you pathetic push-over.* She pulled out the chair opposite Brianna's and plopped into it, its legs or back—maybe both—creaking beneath her weight. "Fine. I accept your apology," she said flatly. *Why? Why!* "But you need to understand how bad you hurt me."

"I do, Rhea, and really, I'm so sorry. I just . . . See, there's a lot going on in my life and emotions are running high. Please believe me, honest, I never meant to hurt you."

I'm supposed to believe that? I suppose there's a bridge in Arizona you want to sell me, too. Maybe some swampland in Florida? "Gimme one of those." Rhea gestured to the chocolate hazelnut candies. "One of the ones in a dark wrapper."

Brianna opened the box and plucked out one of the four darkly wrapped chocolates. She handed it to Rhea, making a point to brush her fingertips on Rhea's palm with a tentative smile.

Rhea jerked her hand away with a frown.

"I want to fix this. *Us*. What if I made it up to you?" She wiggled her eyebrows at Rhea, drawing her tongue across her upper lip.

God yes! "I don't think that's a good idea." *Because it's a great idea. It's a dreadful idea.*

"Oh. Well. Okay." Brianna helped herself to a candy wrapped in white. "I understand. But if you ever change your mind—"

"Trust me, I won't."

"Was it . . . bad for you? 'Cause it sounded to me like you totes enjoyed yourself."

"It was amazing." Rhea dropped her head, rubbing her eyes with her fists. "Which is more reason I won't change my mind."

"Sounds counterintuitive if you ask me."

"That's because you want me to change my mind." Which posed the further question: why? "I won't."

Brianna sighed, "Damn."

While she made her best attempt to enjoy the chocolate, Rhea considered how to tell Brianna she was free to leave at any time.

Brianna cleared her throat. "So I can't help but notice you haven't started packing yet."

"Huh?"

"There aren't any boxes or anything." She chuckled weakly. "It's almost like you're not moving out."

Rhea frowned. "I'm not. I just renewed my lease here."

"But—" Brianna's voice wavered. "You promised me you'd be my roommate. You were the one who suggested it."

"I'm not moving in with you after what you did to me," Rhea cried, her gaze snapping to meet Brianna's. "Are you nuts? Are you actually nuts!"

"You don't need to punish me anymore, okay? Your silent treatment did more than enough."

Rhea slid her chair from the table and rose to her feet. "You know what? All my life I've let people walk all over me. I've let people trample my heart because I was more desperate for their friendship than I had any regard for myself. I've heard since Kindergarten I need to be more assertive. I think that starts now."

"Rhea, please—"

"I don't stand up for myself nearly as much as I should but I'm gonna stand up to you. I'm not saying 'no' to punish you. I'm telling you 'no' to keep myself from being screwed over again."

"Okay, I totally get that and I'm sure I deserve it—"

Rhea blurted words she'd never in her life said: "Don't you interrupt me." She drew in a steadying breath. "Look. Brianna. I'm sorry if you seriously think you're the victim here. I'm sorry if you can't see the difference between me trying to keep myself from getting hurt by you *again* and some perceived punishment."

Rhea set her shoulders and jaw. "No, I take it back. I'm not sorry. I am sick to death of having to apologize for things which aren't even my fault. I have *always* been the one who has to make the first move, to be the one who apologizes when the other person slighted me and never actually apologizes to me for it. It's always been 'Rhea, look at it from your brother's point-of-view.' Or 'try being in your father's shoes.' Does anyone ever take my feelings into consideration? Fuck no. Never."

With a shaking hand, she pointed at Brianna. "You kicked me out of your apartment after you were hurt because I did something that had nothing at all to do with you. I was stranded and it was below freezing out. How can I possibly trust you now?"

"Oh my God," Brianna whimpered, pressing a hand to her lips. "Oh my God, I'm gonna be homeless." Whimpering turned to ugly sobs.

Rhea may have believed such things would serve Brianna right but still couldn't handle seeing her cry. She squeezed her eyes shut, tilting her face toward the ceiling. *It's not fair. She's not crying out of compassion for what she did to me. It's not remorse. She's crying because her cruelty to others bit her in the ass for probably the first time in her life.*

None of that, of course, changed the fact Brianna was going to be without a place to live. *Oh God dammit. I know I'm going to rue being so kind.* She sighed. "You're not gonna be homeless."

"How, exactly?" Brianna said between sobs. "Tell me

how when you're not willing to be my roommate anymore."

"No. I'm not. But . . ." Rhea inhaled. "My community has low security deposit promotions all the time. And the leasing office manager likes me. I'm sure I could talk him into doing a favor . . ."

"Hello? I still can't afford movers, Rhea."

"You don't need them. You don't have much stuff and the majority looks pretty light, I could probably lift it on my own. You can sniff around for some free boxes at local businesses and we can easily get your place packed in a weekend."

Brianna's voice was tiny: "We?"

Rhea choked down her groan. "Yes. *We.* I said I would help, I'll help. We get you packed, put twenty bucks or whatever on a small Budget truck and get you into a place you can afford on your own."

"Oh thanks, Rhea!" Brianna jumped from her chair, racing around the table to give her a hug.

Rhea threw her hands into the air in defense, backing away. "Whoa! Stop. Don't."

"So you're willing to help me move but you won't be my friend?"

"I'll consider being your friend," Rhea replied, "but I don't trust you—I can't—and I'm gonna keep you at arm's distance for my own sanity."

"I wish you wouldn't." Brianna's luscious bottom lip turned outward in a pout.

Front door. Hallway. Coffee table. Famine, locusts, Ebola. Think of anything other than her kissable mouth! That tasty lip—

Well. That worked.

Sarcasm aimed at myself. Really, me?

"Rhea?"

"If you promise again to be my BFF and I brush it off, know it's not you." *Well, it's kinda you.* "It's about all the people who've broken that promise to me before you." Rhea clenched her jaw when Brianna said nothing. "Tell me: What would you do if I'd done such awful things to you?"

"Hey now," Brianna answered. "That's not fair."

"How isn't it fair?"

LEONARD 109

"Because you know I'll say I would have done the exact same things you did. Or worse." Under her breath she added, "I'm not above writing your phone number on bathroom walls at strip clubs."

Rhea gasped. "You didn't!"

"Have you gotten any unsolicited dick pics?"

"No . . ."

Brianna took a deep breath. "That's because I love you too much to have done it, even in my blind rage. Isn't that fact worth something to you?"

Rhea considered changing her phone number anyway and keeping their interactions to social media exclusively. "I'll . . . talk to Steve tomorrow," she said, dropping the subject. "You collect whatever boxes you can get donated to you. Don't be afraid of playing up your rack. You've got assets, use them."

Brianna's eyes darkened but she said nothing.

"And we'll see about getting you moved as soon as possible?"

Brianna nodded. "Thanks for being a better friend to me than I've been to you. I don't know how, but I'll return this favor. I promise."

Rhea waved her off. "Knowing you're not homeless is thanks enough." And that, she considered, was paying it forward from when Huvie rescued her from Brianna's apartment.

———— smile ————

As Rhea settled into bed around ten thirty—mentally praising herself for not giving in to Brianna's seductions—her phone buzzed with a text from Adam.

He said, *I know it's late. If you're still awake can we please Skype? Just need to see your beautiful face.*

She sighed. She was already dozing but wouldn't dream of saying no to such a sweet request. *Yeah*, she responded. *Be there in a sex.* The message sent before she could correct the last word. "Oops." Rhea dragged herself from bed to her desk, lifting the laptop open. "Hurry up," she said to it. "I'm tired."

A couple minutes later, Windows loaded and she opened Skype.

When Adam's window came on, he greeted her, "My sexy girl!"

Rhea yawned. "Hey sweetie, what's up?"

"Brianna just sent me a bunch of messages."

"I'm so sorry, I'll tell her to stop."

"No," said Adam, "don't. She was just telling me what an amazing woman you are. I wanted to thank you to your face. You're doing such a good thing."

Rhea smiled, a little sweet and a little pained. "Thanks."

"She also described to me how lucky I am. How gorgeous you are."

"O—oh?"

"I think she has a little crush on you. How cute is that?"

"Yeah, that's . . . wild." She tried not to flinch, rubbing brusquely at her collarbone.

"Not gonna lie: The thought of you with another woman? Huge turn-on."

Rhea's eyebrows jumped. She didn't ever think he was that different from the average man, at least in terms of his sexual interests. Still, to hear it so bluntly from him, to essentially have been given his blessing to indulge her fantasies gave her pause. *No. I'm not doing that to myself again.*

"Maybe it's something you'd consider some day when we're together? I dunno, as a birthday gift for me? Or something. You know." He shrugged. "Whatever. Never mind. Forget I suggested it."

"Are you so sure you'd be okay with that? I'm sure in theory it sounds good but not so much in practice . . ."

Adam smiled sheepishly. "If I could watch—"

"Did Brianna put you up to this?"

"Honey. The thought's been in my head ever since I found out about your—" He put the words in air quotes: "—girl crushes."

"So it wouldn't be cheating on you if I were to . . ." She circled her hand in the air. ". . . *you* know."

"Not at all!" He shook his head. "Just as long as you tell

LEONARD 111

me every little thing and don't skimp on the detail. Seriously. I'd want to know everything."

That was good to know, Rhea supposed. Though she vowed to never again fool around with Brianna, at least she could stop feeling so damn guilty for what they'd already done. Maybe she would even tell Adam about it sometime, although she couldn't get over the nagging feeling Brianna already did so on her behalf.

"Well. Anyway. I know it's late, get your rest. Okay? I love you."

Rhea smiled. "I love you, too."

Adam left her with two words before he switched off Skype. "Sweet dreams."

*————*smile*————*

"Steve, hi. It's Rhea from 36D." She paced in her kitchen while clutching her cellphone with a sweaty palm.

"*Hi, Rhea. Whatcha need?*" replied Steve.

"Well, I was just calling because I know someone who needs the cheapest unit you've got available before April. Something maybe in mid-March, I guess?"

"*You're referring someone!*" Rhea heard a snap or maybe a clap on his end of their conversation. "*Fantastic. I've got a couple one-bedrooms available next week, and a studio that may be open toward the end of March if the tenants clear out earlier, and assuming they kept their apartment in good shape.*"

"Okay . . ." Maybe Brianna could sleep on Rhea's sofa if things didn't line up just right. It looked as though they might not; on her own, Brianna would only be able to afford a studio apartment. "Um, I was also wondering, if you had the word of a trusted tenant—namely me—could you maybe lower the security deposit? She's a clean tenant, she has no pets and doesn't smoke." *Oh please don't make me regret this.*

"*We're starting a half-off security deposit promotion next month but I'm sure I could make an exception. We're also waiving first month's rent for new occupants.*"

Rhea found it unfair how apartment companies bent over backward to lure in new tenants and conversely did so little to keep the ones they had.

From a business standpoint, it made perfect sense; these companies banked on moves being such inherently sucky things that to avoid doing them was incentive enough for a tenant to stay once moved in.

As a renter herself, she found the policy impressively unfair. Maybe someday she would own a home and all this bullshit would become nothing more than an obnoxious memory.

"Perfect," said Rhea. "Thanks so much. Her name's Brianna Huntington and she should be by to talk to you sometime in the next few days."

"*Thanks Rhea. Have a good evening.*"

"You're welcome—you, too." Rhea ended the call and texted Brianna: *Steve down at my leasing office is expecting you within the next few days. Half off security & 1st month's rent free.* She tossed the phone on her bed to tend her laundry.

Brianna replied at some point before Rhea returned twenty-five minutes later. *Thx Rhea ur the best! IOU 1. XOXO*

Rhea rolled her eyes, nonetheless replying: *You're welcome. Keep me informed.*

Chapter Five

Two months later after only brief and occasional lukewarm interactions made publicly via social media, Rhea arrived at Brianna's apartment by six in the morning, bringing with her two Sausage and Egg McMuffins and a pair of small mocha Frappes.

It was a close call but they made it just in time for Brianna to finish out her lease and start anew at Rhea's complex with the only available studio.

"I thought you might need a boost of enthusiasm for this so I brought some goodies," Rhea said stiffly when Brianna opened her door.

"Oh my God Rhea, you are the actual best. But believe it or not, I was excited for this anyway. Come in, come in."

Rhea reluctantly stepped inside, setting the food on the kitchen table.

"It'll be so good to get away from the place I shared with Travis and it comes with the added bonus of getting to spend all weekend with you."

"Oh?" Rhea faltered. "Oh. Okay. Yay. Well, um, let's eat and get a move on, so to speak."

After eating, Brianna got to work packing her living room and Rhea started in the kitchen, wrapping plates, bowls, and glasses with dish cloths and fitting them into a box. Where Rhea hadn't been left with much following her divorce, Travis left Brianna with less.

In a matter of fifteen minutes, Rhea moved on to cookware, bakeware, and utensils. She finished in the kitchen around the same time Brianna closed her last box of living room items.

"I'll get started in the bedroom. Will you take the bath?" Brianna asked.

Rhea shrugged. "Sure. Why not?"

They went into the bedroom and bathroom, respectively.

The bathroom, with its under-the-sink half-cabinet and complete lack of medicine cabinet took Rhea under ten minutes to pack. The only thing left out was the bottle of soap—with a spit of cleanser remaining—a washcloth desperately in need of laundering, and a half-used roll of single-ply toilet paper. She marked the box and added it to the stacks in the living room.

Upon returning to the bedroom to help finish, Rhea found Brianna sitting on her bed with an open photo album on her lap. "Okay. That's not packing."

"I'm trying to decide if I should throw this out."

"Why would you junk it?"

"I don't need the bad memories."

Rhea frowned. "*Every* photo in there brings back bad memories?"

"No." Brianna flipped a couple pages. "There was this trip to Mount Whitney." She pointed to a picture of herself standing beside her older sister in front of white mountains. With a chuckle, she said, "We actually got along that trip. For most of it, anyway."

"So should I maybe start on your dresser? It'll be easier to move if the drawers are empty, and you've got plenty of open boxes left."

Brianna nodded and replied absently, "Please."

Rhea grabbed one of the empty boxes and pulled open

the top drawer which was filled with bras. She owned a half-dozen of them to Brianna's veritable Victoria's Secret. While she moved the bras into a box, she listened to Brianna tearing photographs from her album one by one.

Second drawer down revealed another array of bras. *My God. She wasn't joking about being obsessed.*

"Oh wow."

Rhea glanced at Brianna as she peeled a photograph from the album. "What is it?" Rhea asked.

"The sleepover at Vegas Comp. Remember that?" Brianna gazed at the picture.

Rhea set the bras into a box and closed it. *Bras*, she wrote on it with a black Sharpie. *Box 1 of __*. She grabbed another empty box.

"You're in this one."

Rhea leaned over to look at it. "Oh yeah. There I am. On my sleeping bag by myself in the corner with my face in a book." She squinted to see which. *Vampire Diaries?* No, she'd read those in middle school. *Valentine?* That was more likely to have been her high school reading.

Brianna cleared her throat. "Trust me. You're infinitely too nice to have been in my group."

Still with the ass-backward compliments? "What's that supposed to mean?"

Brianna crumpled the photograph into her fist. "The brass section was gonna prank you during the overnight. You didn't deserve anything like what they were planning."

"Oh." Rhea turned to the dresser. Third drawer was underwear: a frilly, silky pastel rainbow of femininity. And probably a matching panty for each of her myriad bras. "What exactly were they gonna do?" It didn't matter. They hadn't gone through with it and, besides, that was around eight years ago already.

"You familiar with *Carrie?*"

"Well." Rhea dropped an armful of underwear in the box and regarded Brianna. "That sure as hell would've been something. Why didn't they? Couldn't secure the pig's blood?"

She halfway expected laughter. Or at least a chuckle.

RAYS OF SUNSHINE

"I begged them not to."

"So why do you sound so remorseful for keeping some immature assholes from doing something awful to a girl who was too nice to be in your group?"

"They got so pissed at me," replied Brianna. "I was on the verge of being kicked out of the clique. I would've lost all my friends." She ripped another photograph from the album. "Asshole." Brianna tore another out. "Cunt." And another. "Motherfucking shithead." She glanced at Rhea with red-rimmed, watery eyes. "Got a lighter? I wanna burn these."

Rhea shook her head. "No, I don't. I'm sorry." She returned to her task of clearing out the dresser. "So they ultimately didn't do the prank and they didn't kick you out even though they were pissed at you?"

"Do you remember Jordan? Well . . . I had to give him head to win back their favor." It fell quiet for several minutes. Brianna resumed ripping photographs from the album. "I know he told them all what a freak I was. I know the rumors that circulated about me afterward."

"I didn't hear any." Rhea opened the bottom drawer which revealed a small assortment of vibrators, dongs and socks. *One of these things just doesn't belong, one of these things is not like the other.*

"Well . . . There was the one that I was hot for you."

Rhea swallowed a scowl. "That had to be insulting."

"There was also the one where I was a cock-sucking slut. Which was, strictly speaking, true. So I suppose it really didn't qualify as a rumor. Rumors aren't rumors if they're true, right?"

Brianna seemed a little too accepting of such things. "I did it, yes. But I didn't want to."

"Oh," Rhea whispered.

"I felt so dirty. So. Fucking. Dirty. Like I was allowing myself to be raped and I totally deserved it. I sobbed the whole time. He laughed and called my tears 'more lube,' so . . . Yeah."

Rhea didn't know what to say and so she said nothing at all.

"He recorded it, too, and threatened to upload the videos across social media if I didn't do what he wanted, when he wanted it. There was one time he took me into the band room closet before Monday night practice, pinned me behind the uniforms with his hand over my mouth and then I got to enjoy marching with his spunk trickling down my legs. Only thing worse than the tears running down my cheeks the whole time, I suppose. There was the back row hand job during *Cars*, of all fucking movies."

"Oh my God."

"I started having nightmares. I couldn't tell anyone so I had to figure out how to make him stop before he knocked me up. God only knows how the sperm donor would've taken *that* news."

"Is that why you kept threatening to quit band?"

Brianna nodded. "But I couldn't. Because he needed to have access to me. He threatened me right back."

"You should've castrated him," she blurted.

"Come on, be realistic, Rhea."

Rhea wasn't so sure she'd suggested that in jest. "So how did you make him stop?"

"He wanted a birthday BJ. So I went through with it, the way I always did: Sobbing, gagging, begging him to stop when he grabbed my hair and jammed that Godawful thing down my throat. Only instead of swallowing, I *accidentally* spit it out into his pubes. I got him so messy he had to go to the bathroom to clean it.

"I stole his phone while he was cleaning himself and told him we were through and if he ever said anything to anyone, I'd go to the police and tell them he'd been raping me—which, I mean, he basically was—and since his recordings of me begging him to stop were date-stamped after his eighteenth birthday, he was not only a rapist but a sexual predator because I was only sixteen at the time."

"Holy shit!" Rhea gaped at her. "You should've done that, anyway. He should be in jail. He was assaulting you!"

"Yeah well I didn't exactly see it that way at the time. And I kinda . . ." Brianna sighed. "I don't know. I consented the first time. The first many times. I felt like someone wanted me for *me* and at the time it boosted my self-esteem."

Rhea's jaw fell open and she was silent several moments. "Okay, um, sexual consent doesn't come with a lifetime pass. It expires after each and every act."

"Oh climb down from your soapbox. You seriously mean to tell me you never slept with someone when you really didn't want to? Every time your ex was in the mood, you magically were, too? He always took 'no' for an answer the first time you said it?"

"Okay that's different," Rhea snapped, "we were married."

"How's that different?"

Rhea opened her mouth but no words came out because every reply should could think of was lame as the day was long.

Brianna folded her arms across her chest and looked at her deadpan. "Your silence is real convincing. Y'know, me and Jordan were in a committed relationship, too. I just wasn't in the mood when he was, the same as you and Mark."

Rhea initially recalled never being forced to do sex acts on her husband she wasn't interested in doing.

Except I did. Why else did they cover his penis and balls in sweets? To convince her into doing stuff she didn't want to do. She always dismissed it as being something good wives did for their husbands. Just one of the many sacrifices for marriage.

Oh shit. It shouldn't be like that. Nausea sneaked up on her and for a moment she feared she might vomit in her mouth.

"It all came down to the fact I wanted nothing more than to get away from him. What was done was done and being free from him was good enough for me."

"And all that happened to you because you were protecting me?"

Brianna exhaled. "I didn't want to be a bad person. I didn't want to be my sister's dress-up doll. I didn't want to be the girl with the abusive father. I wanted . . . I wanted to be like you. Good, and . . . and bookish—" She blurted, "not like that's a bad thing. I wanted to be sweet and innocent like you. But I couldn't tell anybody. It was this super-secret dream I had. The more I think about it, the more I realize maybe it *was* a crush. One that never really resolved itself." Brianna gave a single laugh. "Probably the evening we spent together didn't help *that* any."

"You went through hell for me and didn't say a thing to me about it. I sure as hell didn't know, so I couldn't even thank you for it. That's more amazing than you could ever understand. I can never repay you!"

"Rhea, look around. You *are* repaying me. With your friendship even despite what I recently did to you. With helping to keep me from being homeless, for craps sake. Give yourself some credit!"

"I don't see how that's even remotely the same, but okay, whatever. How do you get over that kind of trauma?"

"Pray they someday make a Neuralyzer?" Brianna forced a smile at her before resuming her search-and-destroy of the photo album. "It fucked me up pretty bad. I mean . . . I'm not saying that's what made me bi. I know being attracted to other women doesn't work that way. And anyway, I'm sexually attracted to men, too . . . their eyes, their lips, their muscles. But the sight of actual dick?" She shuddered. "No. Just . . . *no*. I can't. And I think that may be why Travis left me."

Rhea gasped. "Travis left you because you're bi?"

Brianna shook her head. "Oh, no. I never told him. He called me a tease any number of times. I always had to turn the lights off during sex and I couldn't touch his junk. Sure it felt good once he was inside me. I've got more than my fair share of dildos because I love how they feel. But our sex life was bad. Very fucking bad. It didn't help that of course he—like every other man—was all about the BJ's. What a shame 'cause he was hot, too."

She opened the photo gallery on her phone and held it up to share with Rhea. The photo Brianna chose was a selfie taken with her former boyfriend. They were in bed together and her chest was exposed.

It was silent for a while and Rhea was keenly aware of her breathing and heartbeat.

"Honestly? The best sex I've had in my life was with you."

"I'm sorry?"

"There was no terror during foreplay of peen-to-come. No pressure to suck cock. I could fully relax and enjoy myself. I could be vulnerable and intimate with you."

Rhea swallowed. She felt awful for asking—the whole label aversion and all—but once the thought was in her head, she needed to know: "Are you so sure you're not actually, you know, lesbian?"

"Yes! No. I—Don't—I don't know. *Maybe*? I mean, no. I'm not. I can't be. I like Huvie so much I risked screwing things up with you in my jealousy."

"No offense but I think you need counseling."

"I've had it," replied Brianna with a surprisingly chipper smile. "It's the only reason I can have a relationship with anything other than a Ficus or a goldfish."

Rhea took a deep breath. "God. Brianna. I am so sorry for . . . everything."

"Thanks."

"For what it's worth? I don't think I'd have risked my own ass for anyone in high school. You were—and are—a better person than you give yourself credit for. You're better than I am, that's for damn sure."

"Oh, I dunno. You're pretty awesome, yourself."

"So." Rhea straightened and cleared her throat. "We'll be done here in the next hour, I'd guess. We can get the moving truck tomorrow. I don't know about you but I'm beat."

"Sounds like a plan."

"If you want, you know, 'cause everything's gonna be packed here, you can spend the night at my place."

"Really? Thanks, Rhea. You're awesome."

"It's the least I can do." As Rhea began pulling out what little was left in the closet, she said, "You never did tell me where we're taking everything. Did things work out with Steve?"

"Oh, yeah. He waived my security deposit entirely in addition to waiving the first month's rent. I don't know what

LEONARD

you did, but thanks."

She chuckled. "You're welcome." *Wasn't like I had to suck his cock for the favor.*

"He put me in 36C. I was disappointed it wasn't 36D. 'Cause, you know . . ." Brianna gestured at Rhea's chest and waggled her eyebrows.

It was comforting knowing someone quiet and clean was moving in where her good former neighbors lived. At the same time, having Brianna sharing a wall with her would make her too accessible. It would be so tempting, and Adam *had* said she could. He probably wouldn't object to a Rhea sandwich with Brianna. She could think of a few ways that would work splendidly. "Well, 36D is a little occupied."

"Oh. Oh! That's *your* apartment. Doy." Brianna bounced, clapping her hands. "We're gonna be neighbors. Apartment buddies," she squealed. "Like roommates but better 'cause there's extra space and privacy."

"Yep," Rhea chirped. She wasn't sure what they needed the extra privacy for but she bet she'd be plenty thankful for the wall when a lonely night struck and temptation whispered naughty suggestions to sneak into Brianna's room for some X-rated cuddling.

"I'm gonna randomly bring you breakfast some mornings. Pay for pizza to be delivered to your door. Basically? I'm gonna be the best neighbor ever."

"Oh believe me, you don't have to do that. I need a lot more exercise and far less pizza."

"Then I'll join you for morning jogs." Brianna smiled at her. "It'll be my pleasure."

Rhea didn't do mornings—jogs, or otherwise. Brianna would find out soon enough, she was afraid.

Once they finished packing a short time later, Rhea helped Brianna clean the apartment. Rhea may not have been a professional maid service, but anyone coming in after she was finished wouldn't have known any better. It didn't hurt that Brianna was a clean tenant who took great care of her living space. Rhea was relieved to see firsthand what she'd told Steve hadn't been a misrepresentation of facts.

They locked the front door and caravanned to Rhea's

apartment for the night. Rhea ordered Papa John's despite the 'less pizza' mantra and Brianna paid as thanks for all her help.

Conversation during dinner was on topics light and pleasant, and Brianna did more than her fair share of flirting. Rhea was stern when she dismissed Brianna's passes, explaining what her Facebook relationship status of "It's complicated" really meant.

Brianna claimed she knew it all along.

After dinner, Brianna settled on the sofa with one of Rhea's romances while Rhea took a quick shower.

As she dried off her hair, Brianna called for her: "Your phone's buzzing. I think someone's calling you."

Rhea draped her towel on the shower curtain rod to dry, figuring she was going to walk out and find Brianna sprawled, undressed, on her sofa. Rhea'd pretty much *have* to do her.

It was disappointing to find Brianna in flannel plaid pajamas buttoned as high as they could go, hunched over a book and reading. Well, the reading part was sexy. The plaid pajamas, not so much.

Wondering if one more time with Brianna couldn't hurt anything, Rhea checked her phone. There was a missed call from Adam most recently and multiple texts. The last one said: *I'm on Skype waiting for you. Where are you, Sunshine? Everything OK?*

"Oh, shit." She hurried to her computer, texting him, *Be right there hang on.* "I totally forgot it's Skype night." While the laptop booted up, Rhea told Brianna, "Come on in, meet Adam."

"Um . . . are you sure?" Brianna appeared in the doorway and hesitated there.

"Sure I'm sure." Rhea beckoned to her vigorously. "Get in here."

When the video chat came on, Rhea greeted Adam, "I'm so sorry I kept you waiting. Kinda got distracted by helping Bri with her move. She's spending the night here. Wanna meet her?"

"Of course." Adam replied, bobbing his head.

Rhea adjusted the position of her laptop to include Brianna where she sat on the bed. "Adam, Bri. Bri, Adam."

Brianna waved her fingertips at him. "Hey." She retreated into a shrug. "Nice to meet you."

"Pleasure's all mine. So, ladies. How's the move going? Wish I could be there to help."

Brianna and Rhea exchanged glances.

"It's been going better than expected, thanks to Rhea," replied Brianna.

Rhea said, "It's been . . . enlightening. I'll be driving a twelve-foot Budget truck tomorrow. I'm sure that'll be an adventure!"

"Hey, just uh . . . don't make it *too* much of an adventure, okay? I need my girl in one piece, you know." Adam winked.

"I'll be careful," said Rhea.

Brianna corrected: "*We'll* be careful. I want her in one piece, too."

"So, Adam," Rhea said before he raised any questions regarding Brianna's response, "how'd the auction go?" She watched Brianna discreetly slip from the camera's view and settle in the chair beside the desk. Rhea didn't have the guts to ask her for privacy but it was obvious she had no further intention of participating in the conversation.

"It went really well," replied Adam. "I don't have final numbers or anything but all my work went to new homes. I'm not gonna obsess over what they sold for since I've got other things to worry about going forward." He looked down. "I booked my hotel today."

Rhea straightened. "Where?"

He scratched his neck. "Seattle. I leave early on the twenty-fifth and should get there late the next day. I'm gonna do a ten-hour drive Tuesday and another almost eight-hour day Wednesday which gives me all of Thursday to set up. Gary's gonna meet me there to help with everything. But, uh . . . Yeah. This is definitely gonna push back my usual trip to Chicago for another year, I'm afraid."

"Oh. Well. Okay, I guess." *C'mon, at least pretend to be happy for him.* "I'll really miss you." Rhea's voice cracked.

"But I'm so excited you have this opportunity."

"Thanks for understanding, sweetie." Adam sighed. "I promise you, something good will come from this trip." He glanced at her. "If I didn't feel it, deep, deep down in my bones, I wouldn't be going. You know?"

"I know." Rhea choked on her phlegm.

"You know what else? I miss you."

She didn't know how much longer she could withhold the tears. Her words were stiff: "I miss you too."

"If we were together, I'd take you in my arms and hold you tight."

"I know."

"Maybe slide a hand along your thigh—"

"Adam!" Rhea's eyes darted to Brianna, for all intents and purposes hiding in plain sight just beside the laptop. Perhaps he'd forgotten she was present, but Rhea didn't. Or maybe he figured she was within earshot and didn't care. But Rhea did. Her cheeks hot, she reminded him, "I'm not here by myself."

"Oh." He glanced around, rubbing the nape of his neck with both hands. "Well . . . Okay. I could've used some stress relief before I leave for my trip. I understand, I guess. I'll be in touch."

Rhea forced a wavering smile. "Yeah. Okay. Tell me everything when you get home. And um, get me a souvenir from Pike Place?"

Adam chuckled. "I'll see what I can find."

Rhea's eyes stung from blinking around her tears. "Thanks. Hey, it's late here and we've got a super early morning tomorrow and a long day ahead of us, so—"

"Say no more. Love ya, Sunshine. Text when you can."

Love ya? It took a moment for her to find her words. "I will. Love you, too. Bye." Rhea ended the call with a shudder; she had a feeling she'd be sleeping on a wet pillow that night, and not for her damp hair.

"Oh my God," she exhaled. "Thanks so much for being here. I wasn't exactly in the mood to fool around and I don't know what I'd have done without you as an excuse and Lord knows I did *not* want to have to explain why I'm so upset."

"You're totes welcies." Brianna gave her a crooked smile. "It's kind of a shame though. I mean, you know, I wouldn't have minded the show. You could have performed for both of us."

"On a normal day I'd say you have the wrong girl for those kinds of escapades. Today? I don't even know where to start explaining how wrong you are."

"What's a matter?"

Rhea took a deep breath and held it, remaining silent for several moments. She exhaled. "Adam's suddenly absent from my life a lot—I mean more than just not being in the neighborhood, you know—he's making excuses to extend our separation. Call me slow but I'm getting the idea he's only interested in being long-distance friends now."

Rhea rubbed her eyes. "To add insult to injury, I was *so* looking forward to seeing him in four months. And with this change of plans, it'll be over a year before he's here again. And you know . . . it makes sense. Right now maybe he thinks it's too hard to break it off with me because we only recently got together. But think about it: the more time that passes, the easier it'll be for him to just write me off."

She balled her hands into fists, making a motion to punch herself in her thighs without making contact. "God dammit. Why did I have to let myself get so attached to him? I promised myself I wouldn't. I *promised*."

Brianna moved from the chair beside the desk to the bed, patting the mattress. "C'mere."

With a sigh, Rhea hoisted herself out of her seat and plopped beside Brianna.

Brianna pulled her into a tight embrace and held her. "This is a good thing for him, isn't it?"

Rhea nodded. "It's a *great* thing. I just . . . I wish it didn't have to be at the expense of his usual travels. I know I'm selfish, don't remind me."

"You're not selfish. You're loving. But . . . Oh—no, I can't say it, it's not my place."

"What can't you say?" Rhea's eyes narrowed.

"I don't want to hurt your feelings. I only want to help you. So, uh, never mind."

"*What*, Brianna?"

"Maybe if you think he's brushing you off . . ." She took a deep breath and blurted, "don't wait for him. If he's not going to make himself available for you then it's time to move on. This thing you had with him, it was good and enjoyable I'm sure. And obviously it was important for you at that point in your life. But maybe it was never meant to be anything more than a fling. Hot sex, a reintroduction to single life. A reminder that being yourself will attract remarkable people and make special memories."

Brianna shifted in her spot, taking Rhea's hands and squeezing them. "If your relationship with this guy isn't going anywhere, for God's sake, let him go. Your life is here now. Enjoy it! Live for yourself. You deserve to, you've earned it."

"Maybe you're right," Rhea replied, lost in thought.

"Really?" Brianna grinned. "Thanks. I was due." After a moment she added: "And—and hey, I'm available. You're not alone."

*————*smile*————*

Brianna's move went without incident. Tuesday morning before work, Rhea received a text from Adam that he was hitting the road a little ahead of schedule. Wednesday and Thursday were quiet days during which Rhea did her yoga and Zumba classes after work; Brianna joined her for Zumba and proved, of course, to be a natural—much to Rhea's awkwardness and chagrin.

During her lunch break on Friday, while a couple co-workers were getting into a heated argument about the following Saturday's scheduling, Rhea sneaked in a massage with Sheldon. It was hard, as it were, to relax with bickering right outside the door.

Jodie needed the overtime: her daughter lost glasses which cost 300 dollars to replace. Clarence's son had a tooth pulled at the dentist, which cost him just shy of 400 out-of-pocket; he too needed the overtime. There wasn't enough available shift to go around. Therefore, one would get the extra hours at the expense of the other.

"Excuse me," said Rhea to Sheldon. She pulled the sheet tightly around her body and got off the bed, stalking to the door. She threw it open. "Take my shift. *Please.*"

Jodie stared at Rhea's bare shoulders, her face going pink.

Clarence stared hard at her face, as if making sure she knew he wasn't staring at her cleavage. "Is this some sort of joke?" he asked.

"No. I clearly don't need the shift as bad as either of you. So please. Take it and let me have my lunch break in peace. Please." She returned to her massage and enjoyed the silence her small sacrifice created.

When she emerged to resume working, Rhea found Jodie whispering to Brianna in the waiting room.

"Bri?" Rhea asked. "What are you doing here?"

Brianna smiled. "I came for an adjustment. The move fucked up my back something fierce and sleeping on your couch didn't help it any."

"Why didn't you tell me? I'd have done you for free and saved you a copay."

Brianna's smile turned wicked. "You still could—"

"You know what I mean," said Rhea, smacking Brianna's arm playfully.

"My normal doctor referred me to Dr. Kasick."

"Oh. Well, okay then. I hope it's nothing too awful. I'm—" she gestured down the office hall. "—gonna get back to work."

"We on for dinner tonight?" Brianna asked.

"Of course. And apparently—" Rhea forced a smile at Jodie. "—I'm free a week from Saturday, too. So be prepared to find something to entertain me with."

Brianna's wicked smile acquired a suggestive eyebrow wiggle. "Oh, I could think of something—"

"Not *that*," Rhea laughed. She turned to continue down the office hallway, waving over her shoulder. "See you later."

"Bye."

*——— *smile* ———*

RAYS OF SUNSHINE

The knocks came on Rhea's front door much too early Saturday morning. She rolled onto her back in bed, pressing her fingertips to her eyelids before glancing at her clock. *Nine-forty-six? No. Oh hell no.*

"There'd better be a fire is all I'm saying," she grumbled, getting out of bed and padding to her door. Peering through the peephole verified her hunch: Brianna stood outside, rocking in her spot.

Rhea opened her door. "No."

"Rise 'n' sunshine," Brianna sang. "Whatcha doin'?"

"I *was* dreaming." No she wasn't. However, a good coma had been hard to come by in recent nights. And something about Brianna's appearance—hair done in perfect ringlets, war paint on in full effect, skin-tight everything beneath her open coat—indicated returning to bed wasn't in the immediate future.

"Yeah well, 'nuff dreaming, sweet cheeks." Brianna squeezed by her to get inside. "There's a street fair this weekend and since you told me you wanted me occupying you—and you continue to shoot down my sex suggestions, which totes hurt me in the feels, by-the-way—I decided we're going. No arguments."

Rhea groaned. "You morning folk are gonna be the death of me."

"Fevered Pitch is playing there at two. They're my favorite cover band and I'm dying to see them. So get ready while I make you coffee, okay?"

She didn't want to begrudge Brianna her favorite musicians even if she had a terrible case of the not-especially-interested-in-going's. "Fine."

Rhea retreated to her bedroom, first neatening her hair—bless its shortness—and doing her makeup. Brianna looked stunning as always and Rhea—even in her lack of energy and enthusiasm—didn't relish going out as the less attractive friend. She was certainly the fatter one. *As always.*

"Coffee's ready," Brianna sang.

Rhea changed out of her loungewear and dressed in a cheerful yellow blouse she paired with navy khaki pants and a white scarf. She paused to check her phone.

Adam texted her a half hour ago: *Already made my first sale. I love & miss you but I feel confident I made the right choice.*

She sighed. There was no arguing success so she texted in reply, *Hope you sell everything you took with you. Heading out with Bri today, probably won't text much. Love you too.* She took a steadying breath; if she cried, she'd have to fix her makeup and her eyeliner was worn down to a nub already. Not crying seemed preferable all the way around.

"It's a miracle." Brianna announced as Rhea emerged from her bedroom. She handed Rhea a full mug of something she must have thought was coffee. It looked anemic and was probably more cream than anything else.

"What's a miracle?" asked Rhea.

"Shrek went into your room and Aphrodite came out."

Rhea stuck out her tongue. "Gee. Thanks."

"Honest, you look great." Brianna leaned in for a kiss on the cheek. Rhea grudgingly permitted it. "You trying to make me look like a slob next to you?"

"No, of course not." Rhea took a sip of her coffee in an attempt to hide her guilty smile. The liquid may have been closer kin to hot chocolate. That wasn't going to get her through the day; not by a long shot.

"So. Indulge me," said Brianna impishly.

"What?"

"I was thinking it'd be fun to really let our freak flags fly today. I look sexy, if I may say so. And you're hot. So let's mess around with each other and see how many people—men and women—we can make jealous today."

If they spent the day flirting, they'd spend the evening in bed together and Rhea knew it. She was tired of fending off Brianna's advances and her dumb old rabbit was in its death throes the last time she employed it. *Can you die of horniness?* She was afraid of finding out.

Though she didn't let on, Rhea decided Brianna had won this round. It was sex tonight or bust. "Let me finish this cup and we'll get going."

*———*smile*———*

RAYS OF SUNSHINE

The street fair was a sundry collection of local merchants peddling items from salsa to hand knit stuffed animals, and everything in between. There were even booths for local insurance companies and non-profit organizations. It wouldn't have been too surprising to see a kitchen sink thrown in there somewhere.

Rhea got herself a coffee upon their arrival while Brianna poked into a neighboring stand to get churros.

She held a couple cinnamon-encrusted pastries in one hand and texted furiously with the other as Rhea approached. "Hang on—almost done—okay. Okay." She shoved her phone into her purse and held out the pastries. "Work's nagging me about Monday but I'm done. I'm all yours today. Churro?"

"I don't need it—"

"But *I* don't need two. So take one."

Rhea accepted one of the churros with a defeated smile. They toasted each other with them and continued on.

The women wandered from stall to stall, table to table, chatting of the mundane. Attempting to coerce the other into buying any number of items neither needed. Certainly things Brianna couldn't afford. The hung all over each other, smooching whenever they caught someone staring.

They got lunch at a food truck which asserted it served something claiming to be Mexican food before heading toward the stage at the intersection—a couple of Aurora's streets had been blocked off, a makeshift stage erected on the northwest corner of said intersection—as the band Brianna wanted to see began playing.

A crowd gathered while Fevered Pitch played a rock 'n' roll cover of Lady Antebellum's "Where it All Begins."

From several layers of fans away from the stage, Brianna jumped and waved while yelling, "I love you, Kim!"

The bass player—tall, willowy, and platinum blonde—blew her a quick kiss between notes in return.

"Do you know her?" Rhea asked.

Brianna, who had to have the biggest smile of her life on her face replied, "A little. I've been chatting with her a lot through Messenger. If I'm lucky, maybe someday I'll know her a lot . . . Thanks to you."

Rhea tilted her head in question but figured it was better not to ask. That could easily trip into TMI-territory.

Fevered Pitch followed with a twangy arrangement of John Mayer's "Your Body is a Wonderland" and Rhea allowed herself the chance to reflect.

It was a cold early spring day, with a high in the mid-forties and a hazy sky. A moderate breeze carried scents from nearby barbecues along with the sounds of ruffling umbrellas. And she was out with someone who was turning out to be a pretty decent friend. *Or more.*

Her one regret was not taking a heavier jacket; the black one she threw on let the wind cut through a little too easily.

Brianna huddled with Rhea, looping their arms together. "Let's see if we can get closer. I wanna say 'hi' when their set's done."

"Okay."

"Your Body is a Wonderland" blended into a halfway decent cover of "Marry You" by Bruno Mars.

"I love this song!" Brianna squealed, hugging Rhea's arm. "Sing with me?"

She sang along and after a bit, Rhea gathered the courage to join in.

The crowd parted for them as they approached the stage, revealing the sidewalk where there was a vibrantly colored chalk drawing of sunflowers, snapdragons, and lilies. Alongside the chalk bouquet were the words: *Rhea, will you marry me?*

She glanced at Brianna, her mouth falling open.

"What are you doing looking at me for?" Brianna laughed, nudging Rhea forward. "Look *there*."

Down on one knee beside the question mark: Adam L'amoreaux, lifting an open blue velvet jewelry box.

At first, Rhea couldn't process what she was looking at. Then, as the band played out and silence hung in the air, it sunk in.

Her knees turned to jelly and Brianna struggled to keep her on her feet, clinging to her arm. "Don't you faint on me,

Rhea Josse-hopefully-someday-soon-L'amoreaux-if-you-say-yes," Brianna hissed.

Rhea trembled as she lifted a hand to her mouth, her pulse thundering. "Oh my God, Adam—"

His lips lifted into a wavering smile as he gazed at Rhea. He took a deep breath. "The chalk is temporary but my love is permanent. I don't know the kinds of adventures our lives have in store for us . . . But I *do* need to know you'll always be there with me on them." Adam swallowed. "Rhea Josse, will you be my wife?"

"Oh my God *yes*," Rhea shrieked, nodding emphatically. While the crowd roared around them, she added for good measure, "Yes, yes, *yes*, of course I will!"

"You're . . . you're actually gonna have to get down here 'cause I don't think I have the strength to stand—" Adam laughed at his own expense and everyone within earshot laughed along.

"Come on," Brianna said to Rhea. "A couple steps, dear, you can make it—"

Rhea tore herself from Brianna's grip, rushing the remaining distance to Adam and yanking him to his feet. She flung her arms around his shoulders and hugged him while the crowd cheered them on and the band began to play again: A melody Rhea didn't recognize and it had unfamiliar lyrics, but she figured it was for them when the singers—and the crowd—crooned the words *'and she said yes.'*

Adam pulled back, offering her the engagement ring with a trembling hand. "I got it for you."

She sniffled and laughed while watching through watery eyes as Adam slid the ring onto her finger.

"It's beautiful," she said. "Thank you." Beautiful was an understatement; it was perfect. It would have been the very thing she'd have chosen for herself.

He leaned in, pressing his forehead to hers. "Thanks for saying yes."

"You told me you didn't want a girlfriend. You lied to me."

"Hey, I wasn't lying. I didn't want a *girlfriend*, I wanted a *fiancée*. Operative words are crucial."

LEONARD 133

Rhea hugged him again until he grunted from her squeezing. She nuzzled into his neck. "What are you doing here?"

Adam lifted her face, kissing her on the lips. The crowd hooted and whistled. "Um . . . I'm proposing to you?"

Rhea thought she may never stop smiling again. "There never was such a thing as Seattle. Was there?"

"Oh you know there's such a thing as Seattle," he laughed. "I just didn't go there and have no plans to. Not without you, anyway."

A large man who looked like he didn't care the 1970s were over—probably in his fifties or maybe even sixties—approached Adam from a couple feet away, clapping a hand on his back. "Congrats, man. Toldja she'd say yes."

Adam looked a bit sheepish as he nodded toward the man. "Rhea? This is Gary."

"Gary!" Rhea reached out to him without letting go of Adam. They shook hands briefly. "It's so great to finally meet you."

Brianna cleared her throat, joining in by placing a hand on Rhea's shoulder. "You both have an amazing evening together. Kim's gonna take me home." She leaned in and kissed Rhea's cheek. "Congratulations, lovey."

Before Rhea had the chance to reply or introduce Brianna to Adam in person, she disappeared into the crowd.

———— smile ————

Adam and Rhea enjoyed a quiet dinner at an upscale steakhouse followed by a long stroll along part of DuPage River. They headed to Rhea's apartment around sunset.

She gave him the grand tour—all three minutes of it—and he nodded in appreciation of her décor. "I love what you've done with the place."

"Praise from Caesar." Rhea blushed, hugging him from behind. "So . . ."

"So." He folded his hands over hers.

When Rhea orchestrated their reunion in her daydreams, she imagined the passionate stripping of two lovers in romance movies, with clothing hanging from ceiling fan blades, lingerie strewn across the floor in a trail leading to the bedroom, followed by sex too hot for Cinemax 2 AM pornography.

Reality was two adults too shy to make the first move for whatever ridiculous reason.

"Here we are. Alone. And engaged to each other. Together, physically. In the same room." She kissed his neck.

"I can't help thinking there's something we should be doing . . ." Adam released her hands and turned to face her, fishing around in his right pocket.

"Don't tell me you've got another diamond solitaire 'cause I'm really rather fond of the one you already gave me." It was probably half a carat, maybe a little more, mounted in a simple white gold setting. It sparkled like a *Twilight* vampire's chest.

"Not a back-up solitaire, no, but something else I know you wanted me to give you." Adam produced another jewelry box.

"Oh what the hell is this?" she gasped.

He handed it to her. "See for yourself."

Rhea popped open the palm-sized blue velvet box and burst out laughing. "This is *so* not what I meant by wanting you to give me a pearl necklace. But oh my God, I love it. Thank you so much!"

"I know it's not what you meant," Adam replied, tilting his head with a large smile. "But it was *so* worth seeing your reaction." He helped her secure the pearl strand against the nape of her neck. "It'll do for now 'til I can give you the type you meant. Until then . . ." He produced a condom packet from his other pocket. "Lots more where this came from so we'd better start using them."

"Oh. Um, well . . . We're engaged now and I've still got my IUD. So as far as I'm concerned, that's extraneous."

Adam's face lit up and he flicked the foil packet off to the side. In a swift movement, he hoisted her into his arms. "Well then that's more cause for celebration."

Rhea wrapped her legs around his waist, clinging to him as he charged for her bedroom and fell atop her on the mattress.

"Oh you think it was good before—" he kissed her all over her face, his lips traveling down to the side of her neck where he nibbled her. "Mmm, Sunshine, you ain't seen nothing yet."

"Do you get off on commitment or something?" Rhea moaned as he slid a hand along her thigh, caressing her through her khakis.

He snorted. "I get off on you. And you need to get the hell out of these pants." He fumbled with their button and zipper.

"Fine by me. I'll do it."

Adam rolled off her and watched her remove her clothing. She was too eager to get the show on the road to bother with a sexy strip-tease. *Maybe next time.*

"Aw, you didn't go commando. A little birdy told me you were doing that now."

Rhea glanced at him wordlessly.

"What?"

No; this wasn't the time to inquire about conversations he'd had with Brianna.

"If I'd had my way, today would've been in the mid-seventies and I could've worn a certain yellow strappy sundress with a pearly lacey G-string."

Adam looked at her, deadpan. "You did *not* find an outfit like the one from my dream!"

"No." Rhea pouted. "But it wasn't for lack of trying. I don't think I've ever wanted to know how to sew that bad. Believe me, I'll keep looking."

He smiled, pulling her into a brief kiss.

She opened his denim pants and pulled them down. He was happy to see her and she wasn't going by his expression to know it. His boxer briefs followed; since she was already on her knees in front of him, she took him into her mouth, watching as he reeled in sensation. She missed the taste of him, the weight and feeling of his balls as she caressed them.

"Oh God Rhea I missed you—"

After a couple minutes, Adam retreated, pulling her onto the bed with him.

He kissed her on the lips as he shifted between her legs, slipping his hand between her thighs; he smiled against her mouth. "You really didn't know I was here? You didn't see the proposal coming?"

"No, I didn't know, I swear!"

"But it was so obvious—"

Rhea attempted a failed scowl. "Less yap, more sex."

He pulled her forward and sucked her breast into his mouth, playing with her barbell with his tongue as she rubbed up and down his bare member. He slipped a hand between them, repositioned himself and thrust into her with a moan.

As he moved beneath her, she caressed her clit with her fingers and it didn't take long before she came. No squirting this time, not that it was a competition.

And then, so did he—stamina, it appeared, waned where excitement waxed.

They kissed briefly and Rhea dismounted to catch her breath. She rolled onto her side to face him, entwining her legs with his and having to focus on him rather than the feeling of his seed leaking out of her. It wasn't the most pleasant feeling in the world, though infinitely better than wearing jeans with a wet crotch on a freezing night.

"Never done that without condoms," Adam admitted, running his fingers through his hair. "I had no idea it would feel so good. Holy shit. Sorry I didn't last; you feel—oh, you feel amazing. I'll . . . I'll work on lasting longer for you, I promise."

She laughed, caressing his chest. "I could tell how much you enjoyed it." For her, there was no real discernible difference in the act without a condom beyond not having to stop sexual momentum for her lover to dress for the occasion. It would certainly be a fun thing to play with in the shower. Safely and slowly. No potential trip to the ER. Rhea smiled. "I have something I've been dying to tell you in person."

"Oh?"

"I love you."

Adam sighed, caressing her face. "I love you, too. So

much. I can't wait to start our lives together."

Rhea's smile fell. "That's . . . gonna be a bit of a problem."

"What? How? Why?"

"I've got a job here at a place I like. I just renewed my lease for another year." *And oh shit, Brianna.*

"Can't you break it?" he asked with a pout.

Rhea could. Her problem was that she didn't relish returning to California.

"Look," she said, her voice soft to counter the hard reality of what was essentially a rejection. "We just got engaged. We have plenty of time to work this stuff out. Am I right?"

"Yeah. Yeah, you're right. And I knew—I *know* that." Adam sighed. "I was kinda hoping I'd gotten here before you had the chance to renew your lease."

She decided a change of subject was in order. Rhea asked, "So how long are you staying here this time?"

"Two weeks. Two weeks of lazy strolls hand-in-hand with you after you get home from work. Long hot nights in bed with you." Adam kissed her on the lips. "Lots and lots of sex with you. In bed. In the shower. On the couch. Maybe against the kitchen counter? Your hotel room didn't have one of those."

"Maybe against a window?" Rhea batted her eyelashes at him.

"At night with the lights off and the curtain closed?"

"I'll break you down someday. I'm not giving up on that one."

He gave her an awkward smile. "Why don't we start with your car in a deserted parking structure at night."

"That all sounds absolutely wonderful. So, um . . ." She hesitated. "Will you be visiting with your parents? You know, since you're already here?"

"I was planning on it and I want you to come with me this time."

"Of course." Though she didn't relish hanging out at a cemetery, she was thrilled he wanted her companionship this time.

From the nightstand behind her, Rhea's phone buzzed. She shifted to get it but thought better of doing so; anything and everything could wait until after Adam left for California.

"Go on, check. It might be important."

Rhea could've made the argument nothing was more important to her than he was. Instead, she twisted in her spot to grab the phone. When she turned back toward him, she felt the spot of their juices on her bedsheet against her butt and tried not to grimace. "It's a text from Bri. She says to check Facebook. Okay . . ." Rhea switched between apps. "We're both tagged in a post on Fevered Pitch's page."

Adam replied, "We are? Why?"

"Kim here," Rhea read the post. "Fevered Pitch was so lucky to have been involved in the most amazing proposal today." She bit her lip in a smile. "Mazel Tov to the newly engaged Rhea Josse and Adam L'amoreaux! Smiley emoji, smiley with hearts-for-eyes emoji, kissy-face emoji. If you were blessed to be with us at the Aurora Street Fair today and got pics or vid, please share and join us in sending our best wishes for a fruitful union to the happy couple."

Adam leaned in to see the update himself, all smiles. "When was it posted?"

"Five minutes ago." In shock, she noted, "It already has ten replies."

Seven were photos, all of which Rhea saved to her phone. One was a congratulatory comment, the remaining two were videos. They watched through both and butterflies flapped in Rhea's stomach anew. "My God, Adam! How did you even *do* this?"

"Well, after that Skype call when you hung up on me, Cass texted me and told me you thought things were over between us. I knew I had to fix it before I lost you forever. I had a huge amount of help from Gary and Bri." He nudged her leg with his. "Didn't I tell you people are more than happy to help a nice guy?"

"*I'll* say. That was a hell of a production. I just don't understand Bri helping you when she tried to talk me out of being involved with you. She kinda tried to keep me

LEONARD

involved with herself."

"Remember the episode of *Friends* where Chandler pretended to not want to marry Monica when he was preparing to propose to her? We used it as inspiration. I didn't want you ruining the surprise but I also didn't want you finding another guy if you thought we'd broken things off. Bri suggested the idea of keeping you for herself. Or . . . at least trying to keep you for herself."

"Oh my God," Rhea laughed, smacking Adam on his chest. "You used my favorite show against me. I should be so mad at you—"

"But you love me too much."

"I'm crazy for you, you big jerk."

He cleared his throat. "So with you good and distracted and off our scent, Bri and I scoured the calendar for potential events. When we found the street fair and saw Fevered Pitch was gonna be there, she contacted them. They replied with an enthusiastic 'fuck yeah!' and I bought my train tickets that night. Gary worked with the street fair committee to allow me to do the chalk art and he put me in contact with the jeweler who custom-made your ring. When Bri realized you were scheduled to work today—"

"That's why she was talking with Jodie on Thursday." Rhea groaned. "Oh my God, you two got me good."

"What can I say? An amazing girl deserves an amazing proposal." He kissed her softly, muttering against her lips, "Don't ever doubt how much people love you. Especially me."

Rhea snuggled in and they watched as more comments, photos, and videos of Adam's proposal rolled in.

"I can't wait to start my life with you," she whispered. "I love you, Adam."

He replied with a wide smile, "I love you, too, Rhea. Hey, question."

"Shoot."

"There were a few points I got the distinct feeling something happened between you and Bri. Like . . . her act of keeping you for herself wasn't entirely acting."

"That's not a question."

Adam chuckled. "Sorry. How's this: Did you two ever make out?"

Rhea sighed. "What did she tell you, exactly?"

"The only time she ever divulged anything was when she mentioned you go commando. Nothing more. I read between the lines and it put my imagination into a spin."

"I suppose since we're committed to each other now I should tell you the truth. Yes. We did it. We had sex. Once."

"What?" Adam darted upright, his face aglow. "Really? You're not shitting me."

Rhea shook her head. "No sir, no shit. She definitely wanted to screw around again."

"And you didn't?"

"No. Why do you ask?"

Adam shrugged casually, his cheeks going pink. "No reason especially."

"Says someone who has reason, especially."

He laughed a little too hard. "You don't suppose Brianna might wanna maybe join us sometime?"

Rhea smirked, her gaze shifting to their apartment's shared wall. "Well, your birthday *is* coming up." And she was sure they could find an arrangement where Adam kept his parts for Rhea's body only. *A Rhea sandwich. Yummy*! One of her eyebrows arched.

"I don't know what you're plotting but it sure as hell makes me think I've got the best fiancée in the world."

"Yes," Rhea replied smartly, leaning in for a kiss. "Yes, you do."

ACKNOWLEDGMENTS

Ashley (@writer_ag on Twitter), who would need a whole novel to describe how much she's encouraged and helped me with my writing. If you've seen an ad for my book, chances are that was her contribution.

Christina (@ceeleeolson on Twitter), for taking her time to beta-read these tales for me, for being my idea-sounding-board.

Lo-arna (@loarnagreen on Twitter), for her enthusiasm for my writing and her contributions to my romance-lover's giveaway.

Scott (@HaRcTweets on Twitter), for being my inspiration and helping me to write my way out of corners, for beta-reading, for his Photoshop skills, for everything.

Vania (@V_Rheault on Twitter), for her enthusiasm, for being willing to beta-read these tales for me, for helping with the publishing process. If you're reading these words in a paperback, you have Vania to thank. I wouldn't have even considered releasing my work in physical form without her encouragement.

I love you all!

Jewel lives in North Central Texas with her husband, son, daughter, ~~minion of darkness~~ kitty, and a tadpole that will likely never actually frog.

When not chasing the kids or writing, Jewel may be found wielding pointy sticks (knitting hats, gloves, and socks), crocheting, or daydreaming. She has a penchant for all alliteration, costly coffee, fabulous fiber, fanciful flowers, feisty felines . . . and pretty much whatever music she can get her eardrums on. (And yes, she hates that she can't alliterate that better.)

Visit Jewel online by going to her website:
http://www.jeweleleonard.com/

Join Jewel on social media by liking her Facebook page (no frenemies, please):
https://www.facebook.com/Jewel.E.Leonard/

Or chat with Jewel where she's most active on Twitter:
https://twitter.com/JewelELeonard

Made in the USA
Charleston, SC
10 September 2016